BELISHA BEACON
& TABITHA TURNER

RUTH MASTERS

Belisha Beacon & Tabitha Turner
by Ruth Masters

First published 2018, re-published August 2023

© Ruth Masters

Originally published under the author's previous name, Ruth Wheeler

The right of Ruth Masters to be identified as the author of this work has been asserted by her in accordance with the Copyright, Designs and Patents Act 1988.

All rights reserved. No part of this publication may be reproduced, stored in or introduced into a retrieval system, or transmitted, in any form, or by any means (electronic, mechanical, photocopying, recording or otherwise) without the prior written permission of the publisher. Any person who does any unauthorised act in relation to this publication may be liable to criminal prosecution and civil claims for damages.

Cover by The Planet Zarg Design Studio

This book is sold subject to the condition that it shall not, by way of trade or otherwise, be lent, re-sold, hired out, or otherwise circulated without the publisher's prior consent in any form of binding or cover other than that in which it is published and without a similar condition including this condition being imposed on the subsequent purchaser.

ISBN: 9798853349018
Imprint: Independently published

Books by Ruth Masters

Truxxe

All Aliens Like Burgers

Do Aliens Read Sci-Fi?

When Aliens Play Trumps

The Complete Truxxe Trilogy Special Edition

Zealcon

The Extreme Autograph Hunters

The Ultimate Autograph Hunters

Möbius

Belisha Beacon & Tabitha Turner

Order from www.ruthmastersscifi.com

Tabitha

Tabitha knew it was going to be one of those days when her breakfast hatched. She knew that she should have been sceptical after waking up to the shrill sound of her alarm clock, with a craving for egg and soldiers, to find her neighbour Melanie standing on her doorstep, clutching a towering pile of egg cartons. She had barely shared more than a polite, rather awkward nod with Melanie, the kind to which English suburbanites were well accustomed.

Melanie's mother lived in the countryside and had recently visited, bringing her excess smallholding produce with her. Tabitha's neighbour seemed delighted at the opportunity to parade around the cul-de-sac, brightening her neighbours' day with the produce. However, when Melanie's feet and toothy smile remained on Tabitha's doorstep after she had taken a carton, Tabitha realised that the gift was, in fact, no gift at all. Tabitha haplessly retreated into the hallway and fumbled around in her tatty old handbag for her purse and fished out a paltry collection of coins.

"They're free range," Melanie enlightened her, cheerily. Melanie was evidently a morning person. Tabitha was most certainly not.

"I only have seventy pence in change," Tabitha informed her neighbour with a discomfited shrug and a yawn. She didn't want to risk handing over anything larger because Melanie didn't seem to have a spare hand to offer change.

The toothy smile remained, although shrouded in falsity, and the gum-booted feet finally removed themselves from the doorstep as Melanie made her way to her next unwilling customer. "Enjoy," she called back over her shoulder with all the sincerity of a sloppy cashier at a fast food restaurant. Closing the door behind her neighbour, with whom her next exchange would likely be cards containing hollow greetings hastily shoved through letterboxes on Christmas Eve, Tabitha trudged into the kitchen and flicked the kettle switch to the 'on' position.

While the kettle commenced its task, she dropped a teabag into her favourite mug and went about finding a saucepan in the avalanche of cooking utensils in a cupboard that was just out of comfortable reach. She would organise it one day, she thought as she quickly closed the cupboard door. *Bam!* And no one was any the wiser. Only Tabitha was aware of the chaos within.

Tabitha sprinkled salt from the 'hilarious' *Lot's Wife* salt cellar, which had been a house-warming gift from a well-meaning uncle some five years ago, into the bubbling water in the saucepan.

Tabitha opened the egg carton and nearly hit her head on the ceiling strip-light when one of the eggs started to crack. And now, here she was, staring at a slightly gooey baby chicken.

"I'm sorry little 'un," said Tabitha. "You picked the wrong house. I'm afraid that I was never really blessed with much in the way of maternal instincts. But then… you *are* rather cute, I suppose."

As she reached out to pet the new-born, a thought occurred to her. She ran her eyes over the eleven remaining eggs.

"They certainly are free range, aren't they Melanie? They'll all soon be waddling freely around my kitchen!" Tabitha grumbled to herself. She sighed and said to the chick, "I can't risk boiling your siblings alive, can I? It'll have to be toast again today." Tabitha shuddered at the thought of potentially harming any un-hatched chicks as she turned off the hob. The bubbles soon dissipated. Without taking her eyes off the slimy, scrawny little creature, Tabitha slid open the bread bin and placed two slices into the toaster. She pulled off a chunk of crust and crumbled it onto the work surface. The chick made light work of the crumbs and looked up at her expectantly.

"You want more, little 'un?" Tabitha emptied the toaster crumb tray, another task that was long overdue, onto the work surface. The chick feasted, chirruping with delight. "Well that's two birds with one stone. So to speak."

Tabitha flicked the radio on and pondered her situation. A melodic guitar-based song was cut short by overly cheery, brassy broadcasters. What did they have to be so happy about? It was early morning on a Monday, the worst time of day on the worst day of the week. Tabitha had never understood why, on Friday afternoons, radio presenters would seemingly be in the same frame of mind as her, playing upbeat songs and gearing up for the weekend. By the same rule, they should be grumpy on a Monday morning, after all, it was their Monday morning too. If they mumbled sleepily over a cup of coffee and mourned the weekend like most people did, then wouldn't more listeners be able to relate to them? When the toaster finally popped, Tabitha's thoughts were interrupted. She still hadn't figured out a solution to her quandary. She smeared low-fat margarine and the contents of a jar of Marmite liberally onto the toast, and, in the absence of anything to dip soldiers into, cut it into triangles. She leaned on the breakfast bar with one hand as she chewed. Her eyes were fixed on the farmyard animal, which was blocking out the lairy radio DJs with its chirrups and tweets.

"What am I going to do with you then, Chicken Licken?" Tabitha brushed her hands against each other to rid them of crumbs, discarded the empty plate into the sink and scooped up the tiny bird. It was almost weightless in her hands and stood patiently on its orange matchstick legs while Tabitha carried it through the lounge, along the hallway and up the stairs to the bathroom. The chick looked around the large, white tub it found itself in and started cleaning under its wings. Tabitha filled a soap dish with cold water and placed it neatly over the plug hole for the safety of the chick and its tiny legs.

"You'll be fine there for a while," she told the chick. "I need to go out and I don't want you getting lost while I'm gone." As a precautionary measure, she went downstairs and reappeared in the bathroom moments later with the open egg box and a few slices of bread, which she also placed in the bath. "Just in case you have any brothers and sisters in there," she said to the chick. She thought for a moment. "I feel less crazy talking to myself with you around as an excuse. Is this why people have pets? To make them feel less weird?"

The truth was that Tabitha had always felt like she was weird. She seemed to put an inordinate amount of effort into appearing to be normal. She was not sure how far she had the world fooled, but some days trying not to look weird was exhausting. Only the other day, she had dropped her handbag in the supermarket and, thinking she was the only person in the aisle, had pulled a face, puffing out her cheeks and wrinkling her nose, cursing herself as she scrambled after fifty-pence pieces and feminine hygiene paraphernalia. She had looked up and noticed that someone was helping her to gather her belongings and she had still been pulling the face. Flushing with embarrassment, she had mumbled something incoherent, grabbed a fistful of sanitary products off the young man and fled the building. *Normal people just don't do things like that, Tabitha,* she had told herself as she'd scurried off down the street. It was one thing to be clumsy and drop all manner of personal items all over the supermarket, but to be caught pulling faces at her age...

And now she was going to leave the house again. She only needed to collect her car from the garage after its service, but, to Tabitha, the mere prospect felt like an expedition. They would probably be more likely to rip her off not only because she was a woman, but also because they would pick up on the fact that she wouldn't say 'boo' to a mongoose and would be unlikely to protest if they insisted that the car needed further work. Of course, she knew what her friend Ellie would say in moments like this: "Mechanics aren't like that these days, Tabby. They just wouldn't be allowed to be. *I* never have a problem."

Of course Ellie never had a problem. She was achingly slim and naturally pretty and mechanics would be more likely to fall over each other to give Ellie's Clio a service for free than rip her off. She just didn't seem to face the difficulties that Tabitha did. Ellie didn't spend all morning mithering about whether she should be cleaning the house or going for a run. Whichever she chose, Tabitha would feel guilty about not doing the other. Ellie would simply do neither and not suffer any consequences. Her mother would drop in and clean the house and she would still have a body that most women could only dream of. Tabitha wasn't jealous, exactly, she just wished that things were easier sometimes. Everything seemed like such a struggle.

Tabitha dreaded the drudgery of getting up while it was still dark and driving through rush-hour traffic to get to a desk job she hated. Trying her best to respond amicably and professionally to a plethora of customer complaints and still getting negative remarks from her manager was not only exhausting, but utter torment. Nine hours later, Tabitha would be sitting in traffic again with awful chart music crackling through the old car stereo on the only station that half worked. She would come home to an empty house and flop on the sofa, where she would sleep for an hour or so. She would wake up around eight pm, feeling guilty for having slept for so long, and make a start on the housework. She would often feel guilty for neglecting her friends and send them a handful of text messages. Next, she would flick the oven on and dig something out of the freezer for her dinner, which would probably be more full of fat than it should be, but she would excuse herself, feeling that she deserved some pleasure after such a hard day; a few extra calories wouldn't matter, right? The last chip would go from fork to mouth, and, as the guilt of the high-fat meal enveloped her, she would put on her coat and shoes and go out for a walk.

Invariably, the walk would lead her to the Black Swan pub at the end of Ellie's street, and there she would be – Ellie, her best friend, a shining beacon lighting up the whole bar – and all her worries would melt away. Tabitha would decant all the day's woes into Ellie's small, elf-like ears and everything would seem normal again. Her positive view of the world would always put everything into perspective. That is, until the next morning came and Tabitha would have to do it all over again, anxiety and all.

Tabitha wasn't the biggest fan of mornings. The dread of so many things to do and so many calories to try to avoid eating always seemed like such a chore after the promises of the happy, lager-infused evening before. Evenings made promises that they never delivered. Monday mornings in particular had never really got on with Tabitha, but this Monday morning really took the biscuit. She had booked the morning off to go and collect her car from the garage, sort out any issues that might follow and drive into the city to work. But now there was the issue of the unexpected pet. Why couldn't this have happened on a Saturday instead? Saturdays were allowed to be happy and quirky. Anything out of the ordinary that happened on a Monday was just an inconvenience.

Tabitha rounded the corner of Cottonwood Close and continued along the main road, her thoughts flicking between the chick and her usual paranoia. In the morning's excitement, had she remembered to apply her make-up? She couldn't go out without it and didn't understand how other people could. She admired Ellie, whose brimming confidence allowed her to happily leave the house fresh faced, with her bountiful curls pulled back into a quick ponytail, fresh-faced and wearing the first thing she picked out of her vast collection of attire. Tabitha just couldn't do that. She had to choose an outfit that would make her look the least fat for the current season, brush and style her hair and apply foundation, eyebrow pencil, eye shadow, lip gloss and mascara before she would even put the bins out. Ellie had once laughed at the fact that Tabitha wouldn't even sign for a parcel without a full face of make-up.

"You're so vain, Tabby," Ellie had told her, shaking her head and smiling.

"I'm not vain, Ellie!" Tabitha had informed her. "I just don't have the confidence that you do! It's completely different. I can't let the postman see me looking like this." And Tabitha truly believed that she was right. She would have felt ugly and her confidence would have sunk even lower. And what would the postman have thought if a dishevelled young woman had opened the door to him? Vain, indeed! Ellie just didn't get her, sometimes. With a sudden pang of horror, she wondered whether she had greeted Melanie *sans* make-up.

Tabitha sighed with relief as she remembered that she had indeed finished her make-up routine before she went down to make breakfast. She glanced down to check that she was dressed and that her shoes weren't trailing toilet paper behind her. She patted at her handbag to make sure that she had her purse, mobile and house key with her. She was almost beginning to feel at ease when she noticed a gang of three girls walking towards her. They were being rather raucous, pushing and shoving each other off the kerb.

Don't make eye contact, don't make eye contact, she told herself, panic growing inside her chest like the heat from a mouthful of curry that she'd swallowed too quickly. She knew that it was absurd. She was at least ten, maybe fifteen years their senior. Why should she have to be the one who kept her head down? Eyes widening, she realised that she was probably old enough to be the parent of someone of their age.

It's Monday morning. Why aren't they in school? Tabitha wondered. Orly was a nice suburban region, on the whole, but pockets of rougher districts bubbled through it, as they have a habit of doing in most sizeable towns. She hurried along through this particular bubble, not wanting to be delayed, but, inevitably, the gap between the lone pedestrian and the gang of truanting teens decreased. Tabitha would have to walk around them. Why should they all move for one person anyway? Stepping out into the road, Tabitha gave the gang a wide birth. She was almost clear of them, when –

"Oi, what are you looking at?"

"How *dare* you look down your nose at us?"

Tabitha quickened her pace, but a hand grabbed her arm, forcing her to stop.

"Where are you off to in such a hurry?" the first girl asked. She was wearing a pink velour tracksuit and her hair was scraped back into a tight bun, which sat like a turd on the top of her head.

"I'm just going to get my car," Tabitha said simply.

"Ooh, too good for the bus, are we?" mocked another girl, her voice already cracked and suffering from a forty-a-day habit, her t-shirt stretched over a conspicuous bump.

"No, no, I just prefer to use a car," replied Tabitha. *I'm thirty, not thirteen,* she thought. *Why* wouldn't *I have a car?*

"Car key in here, is it?" The girl in the pink grabbed at her tatty handbag.

"No, the mechanic has it," Tabitha said through gritted teeth. She had had enough now. Tabitha clutched the bag more tightly, attempting to loosen the girl's grasp. But it was like playing tug of war with a bulldog – she just wouldn't let go. It looked as though the girl had been experimenting with false nails, although only six of them remained on her nicotine-stained fingers. "Just let go!" Tabitha pleaded as a car whizzed past her, missing her hip by mere inches.

"Fine," said the girl. But as she let go of the bag, Tabitha's mobile phone dropped onto the tarmac with a crash and her wallet landed beside it. Like a vulture, another girl, who had greasy, bleached blonde hair with dark roots and large hooped earrings that would have been better suited as bracelets, swooped down and grabbed her possessions. Tabitha gasped, grabbing at the air weakly as the girl hid behind her two accomplices.

"Keep your shitty old bag," said the girl.

"My wallet! My phone!" Tabitha screamed.

"*Me meee, me meeeee!*" Pink Velour chanted in a childish, mocking tone. She pushed Tabitha to the ground with a jolt. The sudden pain of the hard road hitting her behind took her by surprise and she yelped.

Tabitha saw red. She scowled at the pack of girls, narrowed her eyes and thinned her lips. She rose to a crouching position, placed a hand on the road to stabilise herself and built up the strength in her legs before she swung her right heel into Pink Velour's face, knocking her to the ground. She flung her other leg up k and caught Hoopy Earrings in the ribs with a double roundhouse kick, sending her stumbling, gasping for breath. She dropped Tabitha's wallet and phone and clutched her sides. There was only Pregnancy left. She grabbed the girl's shoulders and ran with her, pushing until she hit a bush, which she crumpled into, her legs flailing pathetically.

Tabitha stood, triumphant. "When I was your age, I was at school studying for my exams. I wasn't parading the streets looking for trouble. Go back to your reality TV, cheap cider and fags. I never understand why people choose to wear tracksuits in the street anyway. Are you on your way to the gym? And I feel sorry for your unborn child," she pointed at the girl in the bush, "being forced to grow up in this environment. Have some self-respect and go to college or something. Stop wasting your life and making other people's lives a misery in the process."

Of course, none of this really happened. Instead, the thirty-year-old woman sat in the middle of the road, crying, with her empty bag beside her. There was the sound of distant taunts and laughter as the band of thieves crossed the road in the direction of the off-licence. Cars sped along the busy road, their drivers honking their horns and giving Tabitha a wide birth, but none of them stopped to ask whether she was all right.

Go after them, Tabitha told herself. *There's still time to say what you want to say, even if you're not really brave enough and skilled enough to knock them all to the ground. But then, why should I bother trying to reason with people like that? They're probably not intelligent enough to understand my point, but they have my wallet and phone! I need to get them back.*

Fortunately, her house keys were still in her jeans pocket, which was something to be thankful for. *I can't believe I've been mugged in broad daylight in Orly,* Tabitha thought. *I was actually mugged!* She got to her feet and rubbed her behind, which was starting to sting. She picked up the tatty bag and waited for a gap in the traffic. *I should phone the police,* she thought, until she remembered that her phone had gone.

She limped across the road and headed towards the off-licence. Perhaps Mr Aurora, the owner, would phone them for her. She slipped into the shop. Her heart stopped as she spotted the gaggle of girls at the counter. Tabitha ducked behind a wall of lager crates.

"Have you got any ID?" came the voice of Mr Aurora.

"Here," said the customer. Tabitha recognised it as the croaky voice of the pregnant girl.

"Miss Tabitha Turner?"

Tabitha gasped from her hiding place.

"Well... you *look* like your picture," the shopkeeper deliberated.

She looks nothing like me! Tabitha's jaw slackened with shock. *She's a pregnant teen with... OK, she has long, dark hair too, but still. Come on, Tabitha. This is it – time to say something!*

She took a deep breath and emerged from behind the wall of lager.

"Mr Aurora, that's *my* ID," Tabitha muttered, trembling from head to toe. "They stole it from me."

"Is that true?" Mr Aurora asked the tracksuited girls before him.

"She's lying!" croaked Pregnancy. "This is my driving licence. Coz... otherwise... why would I have it, like? See?"

"Mr Aurora, I've been coming to your shop for years. Don't you recognise me?" Tabitha pleaded. "Look at the picture, then look at me."

The shopkeeper scrutinised the driving licence. "What is your address?"

"Number four, Cottonwood Close, Orly," Tabitha and the imposter said in unison.

"Which one of you is lying?"

"Obviously the one who doesn't look like me and who is blatantly not thirty years old. Don't let her croaky, older voice throw you." Tabitha's stomach lurched when she vocalised the insult. Her heart was racing. She was further out of her comfort zone than she had ever been before. Was it the trauma of the mugging that was affecting her?

"*What* did you say?" Pregnancy asked, aghast.

"Look, I'm sorry, girls, but I can't serve you. You'll have to put that cider back or buy some Cola-Coke."

"Cola-Coke?" Hoopy mocked the first-generation shopkeeper. "I've not heard of that one. Where do you keep it? In the fridge next to the Bru Iron and the FannyTa?" The girls exploded into mockery and jeers.

"Get out of my shop, all of you," Mr Aurora spluttered, his brow quickly becoming shiny with perspiration, his finger pointing shakily towards the exit.

Tabitha didn't know what to do. She wanted to stick up for the poor man, despite the fact that he had doubted her. Part of her forgave him, mostly because Mr Aurora was far too old to be working behind a counter in a back-street shop.

"Aren't you going to serve us our Cola Coke?" Pink Velour asked, adopting an unforgivably poor Pakistani accent.

"Enough. *Get out, get out! Before I call the police!*"

"All right, all right, we're going!" Pregnancy squealed, heading towards the door. The girls jostled through the exit. Pink Velour, the last to leave, stopped in the doorway and glared at Tabitha and the shopkeeper.

"I don't want none of your stinking cider anyway. Don't know where it's been." She screwed up her face, spouted a string of racist expletives and spat on the doorstep. "Come on gals, let's go 'round mine and see if Kenzie's got any weed."

Tabitha stared, agape. Turning to the shopkeeper, who was visibly calmer in the absence of the gang of teenagers, she said, "If you haven't already, er, I think it might be a good idea if you *did* call the police, Mr Aurora."

"What? Why should I do that? I won't let them back in again, don't you worry. Time is money. Now, do you want to buy anything?"

"I didn't come in here to buy anything; I just want my things back. *Please* can you call the police?" Frustration was now enveloping her in a prickly shroud.

"So, you still claim that that girl has your ID?"

Tabitha nodded impatiently. "And my money and my mobile."

"Very well, hold on," the shopkeeper nodded and scuttled through a doorway behind him, from which hung a strip of multi-coloured ribbons.

Tabitha feared that she would never get to the garage to retrieve her car, let alone get to work. She would have to make a statement to the police, and who knew how long that would take, and, without her wallet, she would be unable to pay the mechanic, so she would be car-less. Maybe she could call on her parents for help. Or Ellie. Surely Ellie would lend her the cash until everything had been sorted. Tabitha was just thinking that everything might be all right. Then something happened that would change everything.

Belisha

Belisha Beacon dropped down from the top bunk and her bare feet touched down onto the cobalt blue floor. She stretched, peeled off her night-suit and stepped into the hygiene cubicle. She closed her eyes as the thin layer of perspiration that had accumulated during her sleep cycle evaporated and was replaced with a feeling of supreme freshness. Her dark locks curled and bowed around her face as the secondary preparation phase gently manipulated each strand into the most fashionable style of the season. She waited while exfoliators, creams, blushers and lash enhancers were applied to her face until she was almost unrecognisable.

Feeling refreshed and reinvigorated, Belisha exited the hygiene cubicle and thumbed through several outfits in her revolving closet. Although her listeners couldn't see her face, let alone what she was wearing, the radio broadcaster always liked to look her best. She selected a shiny green skinsuit that amplified her voluptuous figure and slipped into it. She buckled a chunky gold belt around her hourglass waist and smoothed down the material along her limbs. The familiar hum of the hygiene cubicle's self-cleaning phase kicked into action as she slid her feet into four-inch patent cream heels. Like most sought-after shoes of the season, they were not designed for walking comfortably for more than a few metres, but Belisha had become rather accustomed to them.

She clip-clopped out of the bunk room and into a small, pristine kitchenette, pushed a button on the hot drinks machine, which whirred into life, and opened a pack of protein bars. As she broke her fast, the door to the apartment opened and her flatmate entered.

"Hi, Shan," Belisha mumbled through a mouthful of food and gave a half wave.

"Evening, Belisha. Off to work?"

"Yep. Like spaceships passing in the night these days, aren't we, soul?" She took a small sip of her drink.

"Seems that way. Any of those bars left? I'm too tired to cook anything." Shan disappeared into the bedroom and sauntered barefoot back into the kitchenette without her bag.

Belisha offered her the packet of protein bars. "Hard day?"

"Yep. Long, long day. I'm not sure how much longer I can keep it up for."

"I know what you mean, soul." Belisha dropped the empty packet into a funnel, which seemingly sucked it out of existence.

"I thought you liked it up at the station."

"Yeah, I do, generally. But it's pretty exhausting. It's such a long commute. And you know how much I want to do the morning slot."

"But you get to work on the Möbius Strip, Belisha! The commute and unsociable hours are the price you pay, I suppose."

Belisha nodded. "I suppose so. Right, I'm off. Have a good evening." She brought her fists up towards her collarbone so that her elbows were extended. Shan followed suit and they touched elbows by means of cordial affection.

"See you later, soul."

Belisha teetered out of her luxury apartment and onto the slow conveyor lane. It wasn't too congested; it was twilight and most people were travelling home in the opposite direction, which was a bonus of working the late shift. After a few moments, she found a gap in the median lane and side-stepped across. Taking care not to lose her balance, she stepped across onto the fast lane and held onto the central bar to keep herself steady as she whizzed through the city. Here she would remain until she reached the transport hub in the centre of Hayfen Capital, the main industrial and financial district of Hayfen IV. If the residents of Hayfen IV wanted to find work, then they headed towards the Capital. If budding employees of the entertainment industry were fortunate enough, they could secure a placement on the Möbius Strip.

Shan worked in one of the high-rise office blocks which ran along the eastern perimeter of the Capital. She worked in town planning, so whenever Belisha had a gripe about the city she would invariably air her exasperations in Shan's direction. Shan would routinely tell her that, whatever her complaint was about, it *wasn't her department*. In fact, it had become a long-running joke between the two of them. The conveyor routes, with their illogical (and somewhat dangerous) intertwining paths and confused one-way systems *weren't her department*. The lack of green spaces for people to take time out and relax *weren't her department*, just as the emergent increase in brothels and casinos *wasn't her department.*

Sometimes Shan would get her own back on her flatmate. Why were there no decent songs in the charts these days and why is the radio station riddled with so many adverts? Of course, neither of these issues were Belisha's department. There was little she could do to improve either of these things. Although she was renowned for her position, she was simply a radio broadcaster at Möbius Strip Airwaves.

The grey, repetitive scenery of concrete boxes containing luxurious apartments soon gave way to rows and rows of basic housing, which in turn gave way to the varied, bustling landscape of the inner city. The four outer lanes of the conveyor on either side of her were filling up with the city's inhabitants and commuters. Belisha prepared to change onto the main artery conveyor, Hayfen Capital's biggest highway. Someone to her right was moving into the slow lane, so she stepped into the gap. She stepped to her right once more into the slow lane, alongside which ran a short slip lane which merged onto the main artery conveyor. This was the worst place to make a manoeuvre, in Belisha's opinion; collisions often occurred here. Even after years of using the network, she still breathed a sigh of relief after she transitioned from the slip lane to the fast lane of the main artery conveyor.

Feeling at ease now, Belisha gripped the rail and savoured what promised to be a few uneventful minutes of the journey. Towering above on either side of the main artery in the most illustrious part of the city were offices, eateries, shopping outlets and holographic billboards promoting various wares. The gleaming lights that pierced through the dusk, the hum of the concentrated conveyor system and the hubbub of city life enveloped her as she travelled through the city.

Belisha was almost as confident as her on-air persona. She went through life with her eyes wide open, the very idea of missing out on anything terrified her. If she arrived at work even a minute later than her producer, Oranjer Bannawoo, or her co-presenter, Elliot Earl, she knew that she would most likely miss out on at least three juicy chunks of gossip. She did not like being left out of the loop.

Like her colleagues, Belisha craved constant attention and social recognition; she felt like she needed to be around other people to validate her existence. She had always thought that way. She surmised that it was because she had grown up with so many siblings, all vying for her parents' attention. If she had sat quietly and kept herself to herself, she would have missed out, not only on attention, but possibly on meals. It had been an eternal struggle to be noticed, and that feeling had stayed with her in her adult life. But it was not easy. Belisha had to work extremely hard just to tread water in an ever-increasing sea of media star wannabes.

Belisha couldn't tell effortlessly amusing anecdotes like Treq, who hosted the Second Sunrise Show, and she couldn't get excited about the weather forecast like Ulrahk, but she was confident and conscientious. She put her all into her work and Elliot Earl was her perfect counterpart.

Belisha had been close with Elliot's predecessor, Alexxian Henner. Although they were still in contact, she didn't have the chance to speak to him nearly as often and she would have liked. Belisha hadn't been sure of Elliot when he had first replaced his forerunner, Alexxian, but over the last few months they had developed a kind of kinship. Their ratings had remained consistently high, so the pair must have been doing something right, she just wished that it wasn't so draining. After some shifts, she barely had the energy to eat and sleep, let alone find a relationship.

Belisha had done well at university, found employment in the industry she had trained for and she worked on the coveted Möbius Strip! She lived in one of the nicest apartments in the city, which she shared with someone whose company she enjoyed and who she deeply trusted. But sometimes it felt as though Belisha's life was slipping away from her. There was so much out there she had not yet had the chance to experience; Belisha did not want to miss any of it.

Belisha had been alive for thirty cycles around the primary sun now and she was no better off than she had been eight cycles ago. Certainly, she enjoyed a moderate amount of fame and had friends and a large family on the other side of Hayfen IV, but she was still working on the same radio slot and had a backlog of bills to pay, mainly thanks to her insistence on buying into all the latest fads and fashions.

Her craving to move onwards and upwards was stronger than ever. Her ultimate aspiration was to present the First Sunrise Show. The time when the first sun of the day began to appear over the horizon was when most people were listening. That was where the big money was. Then perhaps she would be able to leave the concrete residential district and be free from the dispiriting commute and move into one of the highly sought, up-scale plots on the Möbius Strip itself. That was the dream.

Belisha was torn away from her musings when the conveyor suddenly halted, which caused what was locally known as 'the domino effect'. Several miles of people on the outer lanes struggled to their feet. Belisha's knuckles were white, her hands still gasping the rail, but she had managed to stay upright and injury free. Standing on her tiptoes, she could make out a pile-up on one of the exit slip lanes ahead. Her exit. She sighed. *Not again!* Belisha checked that the people in her immediate vicinity were unhurt, as was customary, and made her way off the stationary conveyor.

She felt for the people involved in the pile-up, but she was glad that she wasn't among them. She had never been in a bad collision and she didn't relish the idea.

Belisha made the rest of the journey to the transport hub on foot. Her new shoes started to rub, but the alternative was to wait for the conveyor to start moving again, and who knew how long that would take? Belisha couldn't risk being late for work. And Belisha could not be late. The listeners wouldn't wait for her. As her producer Oranjer constantly told her, *your listeners don't care whether you're having a bad day; smile on air and your listeners will smile too.* The advice was obviously good practice, but it wasn't always easily achievable.

Belisha's thin-soled, impractical shoes click-clacked as she hurried along the side path. Like a shoal of fish, she and dozens of other commuters entered the large, glass transport hub. She made her way towards a row of turnstiles which separated four grey spheres from the sea of people. Devices on the turnstiles blinked red or green depending whether passengers were granted or denied access to the inner zone. Belisha nonchalantly pressed her thumb against one of the devices, which turned green as expected, and she stepped through the turnstile and into one of the spheres.

Standing too close for comfort with seventeen other passengers inside the cramped sphere, she waited impatiently for the announcement.

"Please stand clear of the doors. Please stand clear of the doors." Belisha mouthed the words as the electronic voice spoke. "Elevation commences in five seconds. Five, four, three, two, one. Have a pleasant trip." There was a familiar jolt as the sphere began its ascent along the space elevator shaft with a faint hum.

It would be an infinitely more pleasant trip if someone's armpit wasn't trying to devour my face, Belisha thought with irritation. But she knew that she was fortunate. Had it been the morning rush hour, she would not have been able to step straight into an elesphere. There would have been at least a half-hour wait and double the number of passengers. *I'm so lucky,* she reminded herself, although not too convincingly.

Belisha was riding in the world's first space elevator, which transported citizens from Hayfen Capital to the prestigious Möbius Strip. Her thumbprint had granted her access on account of the fact that she worked there. Citizens who didn't work or live on the Strip were not permitted access without express permission. Belisha had often daydreamed about going out on the Strip with Shan and showing her what the esteemed mini-city had to offer. But it was impossible.

"Please mind the gap between the elesphere and the platform. Please mind the gap." Belisha bustled through the door and into the Möbius Strip transportation hub. The immense, glass hub was identical in size and style to the one in Hayfen Capital, except that it was adorned with garish, colourful lights. Tinny pop music transmitted by Möbius Strip Airwaves was being pumped through large, concave speakers from all sides. Belisha recognised the voice of the weather reporter, Ulrahk. It was the final report before her show. She knew that there were three more songs and one advert break to be played before she had to take over the microphone. *I should just about make it*, she thought.

Belisha boarded a conveyor which took her outside of the hub. She stepped into the fast lane and looked down at her feet. Unlike the ones down on the planet, the conveyor was transparent, in keeping with the ground of the entire Strip. Whoever had designed and printed the mathematical masterpiece out in the planet's orbit had obviously deemed it necessary to make its dwellers feel nauseated. Belisha still had not got used to the fact that beneath her she could see the soles of the feet of other commuters travelling along the same conveyor, which was eternally travelling around and around the same plain. The notion made her head spin. The Möbius Strip was vast and long and wide, and it wasn't always obvious that the ground beneath their feet wasn't flat. And the artificially created atmosphere meant that breathing was not an issue out on the Strip. But the transparent ground was disconcerting, a firm reminder of what she was actually standing on.

The perplexing plaza was like a twisted belt suspended in space. It was home to Hayfen IV's glorious, celebrated, and often rather tacky entertainment district. Maybe one day, when she was famous enough to live here, Belisha would remain on the Möbius Strip conveyor. It would take all day, perhaps two, but she would be able to come out one door of the transportation hub and back in through the other without moving an inch. Sometimes, runners would be sponsored to lap the Strip on foot for good causes. Belisha admired them but would never consider attempting such a feat. She had never been particularly sporty, and her ambitions did not lie in physical exploits.

Belisha looked through the transparent ground at the green orb which was Hayfen IV. It looked hazy and unreal through the Strip's thick ground. It looked so peaceful. Shan would be asleep by now, dreaming of her boyfriend and her holiday no doubt. Belisha had long since stopped asking her to listen to the show. She didn't care so much these days. After so many years in the job, she often forgot that anyone was listening at all. It was simply a task to complete out here on the Möbius Strip. A stepping-stone in her path to super-stardom.

Belisha's workplace, the Euclidean Building, was now in sight. She crossed to the slow lane, alighted onto the side path and took the final few steps of her journey. Her thumbprint granted her access to building, where she took the lift to the Möbius Strip Airwave studio on the fourth floor and strode along the familiar corridor to her booth. Nodding at a rather flustered Oranjer, Belisha nonchalantly took her seat next to Elliot Earl, put on her headset and the two spoke into the mic in unison.

"Good evening, Obscurous." And then she blacked out.

Belisha

"What happened?" Belisha Beacon put a hand to her forehead. Why was it hurting so much? What had happened? She kept her eyes tight shut, fearing that it would hurt to open them.

"You all right. No panic, you just fell over. The police are on their way," came a voice so near that she could feel breath on her cheek, the soft scent of spices and cologne.

"The police? Is that you, Oranjer? Oranjer Bannawoo?"

"I think I maybe call the ambulance too."

"What?" Belisha opened her eyes slowly, the strip-light above piercing instantly through them. "It's so *bright*." Pushing herself up onto her elbows, she looked for the source of the voice. "You're... you're not my producer. And where's Elliot?"

"No, I'm a shopkeeper. Mr Aurora."

"Mister...?"

"You were talking to me. Five minutes ago. Do you want glass of water? Cola Coke on house?"

"I don't know what you're saying." Belisha stumbled to her feet, the man who called himself the shopkeeper helping to steady her. The first thing she realised was that her stance was uncomfortably flat – where were her heels? The unfamiliar feeling caused her to wobble. What was she wearing? Where *was* she?

Eyes now wide open, she looked around and drank in her surroundings. There were boxes and metal cylinders everywhere, larger containers filled with more metal cylinders and glass bottles. Rows and rows of glass bottles of all different colours. She licked her dry lips. Had the stranger mentioned water?

"Water, yes, water," she mumbled.

"One moment," said the curious man. He disappeared behind the counter through a peculiar, multi-coloured doorway.

"Is that some kind of portal?" she asked.

"Water, yes, on its way," the shopkeeper's voice called back.

What's going on? Belisha wondered, her mind racing. *One minute I was at work, and now I'm here in this strange, strange place with all these... bottles.*

The shop door suddenly opened and in walked a blonde woman wearing what Belisha considered far too many layers of clothing. She was pushing what appeared to be her offspring, which had its own shock of fair hair, in a small, wheeled chariot. The offspring was screaming, but the blonde woman was paying more attention to the contents of one of the large glass-doored containers. Horrified, Belisha made for the door the oddly dressed woman had come through and left the building. The next thing she realised was that it was daylight.

It was evening. How long was I out for? And where am I? Belisha shielded her eyes and scanned the sky. Where was the second sun? The scuffed, paved walkways indicated that she was not on the Möbius Strip. Was she somehow back on Hayfen IV? Perhaps her older male siblings, who were keen on playing pranks, had turned up at the studio, knocked her out, kidnapped her and left her in a backwards town in the north. But why? And this place was backwards even for the northern hemisphere. They still had personal vehicles here, she noticed as a Range Rover zoomed past. *Where are all the conveyors? What is going on here?*

In a haze of confusion and utter incomprehension, Belisha tip-toed along in unfamiliar shoes along the unfamiliar street, her brain trying desperately to make sense of the situation, to grasp onto *something*.

A loud wailing sound, more irritating and shrill than the child's cry, crescendoed as a vehicle with blue flashing lights whizzed past her.

"What on Hayfen IV is that?" she said aloud. "Why would anyone want to drive that around? I enjoy getting attention, but really, that is going too far!"

Rain started pattering down. Small spots transformed into large, fast, icy cold drops that soaked Belisha's thin clothes. She was almost glad; the water disguised a tear as it ran down her face. But once she had started, she couldn't stop. Soon, she was bawling loudly in the middle of the pavement, tears streaming out of her sore eyes. She just wanted to go home.

"All right, babe? Did you forget your umbrella?" a voice crackling with phlegm greeted her in a sneer. Belisha turned to see a tall, scruffy looking individual. He was obviously awake, although his eyes were unfocused and almost dead-looking. Long fingers brought a skinny, white, papery tube to his dry lips and he sucked on it before blowing foul smoke in Belisha's face. She immediately screwed up her face and tried to walk away, but the man placed a hand on her shoulder. "You tryin' to run away from me, babe? Now that ain't very polite, is it?"

"You're a revolting creature!"

He cackled and took another drag. "Well, I may have neglected my beauty routine this morning, babe, but that's a bit harsh, ain't it? I only wanted to see if you wanted to er… sample some of my wares."

"You couldn't possibly have anything to offer that I would be interested in!" Belisha retorted.

Someone else in this strange and unfamiliar place was trying to get her attention. A young woman with a head of blonde, bouncing curls holding an umbrella ran across the road towards her.

"Tabby!" she said, her expression brimming with concern. "Tabby, come on."

"Wh-what?"

"Excuse me, babe, but we was chatting. 'Less you'd like to buy summat too?"

"What? Oh no. Go away, Kenzie." This new person, whoever she was, seemed to be utterly without fear.

"You know my name?" the man asked her. "So, my reputation precedes me," he said in mocking tones. He cackled again.

"Unfortunately," the girl replied. "Although it's nothing to be proud about. Come along, Tabby."

"Your loss." The man shrugged and went into the shop. When he had disappeared, Belisha found the nerve to speak.

"Who are you?"

"Tabby, it's Ellie. What were you doing, standing out here in the rain talking with that… *man?* Oh, and you've been crying too… has something happened?" The concerned woman's bountiful waves of golden hair tumbled down her shoulders to her waist. Her face was blessed with natural beauty. Long lashes and expressive eyebrows framed her large, blue eyes. She held her wide pink umbrella over the two of them to shield them from the rain. Despite her discomfort, Belisha noticed that the woman's pretty, plastic raincoat reached past her knees. It wasn't a particularly expensive-looking raincoat, but it suited her, and Belisha admired that she seemed to have more taste than the other people she had encountered.

"I don't know what I'm doing here. My name's Belisha," she managed, a little embarrassed about having been seen crying in public. And in front of this beautiful stranger.

"What did you say? You want a tissue?"
The svelte, sophisticated girl took her arm and steered her across the road. "Come on, let's get you in the dry and you can tell me all about it. I thought you were supposed to be at work this afternoon."

"I'm supposed to be at work *now*," Belisha sniffed. She had no idea what was happening or who this person was, but the feeling of her tender, kind arm around hers brought her more comfort than anything had in a very long time. She couldn't be sure how long they were walking for; all Belisha knew was that she wanted to get out of the rain. Unscheduled precipitation didn't occur out on the Möbius Strip, and accurate forecasts on Hayfen IV meant that, if inclement weather was on its way, she was always well prepared. And, as far as she knew, the forecast for the next month predicted dry, warm conditions.

"Where are we?" she asked the girl called Ellie, as she was becoming increasingly convinced that she was nowhere near home.

"We're nearly at mine. Don't you recognise Dew Close?"

"Duke who?"

"Here we are." Ellie steered Belisha up a footpath to a brightly painted green door. Perhaps these were her living quarters. But, instead of pressing her thumb to a pad to gain entry, Ellie disclosed a metal tool that she inserted into a slot halfway up the door and turned. To Belisha's surprise, the entry swung open and Ellie ushered her inside while she pumped the umbrella a few times, shaking off some of the raindrops. Once inside, Ellie disrobed down to another layer of clothing and pulled off a pair of pink patent high-heeled boots. She smiled at Belisha. Her face was full of kindness, but something about her eyes betrayed her. She appeared to be concerned. Distressed, even.

"I'll put the kettle on, and you can tell me all about it," Ellie said in soothing tones.

"You're going to put on what? Is that another kind of coat?"

"What are you talking about, Tabby? Have you hit your head or something?"

"It's quite likely," Belisha complained, nursing her sodden head with both hands.

"Feel free to go and dry your hair – there's a fresh towel in the bathroom. And you can borrow some of my clothes. I know you always complain that mine are too small, but honestly, Tabs, there are only two sizes between us. And you know that I like my clothes to be baggy, anyway."

"Right," Belisha said, distracted. What were these things the girl was speaking of? Towel? Bathroom? Baggy? In truth, all Belisha wanted to do was sit down and gather her thoughts. "I'm all right."

"Your call." Ellie shrugged. "Just a drink then? Usual?"

Belisha nodded, only barely comprehending anything that Ellie said. She simply followed her into another room and sat down on a high stool as she watched the slender woman pour water from a tap and into a bright, metallic container, which she then set onto a platform.

"Did you manage to pick your car up today?" Ellie asked. Belisha looked at her blankly. "You told me that you had booked the morning off to collect it from the garage. I remember because Mondays are my day off and I was going to suggest we meet up until I realised you were going to be working in the–"

"I'm supposed to be at work now," Belisha interjected.

"So you said. But it's not even midday yet. Look… what happened, Tabby? And where is that cute little bag of yours that you never seem to leave the house without? Honestly, Tabs, you look as though you've just dropped out of the sky. No coat, no bag – have you even got your phone with you? Your keys?"

Eyebrows knitted in confusion, Belisha tapped at her pockets, in case any of these items were about her person. She found something small and hard buried in the left pocket of the strange blue rugged trousers she was somehow wearing. It was a tool like the one Ellie had used to enter her living space. She held it out in front of her.

"Well, that's something, I suppose. How about we wait until after the rain stops and then I'll walk you back home? And then I'll help you look for your things. Have you any idea what might have happened?"

"All I know is that I woke up on the floor in… in… well… a man was there, and he said something like the police were on their way and something called an ambulance and…"

"Tabby, have you been mugged? Is that what happened?"

Unable to endure it any longer, Belisha stood up and announced loudly and crossly, "I'm not Tabby!"

Tabitha

"Come on, Belisha!" a wispy voice hissed in Tabitha Turner's ears. "You need to say more than that!"

"Wha–?"

"Miss Beacon, hurry or we're going straight to commercials."

"Where am–?"

"That's it. Cut to break." A glass door opened and a tall, thick set, oddly attired man strode into the room. He loomed over Tabitha like Herman Munster. Anger was manifesting in the angle of his thick eyebrows, the scowling down-turned lips and the slight twitch of his left eye. Tabitha recoiled into the seat in which she had suddenly found herself. A song she had never heard before pumped in her ears. She didn't realise that she was wearing a headset until the enraged man reached down and ripped it off her head.

"Ouch!" she protested.

"Ouch indeed, Miss Beacon! That is what our listeners are saying after being inflicted with seven and a half seconds of radio silence."

"I'm sorry – *what?*"

"Just because Elliot nipped off to the gents, it doesn't mean that you have to disappear off air as well. I can't deal with this, Belisha. Not now. You were thirty seconds late for work, and now this! This is so *unlike* you. You're my star, Belisha. What's going on?"

"I wish I knew!"

"Well you have exactly two minutes and twenty-seven seconds to pull yourself together!"

"Wh-what do you want me to do?" Tabitha stammered, perspiration forming on her perplexed brow.

The man sighed and pressed his thumb and forefinger on either side of the bridge of his nose, as though he was willing himself to calm down. He took several deep breaths. After a few moments, he crouched next to her. A strained smile forced its way across his lips. He picked up the headset and placed it gently back on her head and set the mouthpiece just below her trembling lips. "Look, just do what you do best, soul. Be your usual happy, cheery self and announce the next track. It's all written down on your holoscreen for you, as you know. Then, after the next commercial break, announce the daily competition."

"But–"

The large man exited the small room and reappeared behind a glass screen. Tabitha watched as he brought his fists to his collarbone and extended his elbows in her direction. "You can do it," his voice echoed in her headset. "I'll tap through an auto-cue. Only this once, though!"

What am I supposed to do? Where am I? One moment I had just been mugged and I was waiting for the police to arrive, and the next I find myself in some kind of studio. Did I hit my head? Am I dreaming? Tabitha chewed over the notion for a while and then reasoned; *It must be a dream What else could it be? Well if this is a dream, I suppose I should go along with it.*

An advert finished with a cheerful jingle which advised listeners to "try *Hairgo* – never shave again" and chimed "with no pain." Tabitha was just wondering how her subconscious had conjured up such an obscure, and rather poor, strapline, when she realised that it was the end of the commercial break. *Here goes,* she thought, playing along with her own imagination. She looked around the desk for inspiration and her eyes fell onto a horizontal panel to her right, where blue letters suddenly blinked into existence in the space above it. She read out the lines the monitor fed her.

"Welcome back, listeners. You're listening to *Good Evening, Obscurous*. Next up, this week's number one track, *Where Have All the Seahorses Gone?* by Mistress Halo." *What kind of title is that?* Tabitha wrinkled up her nose.

"Fade it in! Crashing hell, Belisha. The track! Fade in the track!" Herman Munster's voice reverberated in her ear. She looked through the glass at him blankly, down at the bank of nonsensical instruments laid out on the desk in front of her, then back up at the man.

A moment later, someone with striking, spiked blue hair sat beside her. He looked at her for a moment, an expression of puzzlement on his face and mouthed, "*What's going on?*" He shook his head, shrugged, leaned across her and manipulated some of the controls. An unmelodious clamouring poured into her ears. She made a face expressing her distaste and pulled the headset down so that it was resting on her shoulders. The trembling vocals and cacophonous instruments were now pleasingly distant.

"What *is* that?" she cried. How had her brain concocted this awful noise? Was someone using a particularly shrill hairdryer in the waking world?

"Mistress Halo, of course!" the young man with the spikey blue hair informed her. "The song that *you* were supposed to fade in! What's going on, Belisha?"

"That's what I'd like to know." The stocky man from behind the glass appeared in the doorway once more, his face filled with disapproval. "Please don't remove your headset again, Belisha."

"I'm not this Belisha person," Tabitha informed him.

"Well, no, you certainly don't seem yourself today. Maybe you've been overdoing it lately. Look, why don't you go home, get some rest, maybe book yourself a doctor's appointment? I'm sure Elliot will manage on his own for one evening." The bright-haired young man beside her gave a casual nod.

Tabitha shrugged, unhooked herself from the headset and left the room. If this had been real life, she would not have the courage to leave so calmly. Her nervousness would have gone into overdrive and she would have been desperate to satisfy her boss. It was true that her real-life boss never appreciated her efforts, but Tabitha endeavoured to please her and made the effort to do so with a smile, albeit a forced one. But this was not real life, this was merely a strange dreamworld that Tabitha's brain had created, probably as a direct reaction from her traumatic morning. Her brain was trying to protect her from reality and keep her sane. But she didn't feel particularly sane.

Tabitha mithered about what was happening to her corporeal body in the waking world. Was it out cold on the floor of the off licence? Was it covered in bruises after another encounter with Pink Velour and her gang? Or was it slumped in the back of a police car, or worse, an ambulance? Anxiety rose its monstrous head and engulfed her in a sea of worry as she walked along an unfamiliar corridor in a corner of her own imagination.

When she reached the end of the corridor, which was no mean feat in the heels she had found herself wearing, Tabitha saw a set of lift doors that opened in front of her. She habitually stepped into the lift and examined the number pad. *I suppose down is as good a direction as any,* she thought as she pushed the button marked *Ground Floor.* Wincing, she peeled one of the shoes away from her throbbing left foot, which appeared to have a large and painful blister on the heel. *Can you get blisters in dreams?*

Tabitha wondered what to expect when she reached the ground floor. If she knew her mind well, and she hoped that she did, she was being transported to a different part of her dream. She suspected that she would end up somewhere echoing the familiar surroundings of her living room, or maybe her old school or Ellie's house. Or would she find herself on the top of a roller coaster or lost inside a mirror maze? She knew she was dreaming, so perhaps, she considered, she could engineer what was going to happen next. Lucid dreams were always the best kind, after all. She reluctantly pushed the tight shoe back on as the lift came to a halt.

OK, brain, Tabitha told herself, *let's step out onto a long, warm, deserted beach.* But rather than feeling warm sand between bare toes, she was shocked to find that she was still wearing the ridiculously high shoes and standing on a hard, *transparent* surface. She stopped suddenly. She wobbled as though she was about to fall over and held out her arms to regain her balance. What *was* this thick transparent material and why was the whole street made of it? Who were all these people and why were they whizzing back and forth on some kind of supermarket trolley travellator in the middle of the street?

You've surpassed yourself this time, brain, Tabitha mused. *It must have been a really hard knock on the head!* She pondered for a while, lapping up her surroundings. *Maybe this is some kind of ice rink. A very long, wide, strong ice rink with buildings along it. In which case, I won't take off my shoes, no matter how uncomfortable they are.* She looked down, past the long, tapered points of her shoes, expecting there to be a replica in the reflection in the ice. But instead, she saw the vague shape of a portly upside-down man greet the shape of another, thinner, upside-down man and the two proceeded to walk together. Her head suddenly buzzing with vertigo, she looked up again, took a deep breath and told herself to relax.

Tabitha was suddenly conscious that someone was watching her. A middle-aged woman with bright orange hair which clashed with both her leathery, tanned complexion and her burgundy skinsuit.

"Hey, soul, are you OK?" she asked in a voice which was as rough and ragged as her face. "Do you feel faint?"

"I er... no. I don't know. No. Just a bit confused, really."

"Indeed. Do you live out here on the Möbius Strip?"

"On the *what?*"

"Or are you from the homeworld?"

"I'm not sure what you mean." What was this woman talking about? Why was she so interested in her? Tabitha speculated that if she was only dreaming, then speaking to this person would do no harm. So, she said casually, "I'm from England and I think I'm having a rather surreal dream. I'm afraid that you're not even real – my brain made you up," she said with a nervous laugh.

The leather-faced lady's brow furrowed in confusion. Where had the idea for this construct come from? She didn't look like anyone Tabitha knew and the clothes the people were wearing in this dream were unlike any she had ever seen outside of an American seventies science-fiction series. She felt very uncomfortable walking around in heels and a shiny bright green cat suit that emphasised all her lumps and bumps. She stood self-consciously with her arms around her middle, shielding herself from the potential gazes of onlookers. After a few moments of obvious careful consideration, the woman finally spoke again, her eyes wide, shaggy orange eyebrows arched.

"England? As in *Old England* back on the homeworld?"

"England as in England on Earth," Tabitha said, slowly.

The woman nodded. Tabitha looked into her eyes, which were darting around as though she was scanning her or trying to read something etched on her irises. Eventually, she looked away, her mouth slightly agape.

"But it's you! As soon as I laid eyes on you I thought '*That's the girl who presents Good Evening, Obscurous*'. I recognise you from the holographic billboards further along the Strip. But what are you doing out here at this hour, Belisha Beacon? Aren't you supposed to be on air?"

"You recognise me?" asked Tabitha. "You recognise me as this *Belisha* person?"

The woman nodded. "Most souls would. Surely you're aware of that?"

"But I'm not her. This Belisha must be a figment of my imagination, too." Tabitha tugged at her outfit and waved her arms about in exasperation. "My sleeping mind seems to be playing out this strange scenario because of a fever, or in order to figure out something in my subconscious. It's probably a bad reaction to the mugging. My brain has created this alter-ego who wears this crazy costume and lives in this strange place where the pavements are see through and everyone seems to know who I am but *me*. That's just so typical of my brain."

"Why do you think you're asleep, Belisha?"

"Don't you understand what I've been saying?" It was all Tabitha could do to stop herself screaming at the woman. "Look... you seem like a lovely person and maybe you're a reflection of the good part of my psyche or something, but all I want to do is wake up, speak to the police, get my car and my things back and avoid any confrontation with my boss."

"Why don't you come with me and I'll buy you a hot drink? After a jug of souprano, you'll feel calmer and your thoughts will become more rational. You're obviously working far too hard at the station. Those producers at Möbius Strip Airwaves have a lot to answer to."

Partly out of curiosity and partly out of fear, Tabitha agreed to follow her. It was preferable to wandering around the dreamscape alone. The streets were a confusing jumble of people rushing around on travellators at different speeds and there were so many colours and bright lights billowing from the towering edifices lining the Strip that her vision was confounded. She wondered whether her chaotic surroundings were a reflection of her state of mind. Perhaps her brain was trying to figure something out while she lay in, not just a deep sleep, but a coma. Perhaps she should just let it continue so that she could get better and wake up.

"We'll take the conveyor just down the Strip to one of my favourite places. It's far too busy and commercial around here isn't it? Even by Möbius Strip's standards. Have you ever been to a little place called Kello Lumpy's?"

"I haven't been anywhere here," Tabitha informed her. "I don't think I've ever had a dream quite like this one."

"Right. I think you might need an extra-large jug of souprano."

Lumpy souprano, whatever that is, doesn't sound particularly appetising, thought Tabitha. But, in her experience, food and drink never had any flavour in dreams. She followed the burgundy-clad woman onto the moving travellator that she had called a conveyor. Teetering along in her heels, Tabitha made sure she felt as stable as she was going to feel before letting herself take in her surroundings.

"Mumma Toille," the woman said over her shoulder as they trundled along.

"Nice to meet you Mumma Toille. And thanks for helping me."

"Not at all. I'm honoured to help a celebrated person such as yourself, Miss Beacon." A few moments later she said, "We will need to move over onto the median lane, or we'll never get there, soul," and side-stepped to her left onto an adjacent conveyor belt. Tabitha followed suit and found that they were now travelling along at a much quicker pace.

"This is definitely more fun than walking!" she exclaimed.

"You have a strange idea of fun, soul. It's almost as though you've never travelled by conveyor before. Interesting." Tabitha said nothing, instead absorbing the changing environment, which became marginally quieter the further they travelled. "There's no need for us to step onto the fast lane, though. We're almost here." A moment later, Mumma side-stepped back onto the slow lane and onto the transparent pavement. Tabitha struggled to follow her, and it took a while for her to catch up, but she kept her fluffy orange hair in sight. "Here we are – Kello Lumpy's flagship branch."

Tabitha looked up at what looked from the outside like an ordinary coffee shop, albeit larger. The paintwork needed some attention, but otherwise the establishment looked quite unremarkable.

Perhaps my mind is running out of exciting, lavish exteriors after that trip along the Strip, Tabitha pondered. *This place might as well be next to Mr Aurora's off licence.*

Once inside, Mumma Toille advanced towards the counter and pressed her thumb onto a pyramid-shaped device. "Two large jugs of souprano and a bowl of whatever the snack of the day is," she confidently informed the server.

"Today's snack of the day is old-fashioned peanuts," the adolescent female informed her.

"I don't mind what it is," Mumma snapped. "We shall be sitting in that booth over there." Tabitha was taken aback by the sudden change in her tone. Mumma turned on her heel and whisked Tabitha away from the counter to a concealed table at the far end of the L-shaped room. Mumma smoothed down her skinsuit, pursed her lips, narrowed her eyes and looked at Tabitha.

"I know you're not Belisha Beacon."

Ellie

Ellie tapped away on her mobile phone until she found the phone number for her best friend's office.

"Hello, is that that Veronica Vaughan? Hi, my name's Eleanor Price. I'm a friend of Tabitha Turner," she said, in her best telephone voice. "I'm afraid that Tabitha won't be in this afternoon after all. No... no... her car is still at the garage, but it's not that. She's at my house. I'm trying to find out what happened. I think she's had a knock to the head or she's been mugged as... yes, I know it sounds elaborate, but... look Mrs. Vaughan, she doesn't seem to know where she is – *who* she is... well, I'm sorry, but you must understand that... look, I didn't have to call you at all, Mrs Vaughan, but as an act of courtesy, I... right... OK... I'll tell her... back in tomorrow, yes.... right. Goodbye."

Ellie ended the call and slammed her mobile onto the kitchen work surface in frustration. "I don't know how you put up with working for her, Tabs. She's a proper dragon, isn't she? I'm surprised you haven't had a nervous breakdown by now... ah..." she paused for a few moments, before asking, "Is that what's happened to you, Tabs? Has it all got too much for you?"

Ellie gasped, crouched down next to her friend, and placed a hand on the girl's knee. She looked up at her, her eyes searching her face for any sign of recognition. The girl barely acknowledged her. Her own best friend. It was as if she had a stranger in her kitchen.

"Shall I call your mum and tell her what's happened, and get you an appointment with the doctor?"

"I'm fine," said the girl quietly. "I just want to go home."

"But I'm really worried about you now, Tabby."

"I'm not this Tabby person. My name is Belisha Beacon."

"That's what those yellow flashy light things they have at zebra crossings are called. That's not a *name*."

"*Zebra crossings?*" a look of utter perplexity swept over her face. "I'm Belisha Beacon," she reiterated, a little crossly.

"All right, all right. Belisha it is, if that helps." Ellie stood up and went about brewing tea for the two of them. A few silent minutes passed until she brought a steaming cup to the forlorn-looking girl sitting in her kitchen, who seemed to be examining her shoes with a mixture of confusion and revulsion. "Here you go."

"What is it?" The girl sniffed the cup and took a sip, which was quickly followed by a grimace.

"It's what you always have – tea with plenty of milk and two sugars."

"I... I... I usually drink souprano. Do you have any?"

"You don't normally turn your nose up at Tetley," Ellie harrumphed, taken aback. But the girl simply placed the cup on the kitchen table. Ellie looked out of the window and noticed that blue sky was emerging from behind the grey rain clouds. There was even a glimmer of sunlight. She sighed, unable to hide the exasperation in her voice. "Fine. I'll take you home."

The girl followed Ellie through the Orly district and stopped outside a door marked *four*. Ellie prompted her to pass her the key and she let them both in.

"I can't believe you barely even recognise where you live, Tabs. This is really worrying."

"I know where I live," came the reply. "But it's not here."

"Why don't you go and have a sit down in the living room? Oh, can I quickly use your loo before I go?" She ran up the stairs two at a time, hair bouncing behind her. Moments later she shouted,

"Er, Tabs... why are there half a dozen chicks and a loaf of bread in your bathtub?"

Belisha

"So, you believe that your friend might have had some kind of breakdown?" Doctor Molly Wok rubbed her narrow chin between wizened fingers. Her dark eyes glanced over at Belisha, who appeared to be scrutinising a pigeon which had landed on the window ledge outside the small doctor's surgery. It was almost as if she had laser vision and she was trying to cook the thing alive with her glare. She was vaguely aware of the conversation that was happening around her.

"She doesn't seem to know who I am, where she is, *who she is*. And her employer is hardly being sympathetic," said Ellie. "She as good as told me that I was making it up! Why would anyone do that? I think her current state is work related. I can't think of what else it could be. Unless of course she was mugged as I suspected. She doesn't know where her wallet is, her phone... and the worst thing about it is she doesn't seem to care! And that's not like her; she's such a worrier."

The doctor paused for a moment,, before turning her attention to her patient.

"What happened, Tabitha? Did someone hurt you? Did something happen at work? Can you explain what's going through your mind right now?"

"Did I tell you about the chicks?" Ellie interrupted. "In the bathtub with a loaf of–"

"Thank you, Miss Price. You have been most helpful, but I need to speak to Miss Turner now. If you'd kindly wait for your friend in the waiting room–"

"But–"

"*Please,* Miss Price. I appreciate your bringing Miss Turner's condition to my attention, but you don't need to worry. Let me deal with this now."

Ellie opened and shut her mouth several times, turning to Belisha and then to the doctor and then back to Belisha, who was still focussing on the pigeon.

"Fine," she huffed. "Maybe this was a mistake. Maybe I should have taken her to the police station instead." She left the doctor's office, feeling rather redundant.

The pigeon finally decided that there were more interesting places to perch and took flight. At the sight of the sudden flap of feathers, Belisha jumped up out of the chair as though it had administered an electric current through her body. She scowled at Doctor Wok and pointed a finger at her.

"Look, I don't know why I was dragged here. I don't need a doctor. There's nothing wrong with me. I just want to go home."

"Please calm down, Miss Turner."

"I have tried to be calm, or at least to *appear* calm, for the last two hours, since that girl insisted on commandeering me, taking me first to her weird little abode and then to another and now to here – to this place for *sick people*. I'm not sick, Doctor. If anything, I'm homesick!"

"And why would you feel homesick?" the doctor asked, in tones that were becoming increasingly tranquil, which only angered Belisha more. "You live but ten minutes from here." Doctor Wok waved a finger vaguely towards the wall

"I just want to go home."

"Your friend *took* you home when she found you standing out in the rain."

"No. No, she didn't," said Belisha. "And she isn't my friend. I have no idea who that girl is or where I am."

"Do you know who you are?"

"Of course I know who I am. Don't you recognise me? I'm the radio broadcaster for Good Evening, Obscurous on Möbius Strip Airwaves. I'm *Belisha Beacon*!" Belisha stretched her arms out either side of her and paced around the room.

"I see."

"I don't suppose you would recognise me in these terrible, uncomfortable and frankly unflattering clothes." She continued to pace.

"So, does everyone know Belisha Beacon?" the doctor asked calmly.

"Everyone who listens to my show, yes, of course! I'm quite famous out on the Strip. But here on the unfashionable side of the planet, where people still drive 'round in cars and live in hovels, which are even worse than I imagined, where–"

"Where do you think you are, Tabitha?"

"This has to be the northern hemisphere."

"That's correct," Doctor Wok said slowly.

"Then I was right – I *was* kidnapped. I wonder how much the ransom is." Belisha's voice was getting louder as she flooded with rage.

"What makes you think you've been kidnapped?"

"Because I don't belong on this side of Hayfen IV."

"I'll ask you again. Where do you think you are?"

"I told you. The northern hemisphere of Hayfen IV, of course," she all but shouted through gritted teeth.

"I see," said the doctor. "I think you should take some time off work. I'll put you on the waiting list for the cognitive behavioural therapy stress course and I'll contact you when there's a vacancy. Go back out and ask Miss Price to make sure that you get home OK. When you get home, take some paracetamol and rest."

"Home? You mean to that place that girl took me to before? The one that smells of burnt toast, wet towels and farmyards?"

The doctor pressed a button on a device on her desk.

"Mr Smith to see Doctor Wok, please. Clinic six." She looked at her computer screen and said, without even glancing at her, "I hope you feel better soon, Tabitha."

"But–" Belisha stood still, open-mouthed. There was the sound of swift knocking on wood. The doctor responded before Belisha could protest.

"Please go home and rest, as I have advised. Now, if you'll excuse me, I have a back-log of patients to attend to."

As she made her way back towards the waiting room, an elderly gentleman with a halo of grey hair shuffled past her, adjusting his thick glasses and attending to an over-sized shopping bag.

"I don't believe it," said Belisha.

"Unbelievable isn't it?" said a middle-aged man who was also passing by. "You wait for over an hour, you tell them all about your ailments and they fob you off. Did she tell you to take some paracetamols and sleep it off?"

"Yeah," she replied, a little shocked.

"Incredible. Just incredible." The man tutted and continued on his way.

"Tabs!" Ellie greeted Belisha as she stepped through the double-doors into the waiting area. "What did she say?"

Belisha reluctantly left the Orly Health Service building with the bothersome girl in her wake.

A half-full glass of water rested on the bedside table while Belisha slept. Ten tablets remained in the pack of a dozen paracetamol that Ellie had eventually found in Tabitha's sock drawer after searching almost every cupboard in her house. Belisha wasn't used to seeing socks, let alone drawers intended for socks and yet used to store other items.

It was evening when Belisha finally woke up. Noticing her unfamiliar surroundings, she sat up quickly, flailed her arms and knocked over the glass. The water soaked a piece of paper on the bedside table and knocked a pen onto the carpet. Ignoring the spillage, Belisha got out of bed, crossed the cluttered carpet and made her way down the stairs.

"How can I still be here?" she thought out loud. "The joke's over. I want to go home!" *I at least need a hygiene cubicle. I feel as though I've absorbed every odour and every germ in this place.*

Belisha jumped at the sound of a sudden knock on the front door. Tentatively, she turned the handle and opened the door just a little, very aware that she would not looking her best so soon after a long nap. She did not recognise the face of the tall man outside.

"Belisha Beacon. Let me inside. It's important."

Tabitha

Tabitha Turner furrowed her brow so hard that she could almost feel the grooves cutting into her forehead. Her mind was whirring into over-drive. Her gaze moved from Mumma Toille, to the bowl of peanuts, to the floor and back to the hard stare of the leather-faced woman sitting opposite her in the corner booth of Kello Lumpy's café.

A waiter placed two mugs and a bowl of peanuts on the table and left as quickly as she had arrived. Mumma Toille continued to glare across the table at Tabitha. She was beginning to doubt that she was dreaming. It was as though she had crossed into another, nightmarish, reality.

"You *look* like her, you *sound* like her, but you haven't an ounce of decorum, let alone the air of someone so graceful. It's as though a sack of potatoes has been decanted into a priceless vase and it's cracking under the pressure. Just look at the way you stand, the way you walk, the way you wear those clothes. Crashing hell, girl, it's as though they're wearing *you!*"

Tabitha sat open-mouthed as the insults poured out of this stranger, feeling like a jar full of angry bees.

"Do you know who I am?" Tabitha asked softly. Mumma sighed, put the heel of her hand to her forehead and then reached out and took Tabitha's chin between her fingers. Her gnarled digits squeezed her skin, making Tabitha wince. But Mumma held her fast. With each syllable that passed through Mumma's lips, saliva dripped further down her chin.

"You know very well who you are, my dear. You are nothing but one half of the results of the experimentation of Professor Pagter." As the last two words left her mouth, spit flew from her lips and landed on Tabitha's face. Tabitha screwed up her eyes and jerked her head out of Mumma's tight grasp.

"What are you talking about?" gasped Tabitha, her heart thumping almost loudly enough for the entire café to hear. It finally dawned on her that she definitely was not dreaming. Instead, she felt as though she had been plunged headfirst into a living nightmare.

"Oh, you don't remember volunteering?"

"Volunteering for what?"

"For the Experiment, of course!" Mumma grabbed a fistful of peanuts, which she poured into her mouth and chewed without closing her lips. Tabitha gulped and shook her head.

"I didn't volunteer for anything. Why are you doing this to me?" She stared at the woman through a shroud of tears. But Mumma Toille said nothing more. She had stopped chewing and her face had suddenly become completely inanimate. "Mumma?" Tabitha gasped as the middle-aged woman's face began to redden and her brow perspire. Her mouth fell open and the chewed-up nuts cascaded onto the table. Tabitha jumped reflexively. "Mrs… Toille…"

Mumma Toille's body slumped forward and Tabitha leapt out of the booth. Her chest tightening and her lips dry, she skidded across the room, rounding the corner into the main area of the café, narrowly missing the waiter who was carrying a loaded tray. She pushed open the door and click-clacked quickly to the nearest conveyor and let the belt carry her far away from the scene.

What had just happened? Tabitha's thoughts overlapped each other, fighting their way to the front of the queue, holding their hands out, begging for answers. Tabitha was more confused than ever. The woman had showed her kindness, or what Tabitha had believed to have been kindness, then she had turned on her like a woman possessed. Then she just slumped over and died! Had she choked? Or had an unseen assassin murdered her when she blurted out some truth? And who was this Professor Pagter? Whoever he was, maybe he had the answers Tabitha was so desperate for. *That's what I'll have to do,* she decided. *I'll find this professor and perhaps he can tell me what's going on. I can't stay here a moment longer!*

Before she knew it, Tabitha was standing on the central fast lane of the conveyor, hurtling along to who-knew-where and clasping the rail so tightly that her knuckles were white. People weaved in and out of the lanes, casually stepping on and off, creating a blurry buzz around her. She whizzed past the building with a sign that read 'The Euclidean Building' and many other lofty edifices that she had not seen before along the wide, busy street.

What was she doing? Where was she going? What if someone from Kello Lumpy's was following her? After all, she had just fled the scene of someone's death. Tabitha wished that she knew someone she could speak to, someone she could trust, in this demented district. How would she find this Professor Pagter? Would someone at the radio station know where to find him? No, she didn't want to go back there. If she went back, they'd either commit her to whatever this world's version of a mental institution was or, even worse, make her work.

A strange building commanded the view ahead of her, growing larger and larger as Tabitha approached it. The looming glass structure stood out from the other buildings. It was unlike anything she had ever seen before. To her surprise, the conveyor took her through a high archway and directly inside the building, which was home to four huge grey domes.

She stepped off the slow lane and tried to make sense of her surroundings. She was being bombarded by intense, vibrant lights of so many dazzling colours. Terrible, ear-splitting music that she recognised to be the dreadful warbled tones of Mistress Halo resonated through her skull. The song was punctuated by an extra-loud, unnecessarily long note that grated in Tabitha's ears. She was surprised that the glass dome around her didn't shatter into a million pieces. *Wherever I am,* she thought, *these people have the most awful taste in music.* The song was followed by an overly cheery disc jockey, who gushed compliments about the artist who had asked, *where the seahorses had gone?* for at least the second time that evening. He then went on to announce, rather smugly, "Goooooood evening, Obscurous! This is Elliot Earl, broadcasting for your listening pleasure." Tabitha physically cringed. Is that how Herman Munster had expected her to address her listeners? Like some fake, deranged being, high on caffeine or – what was it – souprano? Tabitha knew that she could never be like that no matter how hard she tried. She just wouldn't be able to keep it up. For the second time that day, she found herself wondering about the mentality of radio broadcasters.

So, if this wasn't a dream, was this all some kind of test? Is that why she was here? What was it that that woman had said about an experiment?

"Are you getting in or not?"

Tabitha was torn from her thoughts by a young man, whose arms were loaded with baggage.

"What?" she asked, distracted.

"The elesphere. Are you getting in?"

Tabitha looked at the four domes. She gasped as one of them suddenly dropped through a gap in the glass flooring that she hadn't known was there and plummeted towards the planet below. Its smooth and sudden decent made it seem as though it had been fired from a catapult. Another followed swiftly afterwards. And another.

"Where do they take you?" she asked, still looking down. Tabitha wanted to get as far away from Kello Lumpy's as possible.

The man fidgeted, hoisting a large bag further up his back. He looked confused, as though she had just asked him what colour the sun was. "They take you down to Hayfen Capital of course. Silly soul, you must have been in one before, or else how would you have got up here in the first place? Had a long day, have you?"

"You could say that." Tabitha looked up at the remaining grey dome that was waiting before them. Dozens of people were filing inside. "Is it quiet down there?"

"It's quieter than it is up here."

"That settles it." She stepped inside as another dreadful tune reverberated through the building. As more people piled into the dome, Tabitha was grateful that she had never been bothered by small spaces.

A disembodied voice filled the dome. *"Please stand clear of the doors. Please stand clear of the doors."* The large door closed seamlessly behind them. *"Descent commences in five seconds. Five, four, three, two, one. Have a pleasant trip."* A flash of yellow light filled the dome and a faint, pleasant hum surrounded the passengers. *"Please mind the gap between the elesphere and the platform. Please mind the gap."*

Tabitha and the other passengers spilled out of the elesphere into the centre of another glass building. *Have we even moved?* she pondered. But this glass building was markedly quieter and dimmer, the atmosphere less oppressive. She could hear herself think again. Where did the young man say they were travelling to? Hayfen Capital? Was it anything like where she had just come from? Would she be able to track down Professor Pagter? Perhaps she should have asked someone in the other glass building. There might have been an information kiosk of sorts. Maybe there was one here!

Her stomach feeling as though she had just been through the spin cycle, Tabitha followed the throngs through a set of turnstiles into the what looked like the main area of the hub. Being careful not to inadvertently step onto another conveyor and be whisked unwittingly out of the building, she trotted away from the domes in search of a kiosk, a desk, *anything*. She looked around, not seeing any signs of help. She decided that she would need to ask someone for information about where she could get information. She stood in the middle of the vast room addressing passers-by, "Excuse me–", before they passed by. On her fourth attempt, someone stopped. A woman dressed in a burgundy skinsuit whirled around to face her. Tabitha's breath caught in her chest. For a fleeting moment, she had thought that it was Mumma Toille. But the woman had less conspicuous hair than the dead woman she had left at Kello Lumpy's, and markedly fewer wrinkles.

"Can I help you, soul?"

"I'm...I'm looking for the information desk."

"The..." The woman, whose voice was low and soft, looked puzzled.

"The information desk. Is there one of those big desks with an 'I' above it? Or something similar?" Tabitha asked, hopefully.

"Oh, you want the ArrRobot."

"The R... "

"Over there, soul." The woman pointed a painted fingernail past Tabitha's shoulder. Tabitha turned around and peered through the crowds. On tiptoe in her towering heels, she still couldn't see anything resembling a desk. After a moment, she noticed a shining white, metallic globule that was moving towards her and appeared to be changing its form just for the fun of it. By the time it reached Tabitha, the woman had gone, and the shape-changing lump of metal was in the rough shape of a man. It had even gone to the trouble of forming itself metallic clothes, including a buccaneer hat of sorts, which was balanced rather precariously on its 'head'. Tabitha could not help but stare. And, not for the first time that day, she wondered where exactly she was. Where on Earth would have such a thing? To her knowledge, not even Japan possessed such advanced technology as a shape-shifting mechanoid.

"Arr," said a metallic voice in a comedic pirate accent that resonated from the robot's unmoving mouth. "How can I help ye?"

"Er, hello," said Tabitha. She looked around her, a little abashed, but no one around her seemed to be fazed by the machine. They barely acknowledged its existence.

"Do you have a question *aye* can help thee with?"

"I have more questions than you could ever imagine!" Tabitha blurted out. "Firstly, what accent is that supposed to be?"

After a few moments, the robot replied, "Your accent be Old Middle England, homeworld."

"Old Middle England? Homeworld? Er… What I actually meant was *your* accent, but..." Tabitha thought for a moment. Hadn't Mumma Toille mentioned something about Old England and a homeworld? She closed her eyes for a moment. Mumma Toile. Tabitha gulped as she wondered what had happened following the incident. Feeling guilty, she looked around the station. What if she was spotted by the police here? She admonished herself for being so paranoid and re-focussed her attention on the Robot. Tabitha cleared her throat and began again, addressing the robot in what she felt to be the most methodical fashion.

"OK… Where is the homeworld?"

"Aye, the homeworld be thee third planet from the sun known as *Sol*," came the jolly reply. Tabitha digested ArrRobot's words.

"The third planet from Sol is Earth."

"Earth is thee original English name, arr."

"Do you have to keep doing that?" she asked, a little irritated.

"Arr. I am ArrRobot."

"*Arr*Robot? Oh, I see!" Tabitha giggled for the first time that day. "Your programmers must have had a sense of humour."

"Question not be recognised."

"What? Oh, OK. Then my next question is, if I'm not actually dreaming and if this isn't the Earth, then where are we?"

"This be Hayfen IV."

"I've heard that name before. Is that the name of his area?"

"This area be Hayfen Capital."

"I see. So, Hayfen Capital is the name of this city, but this planet is..." Tabitha gulped as it finally dawned on her. "This *planet* is Hayfen IV?"

"Arr."

"And where is Hayfen IV?"

"It be in the Obscurous galaxy."

"Right. I've never heard of it. I must be a very long way from home. So, what happened to the Earth?"

"It be uninhabitable for the past four hundred year."

Her mind wasn't quite willing to digest the responses. She was still unsure whether any of this was real. Her brain would not let her believe it, yet she craved answers.

"Uninhabitable?" Tabitha reiterated the robot's words. "Why?"

"Accessing databanks. War, famine, greed, long-term damage to thee environment. What other reasons ye be wanting?"

"I suppose it was inevitable. We don't exactly treat the planet with the care it deserves – *deserved* – despite knowing what we were doing to it. But I can't believe it's really gone." She looked away, her eyes glazing over. She turned back to the robot. It was metallic, unmoving, indifferent to her plight. "Then what happened?"

"Project Borrowed Time happened, young maiden. Arr."

"Can you explain Project Borrowed Time?" The words felt numb on her lips. She could not process the fact that the Earth was no more.

"Aye. Ye Earthborns knew that they be living on borrowed time since the year 2000. So, they be building a vast ship to transport themselves to a new planet. Thee greatest scientists, artists, workmen, a great assortment of Earthborns, were chosen to inhabit the nearest Earth-like planet."

"Hayfen IV."

"That be correct."

"But I've never heard of it. The nearest Earth-like planet is at least twelve lightyears away and travelling at the speed of light be impossible. I mean, *is* impossible."

"Do ye have any further questions?"

"Oh yes, many more. Overlooking the ugly fact, for now, that so many people got left behind, I want to know how the first settlers got to Hayfen IV. And how did *I* get here?"

"Accessing databanks." After a brief pause and a soft whirr, the robot explained. "A wormhole linking the Milky Way and the previously undiscovered Obscurous galaxy be first observed in the year 2030. Obscurous was masked completely by Triangulum, therefore it be entirely unnoticed until then. So, the galaxy was thusly named. Probes be sent through the wormhole to Obscurous to explore the galaxy and locate a habitable planet. Hayfen IV be but two lightyears away from thee wormhole."

"It's hard to believe that an entire galaxy was masked by another. That's pretty incredible. And discovering an Earth-like planet is some accomplishment!" Tabitha could not help but be impressed.

"Will that be all?" ArrRobot's metallic hand rose to the hat-shaped metal form, lifted it off its 'head' and offered Tabitha a small bow.

"No!" Tabitha held up her hand in protest. She had so much more to ask. "What about my other question? How did *I* get here? What year is it?"

"It be the year 2418."

"Really? If that's true, then how did I travel here from 2018?" The reality of the situation was beginning to seep into her consciousness. "Will I even be able to get home?" She gulped.

"I be a transport hub bot. My databanks do not have that information. Only transport and tourist information cognition. Arr." Tabitha's shoulders dropped. "Are ye wishing to use the elespheres today?"

"Been there, done that. Look, where can I find out about time travel?"

"There be nothing in my databanks referring to such a mode of travel."

"Doesn't time travel come under the umbrella of transportation?"

"Excuse me, are you going to be much longer?" a stern-faced woman barked over her shoulder. "I need to get to the other side of the city and I'd like to get there before the second sun rises!" she said, her voice wet with sarcasm. "The ArrRobot is for the use of everyone. It's not your personal computer for you to go around asking daft questions. *What year is it, indeed!*"

"Just one more question." Tabitha gave the woman her most amicable smile. "Please."

The woman sighed and crossed her arms over her ample bosom. "Get on with it then," she huffed.

Tabitha turned back to the robot. "Maybe you can help me with this one. Where can I find a Professor Pagter?"

"Databanks be searching through nearest location for 'A Professor Pagter'." The soft whir emitting from the robot's belly was masked by the loud sigh of the stern-faced woman behind her. "Accessing databanks." The whirring seemed to speed up and slow down and then glitch a little. When the robot began to speak again, his enunciation was in an uncertain staccato. "Da... da... da...ta-node corrupt. Data-node corr... corrupt. Smoky Hole... hole..." The robot glitched and jumped oddly in front of her. "Professor Pagter in... Data-node corrupt... Arr... Smoky Hollow. Arr…"

"Smoky Hollow? How do I get there?"

"File corrupt. Arr…"

"Thanks a lot," said the snooty woman behind her. "You've gone and broken the thing now!" Tabitha ignored her. After a soft whir, the ArrRobot stood to attention, having apparently rebooted itself.

"I be a transport hub bot. My databanks do not hold that specific information. Only transport and tourist information cognition. Arr."

"Then what kind of transport shall I use to get there? How far away is Smoky Hollow?"

But the robot simply repeated, "I be a transport hub bot. My databanks do not have that information. Only transport and tourist information cognition. Arr."

"Arrrrrse!" Tabitha said with a growl. She felt like kicking the tin pirate.

"Are ye wishing to use the elespheres today?" it asked again, cheerily.

Tabitha screamed with frustration. The stern-faced woman gasped. She felt like kicking her as well.

"Good luck with it," she said to her. "It seems be malfunctioning."

Tabitha walked away, feeling more confused than ever.

How do I get to Smoky Hollow? Tabitha asked herself. *I don't know how to get out of this strange domed building, let alone get to somewhere I've never heard of.* She gazed up at the interior of the large, glass building and around the bustling transportation hub. Who were all these people going about their daily lives around her? People who were not yet born, as far as she was concerned. So many emotions collided within her. She felt angry that this civilisation had left people to die back on Earth, potentially her descendants. But she also admired the way in which the human race had insisted on continuing and setting up such a spectacular settlement. They may have been their own downfall, but the determination evident around her was nothing less than impressive. She also felt curious. Had they worked out a system to work in harmony with nature rather than destroy it? Had they worked out how to live in harmony with themselves and not destroy each other? Was there a governing body? Was what she saw around her a resounding success? Or was the human race on another inevitable track to destruction?

Don't let your thoughts get in such a tangle, Tabitha admonished herself, as she often did. *One can't learn four hundred years of history of a civilisation in five minutes. Your priority is to get home. You need to find Smoky Hollow. But first of all, you need to determine your whereabouts.*

Tabitha found the nearest conveyor and stepped onto the slow lane behind a man whose large body seemed to be putting rather a strain on the seams of his navy-blue skinsuit. The conveyor trailed out of the building and Tabitha emerged into Hayfen Capital for the first time. As she travelled, she looked around, hoping to see some kind of helpfully placed road sign. They seemed to be somewhat lacking, and her vision was instead loaded with a superfluous amount of less helpful signs and advertisements. The street was adorned with bright, colourful holograms promoting places and products she had never heard of. Teetering tower blocks, interspersed with various commercial outlets, flanked the conveyor. Tabitha remained in the slow lane. There was so much to see that she was afraid she might miss something. Everything was so foreign to her, so *alien*. She was on an alien planet in an alien galaxy surrounded by the descendants of the human race that she had known. The enormity of the situation was alarming.

The conveyor stopped suddenly. Tabitha's breath caught in her throat as she saw a gigantic swell of people drop to the floor, helplessly crushing one another in the process. She let out a scream. Before she could try to leap out of the way, the plump gentleman in front of Tabitha came tumbling down on top of her.

She slowly opened her eyes. Among the unfamiliar patterns of stars, she noticed a curious shape. It looked to her like a ribbon suspended in space. How far away it was, she could not tell. The twisted ribbon was trimmed with strips of lights either side of its width. *The Möbius Strip!* Tabitha thought. She blacked out again.

Belisha

Belisha was so happy to hear another person call her by her actual name that she almost kissed the tall stranger standing in the doorway. She tried to retain her usual decorum and simply offer a half smile, but before she could stop herself, she blurted,

"Please say that again!"

"Let me inside. It's important," he said bluntly.

"No, the other bit. My name."

"Belisha, I really can't risk standing here much longer." A full-blown smile now blossoming across her face at the sound of her name, Belisha let the stranger inside and closed the door behind him. "I believe the custom here is to offer a hot beverage when someone enters your home. I wonder…I don't suppose you have any souprano?"

"Firstly, this isn't my home. Secondly, if it's anything like the other dwelling places here, it's unlikely that the cupboards contain anything as luxurious as souprano. And thirdly, just give me some answers!"

"Calm down, soul. It seems as though you're in need of a jug of souprano even more than I am. Now, let's sit down at least."

Belisha led the tall stranger into the main living space. Although, on reflection, he didn't seem to be as much of a stranger as she had first thought. He knew her name and his accent and diction were familiar. In fact, he was the first sign of normality she had encountered since she had woken up in the building of bottles. She pushed a stack of magazines to one side and sat down on the sunken sofa as he made himself comfortable in a worn armchair opposite her. She stared at the man, wide eyed, willing the information to spout out of him.

"You are not Tabitha Turner, but are, in fact, Belisha Beacon. Is that correct?" he asked.

"Yes. But how did you know?" The stranger did not respond, so she asked, "What am I doing here?"

"You are not here. Only your mind is here."

"Where *is* here, anyway?"

"Belisha, you are on the homeworld, planet Earth, in the year 2018."

"I've... I've... I've gone back in time? Back to the... ugh!" Feeling altogether reviled, Belisha jumped up from the tatty sofa as though it had transformed into a pile of dog mess. She looked around her, rubbing her hands against each other as if to try to claw her way out of her own skin. Not quite knowing where to put herself, Belisha looked back at the tall stranger. "But the homeworld was doomed... it perished! It's... it's *unclean*. It's unfit for human habitation."

"Not for several hundred years from now. Although it is well on its way." The tall stranger looked around, his Adam's apple visibly rising and falling as he gulped. But he didn't get up from the armchair.

"So, what am I doing here? I'm in this awful place when I should be at work at the station."

"Oh, Belisha, such dedication to your role at Möbius Strip Airwaves. You are a celebrated individual, but the Euclidean Building won't fall down without you. In fact, it hasn't even been built yet, so you're not technically missing work at all, right this moment. Except..."

"Except what?" Belisha's throat was dry, her palms clammy.

"Except that someone will be in your place – *is* in your place."

Belisha gasped. "*Who is in my place?*"

"Tabitha Turner."

"*Tabitha?* This Tabby person that everyone here seems to think I am?" The tall stranger nodded grimly. "But why? Who *are* you?"

The stranger ignored the latter question, leaned back in the armchair and offered with an air of nonchalance, "It's all part of the Experiment."

"What experiment? Why is there a backwards Earthborn doing my job?"

"Ah."

"Ah?"

"Well, I understand that Miss Turner wasn't doing the greatest job at the radio station. I believe that she has, in fact, walked out." He leaned forward and gulped a second time.

Belisha clasped her head in her hands, grabbing the matted hair between her fingers, and began to pace the room. Tears of anger were welling up behind her eyes. "Tell me this isn't happening, or *won't* be happening, or... argh! How can we stop this? How can I get back? Did you... did *you* put me here?" She pointed an accusatory finger at the man whose name she still did not know.

"Belisha, I need to know whether you gave any consent prior to your new situation."

"What? Of course not. I didn't consent to anything!"

The man's face fell.

"Look, please tell me what is going on. What is your part in all of this? How did you get here? If you travelled here from Hayfen IV, then you can take me back with you!" A glimmer of hope germinated in her mind. She looked at the man pleadingly. Her eyes pleaded with the man, who's expression was now one of pity. Belisha was not used to people looking at her in this way. She was used to people looking at her with expressions of awe and envy. What was happening to her?

"It's not as simple as that. Once they know I'm here, they'll be after me."

"So, what do I do?"

"Play the game."

"What game?"

"Go to work, socialise, make Tabitha's life worthwhile."

"But that's... that's impossible. Have you *seen* the state of this house? Her friend is insane, and her doctor is even worse. There's no sense of style and the pavements are made of concrete. *Concrete!* The most unmoveable material ever invented! Nothing makes any sense here."

"Play the game, Belisha. It's the only way."

"And?"

"And..." A short gasp escaped the stranger as he turned his head quickly towards the window. He swiftly stood up.

"And then what?" Belisha begged.

Without warning, the man ran out of the room, threw open the front door and was gone.

Belisha ran out into the hall after him, but all that remained was the lingering aroma of stale souprano. She wanted to run down the street and call after him, but she didn't even know his name. What had scared him? Where had he gone?

Part of her wanted to run, but Belisha was not used to high levels of activity and doubted that she would get as far as the end of the road. But she didn't want to stay in the Earthborn's dwelling either.

Oh Belisha, what a mess. She sighed. *So, they want me to play the game, huh? Whoever they are. If I can't find the tall stranger again, then I suppose that the only way out of here is to play along. Right. Then let's start at the beginning.*

Belisha ensured that she had the metal tool that Ellie had used to open the door about her person before she marched out of the house and down Cottonwood Close. She turned this way and that on her way through the neighbourhood, trying to retrace the steps she had been forced to take earlier that day by Tabitha's over-zealous friend.

"Hey, you!" came a sudden shout. "Yesh, you!" The voice possessed the volume and quality of someone who was more than a little intoxicated.

Belisha turned to see a group of girls swaggering towards her.

"Turns out me brother did 'ave some weed in after all, and he let us 'ave some of his voddy, so we are all sorted. Thanks for the cash, though. Might come in 'andy for some fags later." She gave a wicked and croaky laugh, apparently amused by her own words.

"Are you talking to me?" Belisha touched a hand lightly to her chest. She wanted to tell the drunkard in the shabby pink velour costume that she didn't have any idea who she was, but then she realised that people here believed her to be Tabitha. She wrinkled her nose. *Surely Tabitha wouldn't have considered even this rabble of inebriates as friends. If only I could understand this woman's diction. Voddy? Fags? Cash? What?* Before she could think of a retort, another girl, whose belly was plainly swollen with an infant, spoke.

"Knew ya didn't have the guts to call the Old Bill."

"Who?"

"The police, ya dumb tart. The emergency..." she paused to belch, "...servishes."

"Why should I want to call them?" Belisha crossed her arms over her chest, defiantly, eyeing up each member of the tipsy trio. "Yes, thachs right," slurred a girl with greasy blonde hair which was dark at the roots. Belisha glared at the unnecessarily large pieces of metal which seemed to have pierced the lobes of her ears. Her stance was unstable as she pointed a wobbly finger at Belisha. "You jusht remember that. No need to call the Old Bill. No need to tell anyone, 'coz there ain't nothing to tell, right?"

"Did you get your car back from the garage?" asked the first girl. "Because we wanna lift somewhere. Chantelle here is preggers, you see. She can't walk that far, and the bus never stopped."

"Car?" *Did Tabitha own one of those archaic vehicles?*

"If you ain't, then I reckon you should get it back and take us up town."

"How dare you speak to me this way?" Belisha blurted. *How dare they speak to Tabitha in that way?* She thought. *Tabitha seems like an odd character, but she doesn't deserve to be treated like this. Who are these delinquents?*

The three girls broke into peals of laughter, falling about themselves in merriment.

"Bloody 'ell. Who do you think you are? The bloody Queen?" the pregnant girl howled, tossing her dark hair over her shoulder.

"Look, I don't have a car and I don't have time for you. I have a job to do."

"Oh yeah? And what's that then, Queeny?"

"I have to..." Belisha pondered. She considered what the tall stranger had told her. Her task was to *play the game*. So, what was her next move? Was this level one of the game? "I have to put the likes of you in your place," she said finally.

"Ooh, and how are you gonna do that?" asked the girl in pink, a wicked gleam in her eye.

"What are you gonna do? Trying to get this back, are ya?" Belisha watched as the pregnant girl fished a plastic card out of her pocket and flashed it in front of her face. At first, she thought she saw an image of the dark-haired pregnant girl. But the facial features were different. They were more like her own. In horror, she realised that the card bore the name *Tabitha Turner*.

"That belongs to Tabitha!" she gasped.

"It *did* belong to you, ya mean, Queen Tabitha."

"I suggest you return it." Belisha made to grab it before the girl swiped it out of her reach.

"Mek me!"

"I tell ya what, if you manage to get the card off her, I'll give ya back the wallet and phone too. Jusht for fun," the girl in pink slurred.

"She'll *never* do it!" exclaimed the girl with the greasy hair and large earrings.

"I know!"

"I'll tell you what," said Belisha, narrowing her eyes. "Return *all* of the items and I'll allow all of you to walk away unharmed."

The group broke into laughter once more.

"Is that supposed to be a threat?" asked the pregnant girl, tears of mirth rolling down her cheeks.

Belisha nodded curtly. She had no intention of initiating any form of violent struggle, of course. She was not skilled in any methods of combat. She intended instead to employ her powers of cunning and wit.

"What made you steal those belongings in the first place?" Belisha asked the pregnant girl, as she was the first one to stop laughing.

"*I* never stole nothing. It was Keeley what took them. You saw her do it!"

"I did?" asked Belisha. "I *did!*"

"And you didn't stop me, did ya, Queeny? Just sat in the middle of the road and cried."

"Indeed." She said distantly. *How weak is this Tabitha person? Did she not even try to defend her possessions? Did the three of them simply overcome her and knock her to the ground?* She started to feel pity for the girl with whom she had swapped places. "But now I've come to get them back. Or I *will* call Bill."

The three of them looked at each other.

And then Chantelle, t-shirt stretched tightly over her swollen belly, suddenly cried out in pain.

"Aaaagh, bloody hell!"

"What is it, Chantelle?" asked the girl in the pink tracksuit, her face suddenly full of concern.

"I think he's bloody coming, Britney. I think the baby's here."

"Bloody 'ell, shall I call Lee?"

"Don't you dare call that prick!" spat Chantelle. She cried out again.

"He's the father!" cried Britney.

Chantelle recovered from her contraction before shouting, "I don't want him nowhere near baby Finlay!"

"Can I make a suggestion?" asked Belisha. "Let me call the Mergencies."

"The who? Sounds like some crap indie band you and your type listen to. You're not getting your phone back that easily!" Keeley shouted above Chantelle's screams.

"Look, I'm trying to help you. Stop this silliness and hand me the device."

"*I'll* do it," insisted Keeley, reaching into her pocket. She took out Tabitha's phone and dialled three digits.

"Aaagh!" Chantelle stumbled and fell to the ground, pulling Keeley down with her. She cried out again, sounding even more pained, and clutched her distended abdomen. As Keeley fell, Belisha plucked the phone from her hand and spoke into it.

"Is this the Mergencies? I need assistance right away for someone who is having a baby at..."

Belisha looked at Britney, who told her, "March Road."

"...March Road. A crime has also been committed."

Tabitha

Tabitha's mind tried to make sense of the shape. A long, transparent strip. It must have been twenty miles long, a quarter of a mile wide and ten feet thick. The twisted ribbon was populated by grey buildings, so many buildings, festooned in bright lights. A network of fast-moving belts threaded between the buildings, along the streets and connected with each other. The belts were moving faster.

To her horror, Tabitha saw that the ribbon itself was moving. The Möbius Strip was somehow winding around itself faster and faster. It was becoming entangled. She couldn't keep up with it. The see-through strip covered in its many buildings and hundreds of screaming people was beginning to wrap around her legs, pulling her down. It was winding its way through her fingers, tangling in her hair. It pushed down her throat, blocking her oesophagus, suffocating her.

"This is impossible," she choked.

"Belisha?" came an unfamiliar voice.

"Not Belisha!" Tabitha tried to call out. What was happening? She screwed up her eyes, trying to focus on something real. When she opened them, her eyelids were heavy, and her throat was dry. She was lying under a crisp, silvery, paper-thin bed sheet. Dark patches of sweat had soaked through the fabric. Her breathing was laboured.

"Belisha, you're awake!"

"Where am I?"

"You're in the infirmary. You were in a collision. But you're safe now." The unfamiliar voice was coming from an unfamiliar face.

"Was it all a dream?" Tabitha pushed herself up onto her elbows.

"Was what all a dream, soul?" the girl asked. She had a round face that was framed by an abundance of red curls, which had been fixed in place with so much product that they glistened in the bright lights of the infirmary.

"The conveyor, the radio show, the... the Möbius Strip!"

"Yes, all of those things are fine. Oranjer Bannawoo told me that Elliot is doing alright on his own at the station and there's no need to worry about the conveyor. You know how those things are. Dangerous things. And don't try and put the blame on me, soul. You know the conveyors aren't my department." The girl broke into a giggle that made her shoulders jiggle, but her hair did not move a millimetre. "Sorry for laughing, Belisha," she said seriously. "But I'm just so glad that my flatmate is OK."

"Flatmate? Belisha? So, none of it was a dream. I'm still here," said Tabitha sadly, letting herself fall back onto the sweat-soaked pillow.

"Of course you're still here!"

"I think you had better let your friend have some rest. She's obviously rather confused and disorientated. She needs to sleep." A man had entered the room and was busying himself with checking the monitors and various apparatus that surrounded the bed. There were three other beds, two of which were occupied by sleeping patients. The room reminded her of the hospitals where she had visited sick relatives: characterless and drab. It did not, however, seem to harbour the smell of bleach and sickness she usually associated with such places. Instead, she could smell flowers. She recognised the pungent, distinctive scent of lilies.

"Where are the flowers?" she asked, looking around the sparsely furnished room.

"Your flatmate rushed past all of the Mergencies to get here, thinking you were dead, and you ask her for flowers?" the man asked coldly, still fussing with the bedside instruments. "You're lucky to be alive, soul."

"I mean, I can *smell* flowers."

"It's the flower card I got you," said the red-haired girl. "Here." She reached across to the bedside table and handed Tabitha a thin sheet of glass that seemed to be folded in half. "It was only a cheap one from the infirmary shop, but I thought I'd programme one while I was waiting for you to come 'round."

Tabitha's touch brought the glass greeting card to life. The words *Get Well Soon* glowed on the cover in pink and green and as she opened it and the powerful scent wafted afresh from the glass. Before her eyes, the glowing words *from your friend Shan* appeared on the glass, glowing in front of her eyes, expanding and changing form into a soft, pillowy typeface.

"Thanks! I love it. Thank you, Shan," Tabitha said, utterly transfixed. She closed the card, turned it over and opened it again, breathing in the aroma once more.

"Don't overdo it, Belisha. It's only a cheap card, as I said. Anyway, the doctor said that I should let you get some sleep, so—"

"No!" Tabitha protested and hurriedly placed the folded glass back on the bedside table. "I've done enough sleeping. I want reality. Lord knows, all I want is a bit of reality. Stay. Please."

"OK," said Shan. She smiled and sat on the bed.

The doctor sighed and left the room.

"I don't think much of his bedside manner," whispered Tabitha.

"Me neither," Shan agreed. "I think the Mergencies are friendlier than he is. Look, Belisha, I'm glad that you're OK, but you don't seem yourself. I know it was a bad collision and that there were lots of people involved, but you actually sustained very few injuries. I didn't expect you to be…"

"To be what?" Tabitha asked.

"Well, the real Belisha would have been out of bed by now, demanding to go back to work, or home, at least. She wouldn't have whispered behind the doctor's back; she would have said it to his face. You seem different somehow. What's going on?"

"That's the problem, Shan. I really don't know." Tabitha sighed. Should she tell Shan that Belisha was not actually here? Should she tell her that she was an unwilling time traveller and that nothing here made sense to her? Or by doing so would she risk remaining in the infirmary for good? Perhaps she would be moved to the kind of infirmary that dealt with patients who had mental health problems. If no one believed her, she would look insane. She had to know how much she looked like Belisha. Was she a doppelgänger, or had the two girls simply had their psyches swapped? "How do I look?" she finally asked.

"Now, *that's* the Belisha I know!" Shan laughed raucously and patted the silver bed sheet. "Well, I have to be honest. I am your best friend and everything." She paused. "You *have* looked better."

"Right," said Tabitha. That wasn't quite what she had meant. "But do I look like Belisha?"

"Not as the world knows you, soul. If you walked down the Strip looking how you do now, then no one would recognise who you were. It would be the ultimate disguise."

"So, it *was* a bad collision. My face was damaged beyond all recognition?" Tabitha touched a hand to her cheek.

"No, of course not. I would have told you by now if it had been. And besides, the doctor would have corrected it if that had happened. What I mean is that without your hair all perfect and your face naked without any make-up on, you just don't look like… you."

"But I don't look like… anyone else?"

"What do you mean?"

"As far as you can tell, you know that I'm Belisha."

"What is all this about, soul?" Shan asked. "You're not making a lot of sense."

"I'm sorry. I'll be alright in a minute," she lied.

"You're not going to be going off to the station, are you?"

"No, I'm not going back there." Then she added, "At least, not tonight."

"Well, if you're feeling better then you can come home with me now if you like."

"It sounds better than being in here. And it's not as though I'm in any pain."

"Of course not. Your pain suppressor is on maximum," Shan said, pointing to a square patch that was attached to the flesh above Tabitha's elbow. An indentation in the centre was flashing red.

"Can I keep this on?"

"You really are in another world today aren't you, soul? I'll ask the doctor for a stack of them while you get dressed. I'll promise him that you're going home for plenty of bed rest, but, knowing you, I suppose that that's unlikely to be the case."

"You know your flatmate so well," said Tabitha, accepting a fresh set of Belisha's clothes from her.

"I certainly do, soul."

While Shan went to find the doctor, Tabitha changed into another skinsuit. This one was made from a shimmery white material and came with another chunky belt, which she reluctantly clasped around her thick waist under her generous bosom. Tabitha didn't understand. Belisha's body was curvy like hers, yet she wore clothes that hugged every lump and bump. She also seemed to be an overly confident extrovert who didn't mind voicing her opinions. *She's the opposite of me,* Tabitha thought. *Instead of hiding all the things about her that she doesn't like, she celebrates them. And people seem to respect her for it. This is the most alien concept I have encountered yet. I wonder what else I can learn from this woman.*

Tabitha emerged from the infirmary room. She found Shan waiting for her at the exit at the end of the corridor. Shan held up a fistful of pain suppressors and grinned.

"Come on, you scruffy soul, let's go."

"Scruffy?" Tabitha gasped.

"Don't worry, you can jump straight into the hygiene cubical as soon as we get back and you'll soon be back to the old Belisha."

"I'm not sure about that," Tabitha mumbled to herself.

She nodded despite herself and followed Shan out of the building, where they were confronted with another network of conveyors. Tabitha's stomach lurched.

"Do we have to use the conveyors? Can't we just walk?"

Shan burst into laughter and lay a hand on her shoulder. "You are funny, Belisha. Look, I know you had a bad experience, but you're fine. You can't avoid them forever, can you?"

"Evidently not." Tabitha reluctantly stepped onto the slow lane behind Shan. She wished that Belisha's friend had brought her a pair of flat shoes to wear along with the clean outfit, but then supposed that maybe Belisha didn't actually own any comfortable shoes.

Tabitha had no recollection of any of the sights they passed. There were many buildings, but, unlike the Möbius Strip, with its two banks of high-rise structures flanking the conveyor, Hayfen IV seemed to have the qualities of a sprawling city. The district they were passing through lacked the sensory assault of cooking food, bright lights and Mistress Halo warbling *Where Have All the Seahorses Gone?*. It had a more suburban quality.

Tabitha realised that they were passing through neighbourhood after neighbourhood. The first had consisted of grey, compact, box-like buildings. Tabitha thought that the architect who designed them either didn't deem these cheaper homes worthy of an interesting design or was having an off day. The next cluster of homes consisted of markedly more luxurious apartments. Although the three-storey buildings still had the same grey, drab exterior as the boxy houses, it was plain to see that more love had gone into their design and build. Ornamental plants had even been placed in front of most of the buildings. Tabitha was admiring a particularly interesting garden sculpture when she felt Shan grab her hand and pull her off the conveyor.

"Have you forgotten where you live now?"

"I, er, of course not!" Tabitha fumbled. She followed Shan fifty yards or so to one of the apartment buildings and watched as she pressed her thumb to the door of the ground-floor apartment. As the door slid open, Shan lifted her fists to her collarbone and extended her elbows in front of her.

"Welcome home!" she declared. Tabitha eyed the protruding elbows and gave Shan a puzzled look. She seemed to be waiting for something. Was this some kind of greeting? She chose to offer a brief smile and entered the building, leaving Shan standing in her bizarre stance for a moment or two longer before she seemed to give up and followed Tabitha inside.

So, this was where Belisha lived. Tabitha couldn't wait to have a look inside. She didn't know what she was expecting, but she was surprised by the scene before her. It was luxurious, but soulless. It seemed to contain every amenity that anyone could desire: a small, but neat, kitchenette; a large settee, swathed in the same dreadful silvery material she had encountered in the infirmary, opposite a screen that filled an entire wall; and a comfortable, temperate climate. Everything was spotlessly clean. Tabitha suspected that all the other apartments had exactly the same furniture in exactly the same configuration. There wasn't a hint of personality about the place. *Perhaps this is what becomes of us,* she thought. *We all conform to the same way of living. Although, this does appear to be a comfortable home.*

"Do you want to go in the hygiene cubical first?" asked Shan, flopping down onto the large settee. "I'll go in after you."

"Er, sure." Tabitha approached the only interior door, which slid open in front of her. On her left, she saw a set of bunk beds against the wall. The bedding on both bunks was crumpled and there were two sets of night clothes on the floor. *I'm glad to see that they're not entirely perfect!* She smiled to herself. *Now, where is this hygiene whatsit?*

"Oh!" she exclaimed as another door opened beside her. Inside was a windowless, metallic box with the same cobalt blue floor as the rest of the apartment. It wasn't dark inside, although Tabitha couldn't locate the light-source. This was it. She disrobed and stepped gingerly into the small room.

She looked around for a button, a dial, anything. But the walls were smooth save for a few shimmering holes set into the ceiling. She gasped as the hairs on her arms began to tingle. The lights in the cubicle began to throb gently through a rainbow of colours. Then the ultimate feeling of freshness enveloped her. She smiled, lost in the moment of pure cleanliness, warmth and comfort. Yet there was no water. Her body felt dry but moisturised and every single pore felt cleaner than it had ever felt before.

Tabitha gasped again as her dark locks seemed to move all by themselves about her face. She instinctively lifted her hands to touch her hair. It felt softer than it had ever done before. The softness was short-lived, however, for the machine seemed to be styling her hair, setting it in place until it became stiff like Shan's. She wanted to protest, to enjoy having luscious curls for the first time in her life, but she knew no way of stopping it.

Just when she thought it was over, Tabitha felt the skin on her face being manipulated. It was not an unpleasant experience. Her cheeks were being lightly pummelled by an invisible force and a light fragrance filled the air. When she blinked, her long lashes were in her vision. Her complexion and lips felt slightly sticky with make-up and her face felt slightly taught.

A moment later, the lighting stabilised to a pale yellow and the activity ceased. Tabitha felt so rejuvenated that she almost wanted to activate the procedure again. But the door slid open for her to exit and she stepped out.

"That's better!" Shan exclaimed, examining her face. "That's the Belisha I know."

Tabitha gasped and reached for the bed sheet from the lower bunk, which she swiftly wrapped around her naked body.

"Hey, use your own sheet if you're suddenly going to go all shy, soul!"

"Sorry," mumbled Tabitha. She saw that Shan had no qualms about getting undressed in front of her before stepping into the hygiene cubicle herself.

Tabitha explored Belisha's living space while she had a moment to herself. The cupboards were filled with unremarkable packets and boxes of unremarkable food. Then she spied the souprano machine.

I wonder how this works, she pondered. Curiosity got the better of her and she set about pressing various buttons until the machine began to pour a dark orange liquid onto the pristine work surface. In a fit of panic, she opened the only cupboard she had not yet opened, where she found a plethora of containers. She grabbed the one nearest to her and placed it underneath the machine's steaming nozzle. As the liquid began to fill the cup, she searched frantically for something to clean up the mess she had made. But she found nothing suitable to hand.

Tabitha rushed into the bunk room and grabbed Belisha's bed sheet, which she then used to mop up the dark liquid. Why didn't they have any towels in this place? The kitchenette surfaces were pristine once more, but she was now stuck with a pile of filthy, dripping bedding.

It looks like I've murdered someone! Tabitha thought. She gulped as she inspected the soiled sheet. Highly flustered, she dashed back into the bunk room and pushed the sheet under the bed as far as it would go. She tried to justify it to herself. *Well, if there is nothing as basic as a washing machine, what else am I meant to do?*

Tabitha turned her attention back to the souprano machine, which had by stopped spewing into the cup. She realised that it was more of a bowl than a cup. She decided that it didn't matter and took a long sip. No wonder they drank so much of this stuff. It was as though a waterfall of calm was cascading over the furnace of anxiety that had inhabited her mind for so long. For what felt like the first time in her life, Tabitha's jumble of thoughts was finally settling down and simply resting in the back of her mind. The corners of her mouth turned up in contentment. Not just contentment – blissfulness.

She picked up the container again, and before she knew it the bowl was empty and she was lying on the silvery settee, lost in a daze of tranquillity.

"I can't believe you whacked the souprano machine up to maximum, Belisha. You drank a whole crashing bowlful of the stuff!" Each one of Shan's syllables fell like a thousand tiny hammers inside Tabitha's ears. Through dazed eyes she tried to make sense of the scene before her. Belisha's flatmate looked absolutely appalled. "Especially with such a high dosage of pain suppressant. Honestly, soul, I don't know what's happening to you, but you're starting to scare me!"

"I'm sorry. I didn't think," Tabitha managed.

"Did you press every button on the machine or something? I don't know why you didn't buy one of those old-fashioned bathtubs and fill it with the stuff and have done with it!"

"I'm sorry, I suppose I finished the cup. It just felt so…calming."

"And how do you feel now?" Shan planted her hands on her hips, adopting the stance of a cross mother. Tabitha shrank into herself. She had the impression that Shan was about to ground her.

"I feel as though I don't know where any of my thoughts are. It's as though I have to find them all before I feel normal again." Tabitha rubbed her forehead and screwed up her eyes. The pain was unbearable.

"Worse than I thought." Shan shook her head.

"Why do we even *have* that machine?" Tabitha shot the device in question an angry look from her spot on the settee.

"It comes as standard, as you know. But you should have known better than to abuse it. Especially as–"

"–I have the pain suppressor, yes. Which doesn't seem to be working, by the way," Tabitha interrupted.

"I'm not surprised. I think you overloaded it, soul." Shan's face softened and she sat down on the settee, placing a hand on Tabitha's knee. "I think the only way to get the old you back is–"

"–is for me to get lots of sleep." Tabitha interrupted again, stifling a yawn.

"Is for you to *go back to work*. You know you're at your best at work."

"I am?" Tabitha found the idea so amusing that she momentarily forgot about the pain.

"Lounging around here in a souprano coma is not the way to go. It's not like you."

"You're right about that," agreed Tabitha.

"I suggest you slap on a fresh pain suppressor and off you go."

"OK, I'll give it a go." Tabitha sighed. "If you'll come with me," she added, thinking quickly. "Just to the transportation hub. I'll be fine from there. What time is it?"

"It's early evening, nearly time for your next shift. I missed an entire day at the office for you."

"I'm sorry." Tabitha did not know what to say. She wanted to ask Shan more about herself. She wanted to find out what she actually did at the office where she worked, but she knew how odd the question would seem coming from Belisha's lips.

"Never mind, soul. These things happen. At least we're finally getting to spend some time together."

Although her pain was being suppressed once more, Tabitha's nerves were getting the better of her as she followed Shan along the dreaded conveyors on her commute to the radio station. How she wished that she could simply get in her familiar old Fiesta and drive there. Or, better still, drive home. Her thoughts were slowly finding her, and, a little at a time, things were becoming clear again.

As they made their way into Hayfen Capital's transportation hub, Tabitha caught sight of the familiar ArrRobot, which triggered her memory. "Shan," she said. "Have you ever heard of a place called Smoky Hollow?"

Shan frowned. "No, I've never heard of that one. Why?"

"Never mind."

By the time she arrived on the Möbius Strip, most of her memories were back in place. Her usual thoughts had returned, and her lamentations were as wild as ever. She tried to put her thoughts about her appearance to the back of her mind. It wasn't *her* body; it didn't matter. She had to concentrate on the issue at hand. She had to reach Smoky Hollow. She had to find Professor Pagter.

The image of Mumma Toille flashed through her mind. One minute full of anger and bile and the next, gone. Was whoever had done that after her too? Or were they on her side? Either way, she was frightened. She wondered whether anyone at the radio station could help her.

The last thing I want to do is to pretend to know what I'm doing on some alien radio show, she thought. *Or shall I play the game? Just until I know what's really going on here?*

Belisha

"All right, you can have your sodding stuff back," shrieked Keeley, her earrings swinging from side to side absurdly. Belisha almost expected a tiny trapeze artist to leap through them. Keeley hurled Tabitha's belongings at Belisha, her attention leaving her suffering, pregnant friend. "Just cancel that police car. We don't want no trouble."

"I don't wish for any trouble either," stated Belisha.

"Just cancel it!" Keeley shrieked. Belisha did not know how to contact the emergency services herself and did not quite trust the girl, so she deftly made a fake call and pretended to explain to someone on the other end of the line that the matter had been settled.

"Sorted?" Keeley snarled. Belisha nodded.

"The operator on the other end of the line was not in the least bit happy and gave me a lecture about wasting resources, but you have nothing to worry about," she lied.

"Right."

Chantelle's screams were louder than ever as she clawed at the gravel, begging for pain relief. "Gimme drugs! Anyfink to take this pain away!" she cried and let a dozen swear words out into the air. Belisha made a silent vow never to get pregnant.

"Do you want us to come with ya when the ambulance comes?" asked Britney.

Chantelle turned and called back, "Yeah, if you bring some fags!"

"I'm sure they'll give you some of that gas and a load of drugs if you ask 'em to, Chantelle," said Keeley. "Ask for as much of the good stuff as you can. I did when I had my Aisha!"

"Aargh!" A barrage of filthy language sprouted from Chantelle's lips as she clutched her stomach.

"I hope they hurry up," said Britney.

Belisha watched open-mouthed as the motley crew piled into the back of the ambulance, not one word of thanks between them. She hoped that the baby was born with no complications and that all would be well, but she dreaded to think what kind of a life the poor child might have surrounded by such damaging influences. She hoped that maybe Chantelle would grow up and the girls would turn away from their lives of crime and the plants and fags of which they spoke. Maybe. Or maybe not. At least she had helped Tabitha.

She was a hundred metres or so away when a second vehicle rounded on the ambulance and two uniformed men got out. One of them took out a notepad and appeared to be questioning the startled Keeley and Britney.

The phone in Belisha's hand began to buzz. Belisha pressed the flashing green button.

"Hello?"

"Is that Miss Turner?" a male voice asked. He had a lilting, foreign accent that she could not place.

"Who?"

"Tabitha Turner?"

"Oh, er, can I help you?"

"It's Connor here from O'Reilly's Garage. Your car is ready to collect after its interim service, Miss Turner. Technically, it should ha' been ready a lot sooner, but we found some issues with the brakes. It looks like we discovered the' problem just in time, Miss Turner, as I never would ha' forgiven myself if you had driven away and something ha' happened, no I wouldn't. Pat may take his time over his work, but he *is* thorough, I'll say that for the lad."

"I see. And is this going to cost more?"

"I tell ye what, I'll do you a deal, so I will. I'll knock off the price of the' labour on fitting the new brake cable and you can jus' pay for the parts. I'll send you an invoice tomorrow. I ca' be doing with worrying about it now. I want to shut up shop and get to the pub. How does that sound, Miss Tuner?"

"That sounds reasonable," said Belisha. "Can you remind me of the address of the garage?"

An hour later, Belisha confidently climbed into the red Ford Fiesta and tried to work out how to move the two-tonne lump of metal.

She had seen holographic historical footage of similar vehicles. *She pondered, I think I have to start it by turning a key and then there's something to do with a gear stick and those pedals down there. I'm sure I can work it out.*

Belisha kangarooed the car out of the mechanic's narrow and frankly car-unfriendly driveway onto the main road. No sooner had she begun to travel down the street than the drivers of other cars began to beep and parp at her. *Is this some kind of fellow driver greeting?* She wondered and happily responded by locating and hitting the horn button.

Tabitha's phone started to buzz again. Belisha reached over and answered it.

"Thank God you're OK!" It was Ellie. "Didn't you see the note?"

"What note?"

"The one asking you to call me when you woke up. And you have your mobile phone back! How did you get it back?"

Belisha swerved, narrowly missing a cyclist, and almost dropped the phone as she grappled with the steering wheel.

"Look, I can't really speak at the moment. I'm driving."

"You got your car back too? That's great! How are you feeling?"

Didn't the stupid girl hear what she said? Operating one antiquated piece of machinery was difficult enough, but two was nigh on impossible, especially with all the dreadful drivers on the road. As the traffic swarmed around her, the tall stranger's voice reverberated in her mind. *Play the game.*

The way ahead was finally clear as she steered into Cottonwood Close and her thoughts became clearer.

"Where do I work?"

"What?"

"Where do I work, Ellie?"

"Have you forgotten that too, Tabs? Don't worry about work; your boss doesn't know what she's talking about. Take it easy until you're completely better, which you obviously aren't if you can't even remember where the place is!"

"Is there an address somewhere?"

"Um, I suppose that the address would still be in your satnav under Miss Ree Loves Co. from when you went to the interview, if you need it that badly. But–"

"Ellie," Belisha interrupted her, "Soon, you won't have to spend so much time worrying about your friend Tabby. Soon, Tabby will be able to look after herself." She pulled the car to the side of the road and started rummaging through the glove compartment through a pile of crisp packets and dusty, scratched compact discs. She eventually came across a device with the words *Roadguru Satnav* printed above a small screen. She grinned as it illuminated into life at her touch.

"You're making out that you're some kind of burden," said Ellie. "You're not. You're my *friend*. Friends look out for each other."

"Well, in that case, you're doing a very good job. Now stop worrying and let me get to work."

A tinkle of laughter came from the other end of the line.

"It's usually me telling *you* to stop worrying, Tabitha Turner! Anyway, I'll let you go. I'm here if you need me." Ellie hung up and Belisha took to the challenge of setting up the Roadguru. She scrolled through so many electronic pages that were nonsensical to her, tapping icon after icon. 'Navigate to Favourites' – could that be it? Belisha wasn't sure that work was exactly Tabitha's favourite place to be, but she thought it was worth a go. *Now, what did Ellie say? What am I looking for…Misery…Miss…ah there it is.*

"Miss Ree Loves Co.," she said out loud. Belisha frowned as she read the word that followed in brackets, "Hell."

"You have arrived at your destination," the satnav informed her.

"Really?" Belisha slowed the car, which stalled for the eleventh time, and looked around her. She ignored the other drivers, who were parping their horns and swerving around the stationary vehicle. "Ah!" she exclaimed as she spotted a green and gold sign with an arrow pointing across the road that bore the words *Miss Ree Loves Co*. She swung the car across the road, narrowly missing a post van, and parked outside a squat building bearing the same words. Next to the fancy typeface was a logo of a rather sinister-looking crow. She wondered what kind of firm Miss Rees was. A funeral director, perhaps?

"Tabitha! You know very well that this space is reserved for directors only!" An austere-looking woman with brown shoulder-length hair and spectacles reprimanded Belisha the moment that she opened the car door.

"I made the effort to come to work, drove this *thing* all this way and you yell at me the second I arrive?" Belisha retorted. She ducked out of the small car and slammed the door shut.

"As you haven't been well, I'm sure Miss Vaughan will let you park here for *now*," the woman harrumphed. "But, if I were you, I'd move it to the staff car park round the back during your break."

Who was this Veronica Vaughan that Ellie had spoken to yesterday? Was she even more dreadful than this woman? Belisha was not impressed by her first impression of the company.

"Veronica is waiting for you in her office, ready for your back-to-work interview."

"Back-to-work interview? Is that really necessary? I'd rather be left just to get on with things. I am not a child." *What am I saying? I don't even know what I'm supposed to be doing here!* Belisha thought.

The woman responded by simply raising one eyebrow above the rim of her spectacles, which had the effect of making Belisha feel as though she was the size of a flea. The woman turned on her heel and click-clacked through a double door into the building. Belisha gaped after her.

Did she really want to follow her into a hive full of labouring workers only to be confronted with the queen bee herself? Belisha questioned her actions for a moment, and then nodded purposefully. This was for Tabitha. If she could deal with a gang of bullying peasants in the street, then she could handle Veronica Vaughan. How bad could she be?

Belisha

"Sign here," Veronica Vaughan barked, before Belisha had the chance to close the door to the spacious office. "Then we shall begin."

"I'm feeling much better thank you." The sarcastic remark emerged from Belisha's lips before she could stop it. Veronica glowered. She breathed deeply, her chest rising up to her double chin. She pointed a chubby finger at a dotted line at the top of a one-page document on the mahogany desk that divided manager and worker.

Belisha glared at the pens that were standing to attention in a pot on the desk, all in uniform green and gold. She couldn't remember the last time she had used a pen, let alone signed her name. She looked around in vain for a thumbprint recogniser. She realised with horror that she had to sign *Tabitha's* name. She bit her lip, plucked one of the pens from the pot and scrawled something illegible across the dotted line. Veronica made no comment, her piggy eyes still on Belisha's face, burning through to her brain.

"You do realise, Miss Turner, that it is protocol to call in sick personally?" Veronica steepled her fingers underneath her chins, her jowls sagging either side of her face. "I was most disappointed when your little friend, Eleanor Price, telephoned to speak to me yesterday."

Belisha simply nodded, biting her tongue in case any rogue words slipped out. She assumed that Veronica hadn't nearly finished demeaning her employee. And she was right.

"And what was the reason?" She peered down at the document in front of her, which she turned to face her. "I'm afraid that Tabitha won't be in this afternoon after all," she read, "I think she's had a knock to the head, or she's been mugged. She doesn't seem to know where she is or who she is..."

"That sounds familiar, yes," Belisha agreed.

"Indeed!" Veronica barked. "Tabitha, out of all of the excuses I've heard over the years as manager at Miss Ree Loves Co., this has to be the most ridiculous."

"Yet it is true," said Belisha. She thought about Tabitha and how she had been mugged and then unwittingly found herself in Belisha's world, not knowing where she was nor who she was, much like herself.

"And is there any evidence of this mugging? Any cuts, scrapes, stab wounds?"

"I don't think it was that kind of mugging," Belisha admitted. "But I did have a hit to the head, and when I woke up I didn't know where I was. I couldn't possibly have come straight to work in that state."

"Preferring to find sanctuary in the local public house, no doubt!"

Belisha couldn't believe what she was hearing. Surely, this woman could not have the right to talk to her this way, to talk to *anyone* this way.

"Mrs Vaughan,"

"Miss," Veronica corrected her with a glare.

"Of course," Belisha smiled to herself. No self-respecting person would marry this vile being. "If you don't believe me, then I have plenty of witnesses. The man in the shop, Mr, er, Aurora, the blonde woman with the screaming child and, of course, Ellie–"

"And the pub landlord at the local," Veronica interrupted. A wry smile taunted her. "I have seen it all before. They book half a day off for an appointment, only to see that the sun is shining, and decide to spend the rest of the day soaking up rays and getting merry with their *mates*." The words were like poison her lips. Belisha wondered whether this woman had ever had any mates of her own. She doubted it.

"Soaking up rays? Mrs Vaughan, if anything, I was getting soaked by the rain! And I have never got 'merry' in my life!" Belisha threw her chair out behind her and drew herself up to her full height. She wanted to scream, "Don't you know who I am? I'm a very well-respected, high-flying radio broadcaster at Möbius Strip Airwaves, the most illustrious radio station in the system! And you dare to speak to me in this way?" But she pursed her lips to stop the words from escaping; the pressure of her teeth cutting into them in her restraint. The blood was rushing through her body so quickly that her heart felt as though it was going to explode. In her rage, her fists were clenching and unclenching, almost involuntarily.

Mrs Vaughan simply stared at her. Her paunchy middle rose above the desk as she got to her feet. She took a deep breath. "Just get back to work. I don't want to see you in here again, Miss Turner," she barked.

"That's fine with me!"

Her hands shaking as the adrenalin coursed through her veins, Belisha made her way out of the office. Unsure that she could take any more, she headed for the exit, dreams of souprano and her big, comfortable settee nagging at her. How she longed for even a sip of the stuff. But someone was standing in her path.

"Get out of the way," she muttered.

"Hey, Tabitha. How did it go with old fire chops in there?"

"Excuse me?"

"The old dragon, Veronica Vaughan. I see that you made it out alive!"

"Only just." Belisha stopped to look up at the grey-eyed young man. He moved a stray lock of dark hair out of his vision and placed a hand on her shoulder. His touch was sturdy and comforting, and Belisha felt the rage begin to dispel. He smiled at her, an impish cheekiness playing about his mouth, which was punctuated at each end by the most perfect dimples Belisha had ever seen. She was surprised by the feeling that if she looked at his face for any longer that she was going to melt. She smiled up at him weakly.

"But you're going the wrong way. You can't get out of here that easily. Our office is that way."

Our office? Did Tabitha have the fortune to share an office with this man? No wonder she hadn't left the company, despite her dreadful boss. Veronica surely couldn't get away with treating people like that, could she? Perhaps Belisha should file a complaint.

"I... I just wanted some fresh air."

"I don't blame you, but it's probably best if you don't, under the circumstances. You don't want old fire chops emerging from her cave and chasing after you, do you? Besides, if you annoy her, then she'll be in a foul mood and it would make the rest of today a living hell for the rest of us."

"You mean that that wasn't the worst of her?" Belisha whispered.

"You look different today," the young man observed as they walked along the corridor. His voice was deep and Belisha noticed that his Adams apple moved noticeably up and down his throat as he spoke. "I can't put my finger on what it is, there's just something different about you." He turned to look at her and she felt her face redden as his eyes explored her features and then her figure. "Anyway," he cleared his throat and continued. "I heard that you were mugged. Is that true?"

"Yes."

"Are you hurt? Did they take much?"

"My wallet and my phone got taken, but I got them back."

"Oh, that's good. And I'm glad you're not hurt."

"Thanks." Belisha felt her cheeks flush. What was wrong with her? Not many people had this effect on her. Especially primitive ones from place like this. This man was turning the confident radio disc jockey into an incompetent love-sick teenager. How was this possible?

He skipped ahead a couple of steps and opened a double door in front of Belisha, waving her inside, a mischievous smile on his face. But, instead of the intimate office she was expecting, Belisha was confronted with a large, airy room that was home to at least two dozen desks. Her face fell. It looked like the office where Shan worked, but worse.

Belisha learned that the young man's name was Adrian Lee. His desk was at the far side of the room to Tabitha's. Despite the distance between them, she couldn't help but glance across whenever the opportunity arose. She was seated next to a woman called Tricia, although she found out little about her, as she seemed to spend all of her time talking into her desk phone. To her left side was an unadorned wall and in front of her was another row of people who had their backs to her. They also seemed to spend an inordinate amount of time with their ears glued to their desk-phones. The middle-aged brunette woman with thick glasses sat at a desk in the corner, facing the entire room, teacher-like. She glanced up every few moments to run her frowning gaze over her flock and then turned her attention back to her keyboard.

Tabitha's desk seemed to be home to all manner of items – a stapler devoid of staples, three rulers, one of which was broken, seven green and gold pens, two dog-eared handbooks and an empty photo frame. The desktop was barely visible under an ocean of documents, despite the fact that there was a perfectly convenient stack of trays within arm's reach.

Your desk is as bad as your house, Tabitha! Belisha thought. She tidied up the papers as much as she could, stuffing great wads into the already overflowing desk drawers. At least it looked better. She wanted to avoid riling Veronica or her bespectacled accomplice any further today. She grimaced at the state of the keyboard, which looked to her like an old Scrabble board had been emptied into a bread bin. Shaking her head, she turned it upside-down and shook most of the crumbs onto the floor. Some of the keys were sticky and she vowed to wash her hands before she ate anything.

Now what? If only her producer Oranjer Bannawoo were here to assist her. Belisha was good at her job, but she was the first to admit that the support she received from her producer and co-presenter was invaluable.

She glanced around her and noticed that her new colleagues were using the old mouse-click method to operate their computers. She peered over Tricia's shoulder and figured out how to operate the antiquated computer, to some degree. She accessed Tabitha's emails and saw that there were fifty unread messages. Belisha supposed it was a good place to start. She clicked on the first email, which was from a Mr J Hopper.

To whom it may concern, I am writing to complain about the service which we received from one of your engineers.

Belisha rolled her eyes. Her gaze fell onto one of the books which littered the desk. Common Customer Complaints and How to Deal with them Effectively. As she scanned the contents page, she realised she had been wrong. *This* was the best place to start.

Tabitha

"Good evening, Obscurous," said Tabitha in the most cheerful tones that she could muster. She read from the holographic words which bobbed in front of her. "As promised, this evening we have an interview with Mistress Halo. Before I introduce her, enjoy this new version of *Where Have All the Seahorses Gone?*"

Tabitha gritted her teeth, faded in the "singer's" squealing vocals and peered across the desk at the perpetrator. She smiled politely, feigning confidence, and asked the pop singer whether she was ready. She replied with a lofty shrug.

On entering the Euclidean Building that evening, Tabitha had received semi-sympathetic greetings from Belisha's producer, broad-shouldered, hulking Oranjer Bannawoo. He had quizzed her about her health since the domino incident on the conveyor as he ushered her into the studio where the pop star had been waiting. He had informed her that Elliot Earl had kindly passed the opportunity on to Belisha to conduct all by herself. Tabitha wished that he hadn't; she had never felt so out of her depth.

Mistress Halo had been brought no less than seventeen cups of souprano, none of which had been to her liking. They had been too hot, too cold, too weak, too strong or had arrived in the wrong type of mug. She had been showered with gifts sent in by listeners, all of which she had given little regard. The pop princess had spent her entire time at the station impatiently tapping her foot and sighing, as though it was an effort for her even to grace them with her presence. Tabitha found the situation both bewildering and amusing. The woman was like a parody of herself. *Typical mega-star behaviour,* she thought to herself. *Some things never change.*

Mistress Halo was dressed in the most peculiar and over-the-top attire that Tabitha had ever seen, particularly for a radio interview, where she would not even be seen by her adoring public. Tabitha wondered whether there was a webcam or something more sophisticated but concluded that the concept was now obsolete.

She looked across at the singer, who seemed comfortable in her well-proportioned feminine frame, so unlike the half-starved stars Tabitha was used to seeing splashed all over the magazines in her own time. She donned a bright yellow hat that was half a metre wide and was attached at the back to a very short yellow dress made of some kind of plastic. Under her dress, she was flaunting large floral knickers that might have been more suited to Tabitha's grandmother. Her shoes boasted eight-inch heels and were festooned in petals and bows of all colours.

Tabitha tried to avert her eyes from the garish image, but it proved challenging; the woman's ego seemed to fill the entire studio. She had been handed a list of questions that were deemed suitable to ask her interviewee. There was an even longer list of things she couldn't ask.

As Tabitha faded out the last few bars of the cacophony, she took a deep breath and looked into the singer's heavily made up eyes.

"I'd like to welcome you to the show, Mistress Halo," Tabitha read from the monitor. The woman nodded with no audible response. *Well, that makes great radio!* thought Tabitha. "Er, right. We at Möbius Strip Airwaves are big fans, particularly all of us at Good Evening, Obscurous." Tabitha almost choked on her words.

The pop star's mouth curled up at the edges and she eventually spoke. Her speech patterns were crude, almost vulgar, and seemed quite at odds with her flamboyant style. "It's right good to be here too, Belisha. Thanks for 'aving me on an' all that."

Tabitha's heart sank when she realised that the monitor was not providing her with any further lines; she had to conduct the interview unaided.

"Er, judging by all the gifts you've received here at the station, you are obviously well loved, Mistress Halo."

"I'd like to send a big thanks to all me fans out there," she said loudly into the mic, ignoring the pile of presents entirely.

"I'm sure the question on the lips of all of your fans, is, er, how is the next album coming along?"

"I bin down in the studio all week, right. It's not an easy job ya know." The singer flailed her arms about as she spoke, her half-hearted words tumbling from her thickly glossed lips.

"I can imagine that it's not."

"Th'album's gunna be released soon and it's right good. You'll all luv it, ya will."

"So, you have a release date?"

"It's a Friday. No, wait, it's a Monday. The fourteenth. Can I 'ave a cup of souprano?"

How unprofessional is this woman? Tabitha thought. *I have no idea what I'm doing here, but I'm sure Mistress Halo has done more interviews than I've conducted.*

A moment later, a fresh cup was placed in front of the young star. Mistress Halo lifted the cup in her immaculately manicured fingers, sniffed the contents and wrinkled her nose in apparent disgust. She placed the cup back down and glared at the nervous-looking young girl who had served her.

"*Dead air, Belisha?*" A voice in her ear prompted her to continue. Tabitha realised that her jaw had dropped in surprise at the ridiculous display in front of her.

"Er, on to the next question then. Tour dates. I believe that you have a tour coming up."

"I do indeed, yeah."

Silence.

"Can you, er, tell your listeners a bit more about it?" This had to be the worst interview and interviewee situation in history.

"Well, I'll be going 'round all different venues, right, singing all me new tunes."

"Right. And where will the tour take you?" The expression 'like trying to extract blood from a stone' had never meant so much to Tabitha as it did at this moment.

"I 'avent got a list or nothin' on me, but I shall probably be going on a tour of the main venues along the Strip as well as Hayfen Capital, then across the world, like."

"So, you'll be touring the entire planet?"

"Yur. Well, apart from the northern hemisphere, obviously." The singer punctuated her response with a guffaw that merged into a snort. She sounded like a pig snuffling for truffles.

"Obviously," Tabitha repeated.

"Well they got no cash up thur, 'av they, soul?"

"Do you have any other news for our listeners? Are there any other exciting projects in the pipeline?"

"I'm going on me 'olidays soon, but I'm not saying where. I don't want no paparazzi following me and me beau, you know what I mean?"

"Of course." Tabitha had hoped that her interviewee would have elaborated on her answers, but there was nothing more to ask and the screen indicated that there were still five minutes remaining on the interview. "Er…"

"You don' want me to sing do ya?" The singer scowled at Tabitha and then over her shoulder at the producer. "Cause I ain't been paid to do no singing today. Plus, I 'ain't done none of those vocal warmups you're meant to do or nothing."

The last thing I want you to do is sing, thought Tabitha. *Even five minutes of dead air would be preferable to that.* She glanced at the list of forbidden questions relating to relationships, childhood and home life and tossed it aside. Perhaps she could take the interview in a different direction.

"Mistress Halo, if you were an animal, what kind of animal would you be?"

"What are you trying to say, like?" the star got to her feet, her plastic dress squeaking as she did so.

"Nothing. I'm not suggesting that you *are* an animal. It's an abstract question. But which one would you liken yourself to? For example, I think that I'm most like–"

"No one gives a crashing stuff about you. My fans want to know about *me*. Ask me summat else!"

"*She's right, Belisha,*" Oranjer whispered in her ear through her headset.

"*But what else shall I ask?*" she hissed back.

"*Be inventive.*"

But that hadn't worked. This woman was just too stupid. Tabitha sighed.

"Are you a morning or an evening person?"

"Evening, definitely. I mean, look at me. It's evening now and I look right good, dun I? An' I'm in my best mood an' all that." The singer did a twirl as if to emphasise the fact, before taking her seat once more.

"I see. OK..." *Think, Tabitha think.* There were only three minutes left. *What has she never been asked before that wouldn't offend her? What would make interesting radio?*

"*Belisha!*" Oranjer's voice pleaded in her ear. "*Make it a good one.*"

"Mistress Halo." She took a deep breath. This could either be a success or a complete disaster. "Where *have* all the seahorses gone?"

"Nobody's never asked me that one," she replied with her piggy snort. Tabitha wasn't sure, but it was almost as though the strange young star was impressed. "The seahorses, right, they've gone back to the homeworld. It's probably not that obvious from the words, like, but that's where I always thought they went to, any road."

Tabitha nodded slowly. The peculiar woman in front of her might not be the most intelligent or socially skilled person on the Strip and her vocal skills were questionable but had showed some passion for her own lyrics at least. There was some cleverness there, even at a somewhat shallow level.

"And have you ever been to the homeworld?"

"How old do you think I am, like?" Halo gasped.

"But if you had a time-machine, some way of getting there, would you go?" The question seemed to spill out of her.

The singer glanced at a retro digital watch that was strapped around her left wrist.

"I don't get what yer on about, soul. And it looks like your time is up. Cheerio, like."

Tabitha was suddenly alone in the studio, open-mouthed. She eventually managed to engage her mouth.

"Thank you for joining us today, Mistress Halo," she said into her mouthpiece, addressing the empty chair in front of her. "But don't go away, for the new song by Adamus Trent and the Butterflies is coming up next."

Belisha

Belisha was blessed with the ability to read quickly and thoroughly. She had read and understood not only Common Customer Complaints and How to Deal with them Effectively, but the Miss Ree Loves Co. Office Manual and a small selection from the slim volumes that were kept on a shelving unit at the back of the room. The volumes she had consumed consisted of Commerce by Numbers, Basic Washing Machine Maintenance, The Four Ps – Price, Product Promotion and Place, and How to Get Ahead in Advertising. The last one had turned out to be an annotated transcript of a twentieth-century film, but she had read it with interest, wondering with amusement whether Miss Vaughan knew of its presence in the office.

Whenever anyone passed by her desk, she had simply placed a hand over whichever book she was studying and drawn her attention back to the screen. By four o'clock, the number of unread email complaints totalled eighty-five, but now Belisha was better equipped to deal with them. Using her knowledge from the manuals and after a quick search through the computer's database, she began to type.

"Dear Mr Hopper, I am sorry that we have failed to maintain our usual high standards in this instance..."

"Fancy going for a swift half to celebrate your return to work?" Belisha recognised those deep, chocolatey tonnes. She looked up from her seventeenth email and ceased typing.

"But I haven't finished."

"It's ten past five," said Adrian, as though that was meant to mean something to her. He ruffled his dishevelled locks and that cheeky smile of his crept across his cheeks. "I assume that you want to leave the building before the dragon leaves her fiery den? So, do you fancy a quick drink?"

"Of course. But..." Every shred of her being was begging her to go with him. Again, she heard the tall stranger's words echo in her head. *Play the game.* "I don't know..." But what exactly was playing the game? Surely it should entail the fun things too. After all, weren't games supposed to be just that? Fun?

"Unless you have to get back or something. We can go out another time."

Belisha thought about her usual routine when she got home from work back on Hayfen IV. She pictured her comfortable settee, an inviting mug of souprano, her huge holo-screen TV and the fleeting image of Shan as her flatmate left for work, rendering her alone. She then thought about driving Tabitha's rusty little vehicle through miles of congested traffic all the way back to Tabitha's untidy, empty house. Belisha swallowed. The answer was obvious.

"No, no. I don't have to be anywhere."

"Fantastic!" Adrian grinned and Belisha couldn't help but smile back. She felt her face redden once more. He turned away from her and called out, "Tricia, Tabitha's up for it. Turn off your PC and let's go!"

Belisha's shoulders fell in dismay. So, it wasn't going to be *that* kind of evening. She watched, feeling like a fool, as Adrian gathered up the remaining employees like a collie herding sheep. "Come on now, ladies and gents. Well past time. Tabitha is safe and back with us. We have some celebrating to do." *We may not be spending the evening alone,* thought Belisha as she got to her feet. *But this little assemblage does seem to be in my honour.*

Belisha trailed at the back of the pack. On account of the fact that she had no idea where they were going. She was two steps behind Tricia, whose ear was now glued to a mobile phone.

"Yeah, tell me about it," Tricia said into the device. "That's what I thought too, and then I thought, you know what? Stuff 'em. You know? What? Nah I'll be another couple of hours yet. A few of us are going for a quick bevvie after work. Nah, it's no one's birthday. It's that quiet girl, mousey little thing, that Tabitha girl. She got mugged or run over or something and she weren't away for long or nothing, but she's back at work today and, well, it's an excuse for a cider or two isn't it?" Tricia laughed into the mouthpiece and Belisha quickened her pace to catch up with Adrian.

"Hey, Tabitha." Adrian broke off his conversation with a shorter, balder male. "I was just saying to Gerry how grumpy old Fire Chops is these days."

"She needs a good seeing to, I reckon," said Gerry in a thick accent that Belisha had never actually heard in real life but suspected that it was Glaswegian. Gerry emphasised his obvious contentment at his own conclusion with a long drag of a cigarette. "Not that I'd step up to the mark, of course. I might be desperate, but I'm not that desperate. Nae what I mean?" Gerry leaned past Adrian and winked at Belisha. She grimaced in disgust.

"Yeah, all right, Gerry, that's enough. Don't embarrass the girl, you know how shy she is."

"Well, not really," said Belisha truthfully.

"Just at work then, eh?" asked Adrian. "You always seem to have your head down, just getting on with stuff. And clock-watching. You do seem to do a lot of that. Apart from today. Today you seemed a bit more... engrossed."

Had Adrian been watching her?

"I just have a lot to catch up on," said Belisha with a shrug, ignoring the heat emanating from her cheeks.

"Yeah, I suppose you don't want to fall behind. Not with the mood *she's* been in."

"I told you. The sooner Vaughan gets laid, the better!" Gerry gave a laugh that rattled in his throat.

The group reached a building that appeared to be called The Red Lion. A scuffed sign depicting said animal swung merrily from a pole near the entrance. Belisha pondered the significance of the name and wondered whether there would indeed be any lions inside. Big cats had been extinct for centuries in her time. But inside, all Belisha could see were groups of chairs clustered around tables and a much higher, longer table, behind which were shelves festooned with beverages very much like the ones she had seen in the bottle shop. It reminded her of a scruffier, relaxed version of Kello Lumpy's.

"What do you want? The usual?" Adrian turned to Gerry as he approached the high, long countertop.

"Yeah, just get me a pint, pal."

"I don't want Tetley," Belisha said quickly as visions of Ellie and cups of putrid leaf-flavoured water flashed through her mind.

"Oh, I'm buying yours too, am I?" Adrian raised his eyebrows.

"Well—"

"I'm joking. We're here because of you, aren't we? What do you usually drink? Are you driving home?"

"Of course I am," Belisha replied. What did that have to do with what beverage she liked the taste of?

"Aye. Well, you can still have one, lass," said Gerry.

"I'll have whatever you're having," said Belisha with a shrug, assuming that The Red Lion didn't serve souprano. She licked her lips and realised how thirsty she was.

"Right you are," said Adrian and he turned away from her, a small piece of paper clutched in his hand.

Do they still use paper money? Belisha thought, the absence of a thumbprint recogniser suddenly apparent.

"You go and sit down, lass, and we'll bring 'em over," Gerry motioned towards a long, scratched wooden table where some of the other employees were seating themselves. Belisha sat down in the only available seat, which happened to be next to the woman with brown shoulder-length hair and spectacles who had reproached her in the car park and watched the office, hawk-like, all day. She turned and offered Belisha a pitiful smile, her small eyes peering through her thick lenses.

"How are you feeling, now? After the incident, I mean." Was this an attempt at being sincere?

"I'm fine," Belisha replied curtly.

"That's good to hear." Apparently devoid of anything further to add, she turned to the woman on her other side and started talking about work.

Belisha glanced around the table full of the people she had been sharing the office with all day. Was this really what office life was like? Groups of people who didn't have anything in common other than breathing the same air every day for eight hours? At least Belisha's job had variety. She had Oranjer, Elliot, a constant stream of celebrities gracing the station and her listeners. How she missed her listeners. Something nagged at her brain. Wasn't there a special guest appearing on the show this week? Who was it?

Of course, Mistress Halo! Belisha thought with horror. *Which means that... Tabitha will be interviewing her instead, if she still has a job there. Maybe she has already done the interview.* Belisha's eyes widened at the thought. *I hope she did a good job. If she made me look stupid, I'll never forgive her. I hope Elliot conducted the interview. He knows what he's doing. Oh, what am I doing here? Is this some kind of test?* Belisha still had her doubts. Everything still seemed so surreal to her.

"Are you OK?" a large glass slammed down in front of her, breaking her thoughts. "You looked like you were miles away!" said Adrian. He grabbed a chair from another table and pushed it next to hers. If only Adrian knew just how far away her thoughts were from this world. Belisha didn't look up, her eyes instead on the glass, which was filled to the brim with a clear amber liquid. "What is this?"

"Lager. Not the premium stuff, I'm afraid. It's not pay day yet," he said with a laugh.

"Not Tetley?"

"No. Tetley's is a bitter, not a lager," said Gerry and took a gulp of his own drink. "And you said you didn't like Tetley's."

Belisha's brow knotted in confusion. She held the oversized vessel in both hands and took a sip. She grimaced as the unfamiliar flavour of the fizzy liquid hit her tastebuds. She paused, then took another sip. She smiled. Perhaps this was a taste that could be acquired.

Adrian was too busy fumbling around with his wallet to notice Belisha sampling her very first taste of lager. For this, she was thankful.

"Are you looking forward to torture day tomorrow?" one of the other employees called down the table to Adrian. He was a young man with olive skin, a thin face and high cheekbones. Adrian visibly rolled his eyes.

"I don't think 'looking forward' to it is the way I'd put it, Jamil."

Jamil laughed and turned his attention to Belisha. "How about you, Tabitha? Are you ready for whatever Veronica has in store for us?"

Torture day? What was that? Did it entail Veronica Vaughan humiliating the employees of Miss Ree Loves Co. and subjecting them to pain and discomfort?

"It doesn't sound very appealing," she responded simply and took another sip to hide her sudden concern. Maybe Adrian would enlighten her. However, it was Gerry who spoke next.

"It's not even as if Dragon Chops wants tae do this thing. It's only because it's all part and parcel of her management training, and I use that term loosely. If old Miss Ree hadn't made her do it then she'd rather we were strapped to our desks like we are every other damn day, aye."

The horror that Belisha felt must have been evident on her suddenly pallid face, because the eyes behind the spectacles of the brown-haired woman next to her softened and she asked, "Will this be your first ever team building day, Tabitha? They're not that bad. In fact, I quite enjoyed the last one."

"Not that bad, she says!" Gerry cackled and took another hearty swig from his glass. Some of the foam remained in his stubble. "Judith, don't you remember the last one? I still have nightmares about it!" Gerry didn't seem to be afraid of Judith. In fact, he seemed to have a certain amount of affection for her. Indeed, Belisha suspected that Judith was not as hard as she made out. She certainly seemed to have a softer side, out of the context of the office. Perhaps Veronica Vaughan had less of an influence on her the further away she was.

Belisha took a large swig of her drink and felt herself relax a little. Why was she so concerned? She was Belisha Beacon and she didn't have to do anything that she didn't want to do.

"Well, I don't suppose we *have* to go," Belisha offered.

"Not unless you don't want to lose your job of course," said Gerry. Belisha shot a look of desperation in Adrian's direction. Tabitha couldn't lose her job. Belisha was not going to be responsible for that.

"You'll be fine. It's not like you'll be there on your own."

"Where is it again, this team build thingy?" asked Tricia, who had finally removed her ear from her mobile phone. "It's only on my computer calendar and, of course, I won't be going back to the office until next week now. Should've looked earlier, I suppose, but I ran out of time, you know what I mean?"

"It's at Orly Leisure Centre."

"Ah yeah, it's out of town, 'innit? I think I know it."

"Leisure Centres are the centre of everything *but* leisure in my experience," Gerry groaned. "All that gym equipment and people running about everywhere. There's more to life than sweating and swimming, pal," he said into his empty glass and punctuated his speech with a belch that echoed inside it.

"That does sound like torture," admitted Belisha.

"Yeah, can't we have a spa day instead?" Tricia offered. "That'd be more fun."

"It's not a hen do, Tricia," tutted Judith. "It's a team-building day. We aren't going to learn much about each other if we're lying around covered in mud."

"Och I dae know, Judith!" guffawed Gerry. As Belisha swallowed the remainder of her drink, she wasn't sure, but she thought that Adrian was looking her way, that naughty smile of his playing on his lips. She felt her heart leap, and when she set the glass down she avoided looking at him, instead letting her gaze fall towards the other end of the long table, where one or two people were starting to put on coats and unhook bags from the backs of chairs.

Gerry was the next to stand up. "Well, that's me. I'd better be getting back for my tea. See you all tomorrow." He gave a lengthy wave to the group and made for the exit.

"Yeah, early start tomorrow. We'll all need our strength for torture day," said Adrian as he got to his feet.

Belisha realised that her glass was empty and pushed her chair back. If Adrian was leaving too, then she had no reason to stay. She did not wish to sit next to Judith for longer than she had to, even if she was trying to treat her like a human being. A wave of fatigue washed over her, and the thought of even Tabitha's bed was inviting.

"Will you be OK driving?" Adrian's face was suddenly full of concern.

"You're not on any medication after your incident, are you?" Judith asked her. "Because even one pint can affect you if you're on painkillers, you know."

"No, I haven't had any today," she said truthfully.

"You *do* look a little wobbly, love," said Tricia in tones that weren't entirely sincere.

What were they talking about? What did they mean by 'wobbly'? What did that have to do with anything and what did it have to do with driving? It's not as though she'd had an entire jug of souprano. *I'm sure I can handle that old wreck on those roads,* thought Belisha. *I got here alright didn't I?*

"I'm just tired. I'll be fine," Belisha insisted.

"She'll be fine," Adrian agreed and smiled firmly at Tricia and held the door open for the three women as they exited.

By the time she reached Tabitha's old Fiesta and had breathed a few lungfuls of fresh air, Belisha felt awake again. She almost regretted leaving The Red Lion so soon. If only Adrian would have stayed with her. Maybe he would have if she had asked him to. *Maybe tomorrow,* thought Belisha hopefully.

Tabitha

"That was fantastic, well done, soul!" Oranjer Bannawoo bounded into the studio with such bravado that Tabitha was taken aback for a moment, for the producer did not look like the kind of person who would bound anywhere. Tabitha's performance had obviously swayed him to do so.

"It was?" Tabitha looked up at him. "I felt it was all a bit… well… awkward. I bet the listeners were cringing."

Oranjer laughed. "Mistress Halo is notoriously difficult to interview. You should know that from last time she was promoting a tour. And she's so ridiculously common! What kind of accent is that anyway? But you were brilliant. You kept your cool, avoided the taboo questions and actually seemed to engage that moody… er… *singer*. I was waiting for you to snap back at her like you do with some of our other guests, but that was pretty good! Until the end, anyway. Time travel, Belisha? What was all that about?" Tabitha bit her lip. She knew it had been an odd thing to say.

"Well, at least you didn't ask her about *the breakup*," he said, as though he was referring to a milestone event in the history of the planet. Tabitha nodded slowly.

"I suppose that would have been a bad move?" she guessed.

"Absolutely!"

Oranjer sat down on the edge of the desk. Despite its robustness, it creaked slightly under his immense weight. "I like your new style, Belisha. You seemed more laidback with your technique than usual. It's almost as if you've reinvented yourself." Below his ample forehead, his narrow eyes were scrutinising her face, as though he was trying to figure out what was different about her. "Keep it up and you never know, the morning slot may soon be yours."

"What? Mornings?" gasped Tabitha, the word practically burning her mouth.

"In fact, how about I talk to the producer of the First Sunrise Show about giving you a trial? Elliot and I would miss you up here in the evening slot, of course, and it's a tough slot. It'd only be a trial. But you never know!"

"Um…"

"This is the opportunity you've been waiting for, Belisha!" Elliot Earl leapt into the room, knocking one of Mistress Halo's many unwanted mugs of souprano flying in the process.

"It is?" Tabitha asked tentatively, looking up at the fresh-faced young man. The indigo skinsuit he was wearing emphasised the bright hue of his hair.

"You know it is! Don't pass it up on my account. Go for it! The morning slot is the slot that every broadcaster wants and has done since radio began!"

"*It is?*" she asked again. Was setting your alarm to get up for work at two o'clock in the morning really what all daytime DJs craved? She raised an eyebrow. Perhaps Oranjer and Elliot were right. Maybe it *was* a good opportunity.

"And think of the money. If you can make it on to the First Sunrise Show, you'd be able to move to the Strip!"

"I would?" Tabitha said, autonomously, her brain whirring through a hundred thoughts. Would it be a good thing if Belisha moved to the Strip with the other high-flying celebrities? What about Shan? What about Professor Pagter? She needed to stay focused.

"You don't have very much to say about such an exciting prospect! Hmm…perhaps you're in shock. Is that what it is? OK, introduce the next track and I'll get on the line to Rusabelle West."

"Who?" Tabitha asked, distracted.

"Belisha Beacon! The producer of the First Sunrise Show, of course!" Oranjer beamed.

"And I'll go and fetch you a large souprano. For the shock," Elliot added.

"Right," she said, and turned back to the desk before clumsily fading in the next track, which was all cymbals and screams.

Tabitha got through the next few hours with surprising ease, playing track after track and putting as much enthusiasm as she could muster into the lines she and Elliot read from the holographic cue screen. She felt comfortable enough to add her own patter now, even insert a little fake banter with her co-host at times. And she managed to steer clear of the subject of time travel or let any of her real thoughts make themselves known.

As Elliot faded in the penultimate track, Tabitha's thoughts were centred on the idea of her succeeding in getting a promotion for Belisha. Perhaps Belisha was doing the same for her at Miss Ree Loves Co. Tabitha snorted. If what she knew to be true about Belisha from literally walking around in her shoes, then there would be no way that Belisha would have put up with being treated how Tabitha was at that place. She had probably let her mouth run away with her and got her fired. Or burned the place down. No. Belisha wasn't that kind of person, was she? But if she had got Tabitha fired, then it would mean that she would not be able to admire Adrian from afar ever again.

She sighed at the realisation that that would be about all she would miss about the job. Sure, Adrian had talked to her. On a daily basis, in fact. But he didn't really know her. No one did, really. No one apart from Ellie. And even if Tabitha no longer had a job back in the real world, would she ever be going back there? If she moved to the First

Sunrise Show, would Belisha ever come back to appreciate it? Would either of them ever get home?

The DJ for the night-time slot entered the studio to take over from the duo's duties and Oranjer prompted her to wrap up her show.

"Thank you for listening to Good Evening, Obscurous. I shall soon be handing you over to Reety Reeterson for The Moonlight Show. But first, here's a track from the Möbius Strip's latest boy band. Yes, it's *Conveyor of Love* by The Strip Boys. Good evening, Obscurous!"

She shook her head as she faded in the song. She turned to Elliot. "The Strip Boys? Really?" she choked. "That sounds like a manufactured band if ever there was one. Or a poor man's Chippendales." Elliot shrugged as Tabitha disengaged herself from the headset and let Reety take her seat. He smiled cheerily at them and placed the headset over a thick mop of ginger hair. He immediately began to alter the settings on the apparatus in front of him and tapped his foot along to The Strip Boys' song.

The door to Oranjer's booth opened and he beckoned her over with a hand as big as a dinner plate. "Belisha, have you got a moment?" Tabitha gladly followed him into the soundproof room. This could be the perfect opportunity to ask him whether he knew anything about Mumma Toille and the whereabouts of Smoky Hollow. Shan couldn't help her, but it didn't mean that no one else could. He had to know *something*. She took a seat next to him. Through the pane of glass that separated the studio from the producer's booth, she could see Reety Reeterson happily talking away to his listeners.

"I'm glad you called me in. I needed to speak to someone," she said.

"I spoke to Rusabelle West," Oranjer enthused, ignoring her words completely.

"Already?"

"Yes. And she said yes! The producer of The Sunrise Show is happy to give you a week's trial, Belisha Beacon. But she needs you to start tomorrow morning!" His enthusiasm seemed at odds with his serious, bulky frame, but Tabitha couldn't help but smile back. His face fell slightly as concern washed over it. "Of course, that doesn't give you much time to prepare..."

"Or sleep," added Tabitha. "But I have something more pressing. I thought you might be able to help me."

"More pressing than preparing for your first public appearance on The Sunset Show?" Oranjer asked doubtfully.

"Well, it's just—"

"Reety, don't forget to mention our sponsors!" Oranjer said into his mouthpiece. He paused as Reety responded and then turned his attention back to Tabitha. "You were saying, Belisha?"

"Have you ever heard of Professor Pagter, specifically about an experiment that he might be involved in?"

"Is this some kind of new show?"

"What? No!" *Not everything is related to entertainment.* "He's a scientist or something and someone was trying to tell me about him. A person called Mumma Toille. And something happened to her. She died, right there in front of me! And the ArrRobot, he said something about a place called Smoky Hollow and... do you know where that is?" she blurted.

Oranjer waved through the glass at Elliot, who was just leaving the studio, and then spoke into his mouthpiece again, "Reety, you need to move faster between these tracks, or we'll never fit them all in. Less of the chatter and more tunes, yeah?" Another pause. "Nice one, soul." He turned back to Tabitha. "Sorry about that. Look, Belisha, are you still on a high dosage of pain suppressor? Believe me, you have done a fantastic job this evening, but you're still recovering from the collision and as you said, you do need to get some sleep before your next shift. There are only eight hours until you need to be back here! I think it would be a good idea if you went home and made the most of the time."

"But—"

"Look, a lot of people get killed in conveyor collisions. You were lucky to be near the end of the domino effect. I'm sorry that you were involved, but that's the way it is. Until they improve the damn system then there's little we can do other than simply not use the things."

"I wasn't talking about the collision!" Tabitha protested. Was he even listening to her at all?

"Reety–" Oranjer spoke into his mouthpiece again.

Tabitha sighed. "Don't worry about it." She stood up to leave.

"I'll speak to you tomorrow, Belisha, to see how it went. Oh, and good luck. You'll be great!"

As she left the Euclidean Building, Tabitha puzzled over Oranjer. On the one hand he seemed so helpful and encouraging and she felt that she could talk to him, but on the other he had been so dismissive. Or had he just been busy? Was one side simply his show-biz persona and the other the real Oranjer? She was confused. She was not used to being praised for her work, let alone being promoted. Was Oranjer being sincere?

Tabitha realised that she was even forgetting who the real *Tabitha* was anymore. She was even answering to the name Belisha now. She sighed again. Whatever was going to happen, she needed some sleep.

Belisha

Tabitha Turner's battered, red Fiesta rolled into a vacant car park space at Orly Leisure Centre. It was looking particularly battered after an encounter with a bollard and another with an exceptionally high kerb. Belisha Beacon stepped out and surveyed her surroundings. Although it had barely been worth driving to the location which had turned out to be less than a mile from Cottonwood Close,

Belisha knew that she would not have been able to find it without the satnav.

The leisure centre looked quite unremarkable; a dark green corrugated metallic box-shaped structure with yellow double doors and yellow-framed windows that had seen better days. The squareness of the building reminded Belisha of the houses in her neighbourhood. She supposed that the place might have had an air of the avant-guard several decades ago. But, to her, the building was practically prehistoric. The faint smell of chlorine wafted out from its interior whenever the doors opened.

Belisha pondered the possibilities of the day ahead. What lay in store for her and Tabitha's colleagues, and what could they possibly gain from coming here?

"Well, this is pretty grim!" said Tricia, who had just appeared next to her, to no one in particular. Belisha was about to respond when Tricia strolled ahead, her buzzing mobile phone suddenly flying to her ear in a perfectly manicured hand. "Oh, hi, Diane. Yeah, I just arrived. It looks like it's going to be a long day! So, how's it going with what's-his-face?"

Belisha shook her head and entered the leisure centre before the door had chance to close behind the talkative Tricia. A reception desk took the length of the wall ahead of her and a handful of patrons were milling around the foyer.

"Can I help you?" the receptionist addressed Belisha, as Tricia was too busy snorting loudly into her mobile.

"I'm here for the torture-day. I mean, *team-building* day," she said.

"Are you Miss Ree Loves Co.?" the brunette asked her, without looking up from her screen.

"No. I'm Belish– Er, Tabitha Turner."

"We only have one team-building session scheduled for today. Are you sure you're not Miss Ree Loves Co.?"

"Well, I've been working for the company if that's what you mean."

The receptionist glared at her over a pair of purple-rimmed reading glasses. What was her problem? The receptionist pointed at a door to her left. It was painted green and sported a small, circular window slightly too high to actually look through. "Through that door and up the stairs. Turn right and you'll be met by Alison in the yellow polo shirt."

As promised, an employee holding a clipboard and wearing a cheery, sunshine-yellow polo shirt was waiting to greet Belisha and her colleagues. Her forced grin did not relax for one moment as the group entered one by one. She repeatedly clicked the end of the ball-point pen she was clutching. There was something rather unnerving about her.

Belisha smiled as Adrian entered, the last to arrive. He gave her a wave, but if he had wanted to speak to her then he wouldn't have been able to, as Alison finally spoke and took a register. Belisha noticed that Veronica Vaughan wasn't present. Her name had not even been called out. Wouldn't Veronica be the one who would benefit most from bonding with her employees? Surely she was the one who needed to develop her people skills and try to get along with people.

Alison looked down at her clipboard and informed the group in saccharine-sweet tones, "The first task of the session requires getting into groups of three."

Belisha noticed Tricia pocket her phone and grab Adrian's arm with one hand and Jamil's with the other in one swift move. She watched as Tabitha's colleagues effortlessly grouped into trios. Adrian offered her a half-shrug and an apologetic smile before Tricia steered her prey over to where Alison was waiting.

"It's like being picked last for the football team all over again, isn't it, lass?" Gerry's raspy voice croaked behind her. "Obviously, it would have been netball in your case. Want to team up with me and Judith?"

Judith peered at her through her thick lenses.

Do I have a choice? Belisha shrugged. She had no concept of being chosen last for anything.

"Ace! Well done guys," Alison all but squealed with delight. "You're bonding already. That's ace!" She clicked the end of her pen several times for good measure.

Belisha bit her lip and glanced at Gerry, who raised an eyebrow in apparent bemusement. Judith was preoccupied with cleaning her glasses. Belisha noticed how tiny her eyes looked without them.

"Ace. Well, now you're all in your groups, let's go across to the sports hall. On your way, grab one of these batons from me. You'll need one per group."

"Batons?" Gerry muttered out of the corner of his mouth. "Is that to whack the silly lass over the head?" Belisha stifled a laugh.

"I assume it's for a relay race of some kind," said Judith, replacing her spectacles.

"Come along, teams," Alison chirruped. "It's relay race time! I hope you've all brought your trainers with you."

Gerry groaned. "I have nae brought my lungs with me, let alone my trainers, know what 'm saying?" He emphasised his point with a raspy cough. "Are they trying tae kill me or something?"

"That's not the right attitude. It'll be fun, you'll see!" Alison said through two rows of perfectly straight teeth. Belisha guessed that this woman was more used to addressing classes of schoolchildren than a score of fully-grown, fully qualified adults.

"Wannae bet?"

Belisha decided that she liked Gerry. He voiced his thoughts and wasn't afraid to do so, but he wasn't cold and cruel like Judith. She was surprised that Judith was in attendance. Perhaps she wanted to keep her watchful eye on the workforce and ensure that they were having as little fun as possible. Belisha thought Tricia was just plain irritating, but Jamil was pleasant enough and Adrian... Adrian made her smile. Far more than she dared to admit.

She gave little regard to the rest of the assemblage, a mass of worker drones who reminded her of the less popular pupils at her old school. Besides, Belisha did not plan on being here for long enough to get to know them all. It was plain from the way that others related to her that Tabitha, who had obviously worked there for several years, had little regard for them too. She decided that it wouldn't be her place to change anything. Apart from perhaps getting to know one or two of them a *little* better…

"What are you grinning at, lass?"

"What?" Torn from her thoughts, Belisha blushed. Had she been grinning?

"Here, this'll soon take the smile off your face." Gerry winked and handed her a metal baton. It was coated in thick, shiny red paint that was flaking off at both ends. Alison's girlish tones rang through the sports hall,

"If any of you have neglected to bring along suitable footwear, then we have a selection here at the centre if you need to borrow some. There are also shorts, polo shirts and towels if you need them." Alison glanced around at the group. Belisha looked down at Tabitha's terrible flats and cringed. She wasn't sure what was the worst prospect – suffering Tabitha's lack of fashion sense or delving through a box of smelly second-hand footwear. Alison continued. "As I'm sure a lot of you will remember from your school days, a relay race involves staggering team-mates around the track. When I blow my whistle, the first runner will run as quickly as they can around the track and then hand the baton onto the next runner. Let me make it clear that the second runner cannot run until they have the baton. The second runner will then run as quickly as they can to the final runner and hand the baton over to them. The final runner will then complete the lap. The first over the finish line wins the race. Of course, all the pressure is on the final runner. Don't let your team down! Any questions?"

"Aye," Gerry raised a hairy arm. "What happens when the first runner reaches the second runner?"

"They hand the baton to the second runner."

"I see. And what happens when the second runner reaches the third runner?" There was a twinkle in his eye that suggested to Belisha that Gerry was joking, making fun of the infuriatingly cheerful girl.

"They hand the baton over to the third runner," she said, trying to remain cool, but her eyes betrayed her.

"I see," Gerry continued. "So, why can't we all run at the same time. It might be quicker, aye?"

Belisha thought that Alison was going to explode. She bit her lip to prevent herself from laughing aloud. Alison raised her voice just a touch and reiterated,

"Because it's a team game. And the next runner cannot run until they have the baton!"

"Aye. I think I've got it now. Cheers."

Although obviously annoyed, Alison managed a forced "Ace!"

Belisha's eyes were watering with mirth. Gerry's dead-pan expression and Judith's look of disgust only made her laugh all the more.

Five races later, Alison blew long and hard on the whistle, which signified that the game was over. Belisha slumped to the ground, hoping that her breath and her sanity could be found somewhere on the dusty sports hall floor. Gerry collapsed next to her. Once he had got his breath back, he spoke.

"Well... we may be consistently bad, but at least we're consistent, eh?" he wheezed as he mopped perspiration from his brow.

"That was a pretty poor show, team," Judith admonished. "I'm at least ten years your senior, Gerry, and twenty years yours, Tabitha, and I can run faster than both of you!"

"What's your secret, Judith?" asked Gerry.

"Zumba. Every Tuesday evening without fail!" her seriousness was at odds with Gerry's devil-may-care attitude to such an extent that Belisha found herself laughing again, despite her breathlessness. "I can't believe we came last in every single race!"

"So what's next?" asked Gerry, ignoring her. "Pub?"

"Right, teams, that wasn't bad. It's interesting to see how you all work together, no matter what your... abilities are," Alison chirped.

"Is she looking at us?" whispered Gerry.

"I think she might be!" giggled Belisha as they got to their feet.

"Ace! Well, that's part one of the session complete. Next, we have basketball!"

An audible groan rose from Gerry's throat. Whatever basketball was it obviously involved further energy expenditure.

Tabitha

The wail of Belisha's alarm clock pierced through the darkness. Tabitha's brow creased in annoyance, her eyelids begging to remain closed and her mind longing to fall back into blissful slumber. Yet she managed to force herself into a seated position. She yawned as she dropped down from the top bunk and silenced the alarm. Shan mumbled contentedly at the resumed hush of night and rolled over. The crumpling sound of the ample sheet that enveloped her sleeping flatmate only served to exacerbate the cold discomfort that Tabitha felt. How she envied her, warm and comfortable with several hours' sleep ahead of her. Tabitha looked yearningly up at her bunk, placing a foot on the bottom rung. She yawned again and shook her head. No. She had to get up. It was dark and she was tired, but sleep was not going to help her to get home. She thought of her duvet and central heating and hot water bottle.

She needed to find the professor. She considered the First Sunrise Show and pictured Oranjer's face. This might not be her real home, but she couldn't let him down, could she?

In an attempt to rouse herself from the nagging tiredness, Tabitha stepped into the windowless, metallic hygiene cubicle. Within moments, the hairs on her arms began to tingle and the lights began to throb through the colour spectrum. She managed a smile as the feeling of warmth and freshness engulfed her body. Then came the uneasy feeling of her hair moving around her face, creating a style pre-set by the machine. Her many strands were curling and twisting and intertwining and *ouch!*

The smell of burnt hair instantly filled the cubicle.

A stark, oppressive light flooded the small room, making Tabitha feel very exposed. An alarm screeched. She covered her ears, screwed her eyes shut, crouched in the middle of the floor and screamed.

"What's going on?" she cried.

"Belisha?" A bang on the door caused it to open at once and Tabitha felt the warm air dissipate as she remained huddled, shivering and utterly naked in the centre of the hygiene cubicle. The alarm ceased. "Oh, soul, let me get you some clothes!" said Shan, suddenly awake. Tabitha felt the weight of material being dumped on her shoulders. "This stupid machine. We only had it fixed last month, didn't we? I'll have to call the engineer out again. I hope he doesn't charge us, though. What are you doing up so early anyway, Belisha?"

Shan remained in the doorway as Tabitha, her goose-pimpled skin still slightly damp, stepped into a crimson skinsuit. It was not a colour or style that Tabitha would have chosen but getting warm was her priority.

"I'm working on the First Sunrise Show," she said quickly.

"What? You didn't tell me!" Shan's eyes widened in delight.

"It's just a trial," Tabitha explained as she emerged from the broken cubicle, now fully dressed and a little warmer. "I didn't have time to tell you because you were already in bed when I got back last night."

"Of course. Crashing hell, you haven't had much sleep, have you?" Shan looked at her. "And the hygiene cubicle couldn't have picked a worst day to break down. You can't go up to the Strip looking like that!"

Shan may have been shallow, but she was probably right. Tabitha raised a hand and felt her hair. Half of it was sticky with some kind of setting product and the other half was damp, limp and singed at the ends. Not to mention that her face wasn't made up. And Tabitha had not left the house with a naked face since she was fifteen years old.

"What am I going to do, Shan?"

"Well, you probably don't have time to wait for the engineer to get here, so we'll just have to do the best we can the old-fashioned way."

"You're going to help me?" Tabitha asked, trying to detangle her hair with little effect.

"Of course! I have some brushes and powder lying around somewhere. I'll make some souprano and grab it."

"None for me, thanks," said Tabitha.

Shan shrugged and went about searching through one of the bunk room drawers. "Go on through and I'll be with you in a minute."

Tabitha wandered into the main living space. Her stomach had not yet woken up and her thirst had somehow been quenched from the first part of the cleansing process, so she simply sat and waited. Moments later, Shan appeared with handfuls of beautifying paraphernalia, some of which was familiar to Tabitha.

"I don't even know how to use half of this stuff. Most of it was my grandmother's and is probably dried up by now." Shan made a face as she unscrewed the lid of a tube of mascara. The contents flaked off the wand and onto the floor.

"This looks like it might still be OK." Tabitha picked up a lipstick and wound the waxy, bright crimson stick to the top. "It matches my outfit, at least." She located a small mirror among the pile of tubes, brushes and sticks and got to work.

"Well, if you know what you're doing with that lot, then I'll try and make some sense out of your hair."

Tabitha winced as Belisha's flatmate pulled and plucked and brushed and gathered her hair into the oddest style that Tabitha had ever seen. Shan made a face.

"It's a bit 2417, but it'll do. It's all the singed bits. You'll just have to wait for the strands to grow back." Shan smiled and said, "you've done a great job with your makeup! I might have to try some of this stuff out myself. You look gorgeous. It distracts from your hair, at least."

They both giggled. Tabitha couldn't remember a time when she had done anything as girly as play with hair and makeup with another person. It wasn't something that she and Ellie had ever really done together. Besides, she would have felt far too self-conscious for even her best friend to see her naked face. Even after all these years. She considered how odd that seemed now.

"Thanks, soul," she said, adopting the term for the first time. She got to her feet. Shan wrapped her arms round her.

"You're welcome. Now, hurry up or you're going to be late for your first First Sunrise Show! I can't wait to hear all about it when you get back. We might even be able to eat dinner together for the first time in months."

"You never know!" said Tabitha as she hobbled out of the door in Belisha's ridiculous shoes.

But as she made her way to the conveyor, at the forefront of Tabitha's mind was Professor Pagter and the longing to return to her normal life. Shan had been kind and, with the confidence boost that Oranjer Bannawoo had given her, Tabitha had felt like she could actually be someone here. But she could never be herself. She was trapped inside the body and the world of a stranger. Tabitha could never succeed here. She was out of her depth. She decided that she wouldn't go to the studio after all. She would go and find the professor. But where would she start?

"*Belisha Beacon*, is that you? What are you doing so far from the Strip?" A young woman with blonde hair dressed in grey-black attire stepped onto the conveyor in front of her. She had a sharp jawline, red lips and her hair was fashioned in a kind of vertical style that made its wearer look eternally surprised. She seemed very full of energy for someone who was up and about at this time in the morning.

"I live out here," she said, and then silently cursed herself for offering that kind of information to a perfect stranger.

"I see. Jennie Christian!" The woman lifted her hands to her collarbone and pointed her elbows at her in an enthusiastic greeting. "Pleased to meet you!"

Tabitha tentatively followed suit and bumped elbows with her – albeit a little harder than she would have liked.

"I'm a huge fan of yours and I just wanted to say how much I like your new look. It's... it's inspiring!"

Tabitha, who was used to playground taunts and the sneers of strangers, dropped her elbows, laughed nervously and looked away.

"No, really! It's sensational. What do you call it?" she grinned at her, so full of beans (And, possibly, souprano) that she could barely keep still.

"What do I call what?" Tabitha wished the woman would leave her alone. She needed to work out a plan and figure out which way to go next. Perhaps if she got off at the next junction…

"The look, of course!"

"What? Oh, it's called the Tabitha look," she said with a shrug.

"The Tabitha Look?" Jennie repeated. "That's unusual."

"It's named after someone very close to me," she said, looking, not at the woman, but for signs, any signs, to somewhere she had never been. The conveyor was the quietest that she had seen it. There was no one about since it was still the early hours. No one apart from Belisha's super-fan that is.

"So, are you off to the Strip?" Jennie gushed. "I'm sorry, I'm not stalking you, I'm really not. I'm a genuinely nice person. I was just surprised to finally meet you. I have never been to the Strip, so I've never had the opportunity to go to the radio station." Her words tumbled out of her mouth uncontrollably like half-digested Alphabetti Spaghetti. "Not that I'd hang around the station. As I said, I'm not a stalker. Oh dear. I'm not painting a very good picture of myself, am I?" She paused and took a breath.

"You don't by any chance know the way to Smoky Hollow do you, Jennie? I need to get there," Tabitha asked her, hopefully.

"You need to get to Smoky Hollow?" She looked taken aback. "No, no I've never heard of it, sorry. Is it a place on the Strip?"

"I have no idea where it is. Even the ArrRobot doesn't seem to know. Some help he was."

"Oh, I'm such a huge fan of your show Belisha. I know all about you and Elliot Earl. For example, I know that the ArrRobots use synthetic voice patterns originally recorded by Elliot's uncle. Did you know that about him? I suppose you would, working with him and all. But I don't expect you'll be working with him now that you're moving to the First Sunrise Show. It's all over the holopapers. Have you seen the holopapers this morning, Belisha? Do you think Elliot will be joining you on the First Sunrise Show or do you prefer to work alone? Oh, I'm *so* excited for you, Belisha." She spoke so quickly that all of her words ran into one another and Tabitha struggled to keep up with her. However, Tabitha could not help but be amused by her.

"So, you know all about us, do you? Do you know whether Elliot's uncle was a pirate?"

"No," Jennie said seriously. "He's a professor."

Belisha

The leisure centre sports hall was filled with Miss Ree employees waving multi-coloured ribbons and chanting,

"We can achieve anything that we want to when we work in a team" for the twelfth time. Jamil had been right. This was definitely a form of torture. Just what any manager thought their employees could get out of such humiliation and stupidity was beyond Belisha's reckoning. Such cruelty. Such utter pointlessness!

"Say it like you mean it, team!" Alison's voice peeled loudly, echoing through the sports hall. The overall volume increased a few decibels, although it was obvious by now that arms were aching, and spirits were crushed. "Ace!"

Belisha could stand it no longer. She addressed Alison. "This is ridiculous!"

Belisha heard her colleagues gasp and saw the shock shatter Alison's perfectly calm expression.

"Excuse me?" Alison squealed. "This session is not yet over. We have another fifteen minutes scheduled."

"And what can we possibly achieve in fifteen minutes?"

"Stronger core muscles and even stronger bonds with your team-mates. We're going to be hula-hooping!" The woman's swollen sense of optimism coupled with the crazed look in her eyes made Belisha explode into giggles. Gerry guffawed.

"I'm sorry lassie, but I draw the line there! You've had us running, playing basketball and waving ribbons like a bunch o' wee'uns. And now you want us tae literally jump through hoops? There's no way. I'm going to have a nice long shower then I'm off tae the pub. Anyone else coming?"

A ripple of exhausted cheers ensued, but Judith did not join in. She huffed and protested profusely. Belisha grinned at the realisation that Judith seemed powerless to prevent them from leaving.

"It looks like your mission has been accomplished, Alison," she said. "This team is closer than ever!"

Alison and Judith were left open-mouthed as the employees of Miss Ree Loves Co. high-fived and made their way to the showers. Gerry added insult to injury by hurling his rented trainers across the floor in the vague direction of the spare clothes basket.

Thirty minutes later, Belisha and the Miss Ree employees reached a building called The Black Swan. A handful of them lingered outside, inhaling nicotine and tar, while the rest hurried into the warmth of the pub. Belisha found herself inside yet another rough-looking room with tables and chairs and no animals of any kind. Much to Belisha's confusion, once again, there wasn't a single swan in sight – black or otherwise. She had noticed that they had walked past Ellie's house on their way, so she knew that she wasn't far from home. Or Tabitha's home, at least. Perhaps she'd be able to relax a bit more than she had been able to the previous evening, knowing that she could simply walk home at whatever time she pleased. Perhaps she'd even get to sit next to Adrian. She smiled to herself. Perhaps she should buy him a drink this time.

Belisha sighed. How she wished that her thumb print would grant her access to her money back at home. She hoped that Tabitha wasn't spending it all. Not that she had much surplus cash once all her bills had been paid. But Tabitha worked too. Surely, she wouldn't mind if Belisha used a *little* of her money?

She felt around in her bag and found Tabitha's wallet. On close inspection, she discovered that, thanks to the gang of ruffians she had encountered, it was devoid of any of the paper money she had seen Adrian use. She looked around and noticed Tricia waving a plastic card around at the broad, middle-aged man who was serving drinks. The man informed the group that,

"Contactless is buggered. You'll need to use the ol' chip and pin I'm afraid." Belisha watched as Tricia inserted the card into a slot on the machine, she pressed five keys and handed the device back to him. He returned the card and placed two beverages in front of her, which she took without a word and clip-clopped away.

Belisha had forgotten that people used to use cards with codes as currency to save carrying all that silly paper around with them. She thumbed through Tabitha's wallet and, behind a pale pink card with a photo and some writing on it, gleamed a blue and silver card, much like the one Tricia had used.

"Is it your round, lass?" Gerry's smoky breath wafted in her direction. He had brought not only the cold, but the stench of his bad habit inside with him. Belisha coughed and took a step backwards.

"Yes," she said. "If you save me a seat." She pointed to the vacant spots near to where Adrian was sitting.

"Nice one!" Gerry grinned, nudged her arm playfully and made his way over to the table. Now, where would Tabitha have put it? She seemed to be a bit scatter-brained. Would she have written it down somewhere?

Belisha checked every corner of Tabitha's bag and every nook of her wallet. The sound of her mobile phone startled her, and she plucked it out of the bag. Ellie! Just the person.

"Hi Tabs," said Ellie cheerfully.

"Hello."

"I can hardly hear you. Where are you? It sounds pretty noisy!"

"I'm at The Black Swan," she said loudly into the mouthpiece.

"You're at our local? You didn't tell me you were going!" Ellie sounded disappointed.

"I didn't know I was coming here until five minutes ago."

"What? Sorry, I can barely hear you. I would join you, but I have a tonne of stuff to get sorted for work tomorrow plus a pile of ironing. Oh my God, I'm starting to sound just like my mum!" Ellie laughed so hard that Belisha had to hold the phone away from her ear. Did Ellie really need to be this big a part of Tabitha's life? Was she incapable of doing anything without consulting this woman first?

"It's OK," said Belisha, trying not to let the irritation seep into her voice. "Anyway, I want to try and talk to Adrian."

"Adrian. That cutie at your work? Are you actually going to finally pluck up the courage to speak to the guy properly?" Ellie laughed again.

Could you sound any more condescending? Belisha thought. No wonder Tabitha had no confidence if even her best friend mocked her.

"That's the plan."

"Well, I'll leave you to it. I only rang to see how you were recovering. And, Tabs, don't blow it! I want to know every detail," she said the last few words in a loud whisper.

"Wait, I want to buy him a drink. What's my chippenpin?"

"You've forgotten your pin number now, Tabs? Is your memory still not fully recovered?" she sounded concerned. Belisha decided to play on Ellie's sympathy.

"It doesn't look like it," she said softly. "Do you know my number?"

"You've never told me your code, Tabs. It's not really the kind of thing people do, is it? It's supposed to be secret. Did you store it in your phone somewhere? Maybe it's under 'Bank' or 'Code' or 'Number' or…I don't know. Just have a look through your contacts list and notes and things. You never know."

"I'll do that, thanks." Belisha hung up and scrolled through the various menus on Tabitha's phone. After a couple of minutes of searching, she came across a suspiciously named contact called 'Mr Chips'. Mr Pin's number seemed to be far too short to be a phone number. In fact, it was only four digits long. Belisha smiled.

Tabitha

"A professor?" gasped Tabitha. "Professor Pagter?"

"Yes, that's the one. Poor guy went missing apparently, a few months ago. It was all over the news at one point, don't you remember? Elliot must have told you about it. I don't know whether they ever found him. I suppose it's old news now. It's all about immigrants from the North these days, isn't it?" mused John.

"So, he could still be missing?"

"I don't know how anyone realised he had gone missing to be honest, do you? After all, he's known for being a bit elusive. No, 'elusive' is the wrong word. *Reclusive*. Nothing has been heard from him since his latest experiment was commissioned some months ago. Something that's been his ambition all his working life apparently." John shrugged.

Tabitha's heart skipped a beat. "Did you say experiment? What kind of experiment? Has the professor been experimenting on…people?"

"My knowledge of his work isn't that extensive, soul. I know he provided the dialogue for the ArrRobots and that he's Hayfen Capital's most famous scientist, but I don't know the details of any of his latest work. You'll have to ask Elliot about that."

"Perhaps I will." Mumma Toille's words echoed in her ears. *You, my dear, are one half of the results of the experimentation of Professor Pagter.*

"Here I am, meeting my favourite broadcaster for the first time and I'm jabbering on about some old professor."

"Don't apologise," said Tabitha. "You've helped me out today. Thank you."

"I have? Well, I had better let you go then, hadn't I? I will tune in to the show as soon as I get to work!" John stepped off the conveyor. He called after her, "It was great to meet you, Belisha Beacon!"

The first sun had almost risen when Tabitha reached the Euclidean Building. She had gone against her best judgement to begin her quest to find Smoky Hollow alone and travelled up to the Strip. What else could she have done? She might as well help Belisha out and see if the new post at the station was any good. And, if Elliot was around, she could ask him about his uncle.

She patted her oddly styled hair, chuckling to herself at the term 'The Tabitha Look' and entered the building. A woman was standing in the entrance, her hands clasped in front of her. For a moment, she thought that the slender woman was Judith from work, but she was less angular and definitely less beige. She greeted Tabitha at once.

"Belisha Beacon!"

"Hello."

"Rusabelle West. Delighted to meet you. *Finally*." Her voice was low and gravelly, and she seemed strict although strangely amiable.

"Have we never met before?"

"No. But not for want of trying. Our shifts have always been at the opposite ends of the working day, haven't they?" Rusabelle placed a hand on the small of Tabitha's back and steered her towards the lift lobby. "I bet you haven't been up to the sixth floor before, have you, Miss Beacon?" she asked as they ascended. Tabitha shook her head. "Well, you go on up. I need to stop off at the third floor to organise something for tomorrow's show. I'll be there shortly," she said curtly. Tabitha was not sure what to make of her.

"But isn't the show starting soon? I don't know what to do!" Tabitha protested.

"Oh, you'll be fine, a girl with your experience. Just slip on the headset and introduce the show. The commercial break is just finishing, and the next track is a six-minuter, so you have plenty of time to get settled."

"But–"

The lift door opened. Rusabelle waved dismissively at her and stepped out into a long, grey corridor. The doors closed once more, and the lift continued to rise almost as quickly as Tabitha's anxiety levels. She watched the display as the numbers rose from three, to four, to five, to six, to seven, to…

"Hey!" Tabitha called out. "You were supposed to stop at six!" She banged on the door, but still the carriage continued to ascend. *Great. I'm going to be even later,* thought Tabitha.

The door pinged open at level seventeen. A short man carrying a tray of steaming hot drinks stepped in and acknowledged her.

"Going up?" he asked.

"No, I was supposed to get off at level six, but the lift carried on going."

"Oh, these damn things. They're always playing up."

What was it with technology today? Tabitha would have hoped that all these problems, like disobedient lifts and dodgy showers, would be obsolete in the future.

"Well, I'm only going up to the next floor. You don't mind, do you?"

"Well actually I–"

"Good," he said, without even looking at her. "These drinks won't stay hot."

Tabitha could feel her blood beginning to boil. Why had she always let people treat her like this? It was time for her to stick up for herself. "I do need to be on air any minute now," she informed him.

"I'm sure a few extra moments won't hurt," he said.

I don't think I'll ever be the kind of person that people listen to, thought Tabitha. *Even in someone else's body, I appear to have the word 'doormat' written across my forehead.*

Tabitha fumed silently as the man and the tray of drinks disappeared up another grey corridor. She was left alone once more. She selected level three and waited for the doors to close. But they didn't budge.

"Oh, just perfect!" she said aloud. "Today is not my day."

Another man, who looked as though he was in his late seventies, rounded a corner and stopped in the doorway. He looked surprised to see the girl standing there, not going anywhere, talking to herself. "Belisha! Aren't you supposed to be on level six?" He tugged at a weather-worn cap.

News seems to travel quickly here at the station, thought Tabitha. Was her new position common knowledge?

"Yes," she replied. "But the lift has other ideas."

"It's broken? Oh dear, that won't do," said the man. "The stairs are at the wrong side of the building. It'd be quicker to use the pole."

"The pole?"

"Yes, the emergency pole. Haven't you used it before? I'm surprised, with the number of times that this thing fails. It wasn't like that back in my day of course. Back in my day—"

"Please can you tell me how to get to this… pole? I don't mean to be rude, but I really am running late!" Tabitha could feel her cheeks flushing with frustration.

"Yes, of course, Miss Beacon. It's straight down the corridor, then turn left, then left again so that you've almost come back on yourself and it's in the room to your right."

"Really? That far away?" Surely, six minutes must have been up by now. "Well, thank you sir, and have a good morning," she said as she brushed past him. She couldn't help but notice the smell of stale urine.

"Sir? Now, there's a new one!" the old man chuckled.

Tabitha stopped halfway down the corridor to remove her uncomfortable shoes and ran the rest of the way barefoot. She reached a small room, in which a circle was cut away in both ceiling and floor to make way for a pole. At the far side of the room, underneath a small window, stood an odd little table with a dozen or so gloves stacked on top of it. Tabitha looked up and down the length of the pole, which appeared to span every one of the building's many floors. She gulped.

Tabitha hadn't slid down a pole since she was eight years old. She remembered it well. It had been in the centre of a dome-shaped climbing frame in a playground her family had taken her to when they were holidaying by the coast. It had terrified her. She had wanted to climb back down the way she had come up, but the children queuing behind her were goading her to hurry. So she had grabbed onto the pole, wrapped herself around it and dropped. However, the boy who was next in line had been so keen to take his turn that he hadn't waited for her to reach the bottom. The result was a bruised shoulder, grazed knees and a muddy face. She had not used one since.

Faced with the longest pole she had ever seen, Tabitha held onto the cold metal with one hand and peered down through the floors. She would have to step off – jump off, even – at the correct floor. Tabitha pushed her feet back into Belisha's shoes, took a deep breath and thought for a moment. She was on level eighteen and needed to get to level six.

That's thirteen stories! She thought with horror. *Thirteen. Unlucky for some, and most certainly for me. I'll never make that. I'll burn up in the process! The momentum that'll build up will be huge. Not to mention the blisters on my hands.*

Realisation struck her. The gloves! She helped herself to a pair. They were rather large, green and made of a soft fabric. Soft fabric meant little friction.

She looked up to the top of the pole to ensure that there was no one hurtling down above her. There wasn't. It was clear. "Well, here goes!" she said out loud.

As she began to slide, a scream crescendoed from her throat. She wondered why there was no one else using the pole, since the lift was out of order. Then she wondered how people were expected to get *up* the pole in the absence of a lift. The last thing she thought was *ouch!* as her posterior hit the hard floor. She had forgotten to get off!

Rubbing her behind grumpily, Tabitha looked up the pole shaft and saw several faces peering down at her from different levels. All of them were laughing. She looked around and realised that she was in the corner of the lobby.

Three young women scuttled past, giggling behind their hands.

"What are you *doing* Belisha? This is most unlike you!" Rusabelle West had appeared in front of her, arms folded across her chest, giving off the air of a disapproving headmistress. Rusabelle West was not laughing. "This isn't a playground. You're supposed to be on level six!"

"I…I…the lift is out of order. The old man. He told me to use the pole."

"You know that the pole is strictly for emergencies, Belisha. It is not for hanging around on like a zoo monkey. And the lift is working perfectly well now, so get a move on," she said crossly.

"I'm sorry," Tabitha pleaded. "I didn't know. He must have been playing a trick on me."

"Don't tell me you listened to Senile Sid!" Rusabelle tutted as she ushered Tabitha in the direction of the lift. "I don't know why they keep him on here. My cat could do a better job as caretaker."

The lift journey seemed to go on for hours. Tabitha prayed that it wouldn't break down again and leave her incarcerated with her cross boss. She breathed a sigh of relief when the doors finally opened and followed Rusabelle to the studio. Without a word, the producer slammed the door to her booth and seemingly expected Tabitha to get on with it without any assistance.

Tabitha glanced at the clock on the wall. Had her listeners really been exposed to four whole minutes of dead air? Wasn't there a fail-safe in place to stop these kinds of things from happening? Or was Tabitha so incompetent that these things never normally happened?

She put on the headset and adjusted the mouthpiece. Hopefully there was someone out there still listening. She was so grumpy by now that all concern had escaped her. Her feelings were evident in her voice.

"This is Belisha Beacon, broadcasting for the first time on the First Sunrise Show. I got here eventually. Sorry about the silence. But I suppose four minutes of silence is preferable to listening to *Where Have All the Seahorses Gone?* for the hundredth time, anyway." Had she gone too far? She didn't care. "Look, I've had a pretty dreadful start to the day, listeners. First, I got up at crazy o'clock. Do you know how early I had to get up to be here today? This may be the First Sunrise Show, but it was still dark when the alarm went off. Not that I could tell, as there are no windows in my bedroom. I was so, so tired. And guess what happened next? In an attempt to wake myself up even one iota, I got into that loony hygiene cubicle and the stupid thing broke! So, there I was, cold, naked, no make-up, my hair stuck up like a mad duck and looking worse than I had when I had got in the thing!" Tabitha didn't know why she felt the need to tell the world every detail, but she was enjoying herself too much to stop. "After a half-arsed attempt to rescue things with real, proper make-up, some hair products and a sympathetic friend, I managed to get out of the house looking half reasonable. But it was still dark, and I was still tired and annoyed. And *then* I bumped into a fan who kept me talking for ages." She was careful to omit the content of the conversation. She could see Rusabelle West waving her arms angrily through the glass. She was shouting through her earpiece for her to stop. But Tabitha ignored her and continued. "And when I finally got to the Strip, the lift took me up to the wrong floor! By this time, you were probably all listening to silence and I was getting more and more stressed and visiting half the floors of the Euclidean Building but the very one that I needed. Then the lift stopped working altogether! And next, an old man who reeked of urine told me to use the pole to get to the lower floors and I stupidly listened to him." By now, the producer was trying to get out of the booth, but it seemed that the door was behaving as badly as the lift, as it appeared to be jammed. Tabitha could hear her furious cursing through her headset. But still she continued. "I have never heard of a fireman's pole being anywhere but a playground or a fire station before, so how was I to know that I shouldn't have listened to Senile Sid, as he is apparently known, and simply should have waited for the lift to start working again?" She ignored the rants, swear words and screams in her ears. She simply raised her own voice. "Because I didn't want to be late for work, that's why. I didn't want to let my new boss down. But I don't think I impressed her when I landed on my bum in the middle of reception when I was supposed to be playing Mistress Halo." By now, Tabitha was laughing manically into the mouthpiece. "And that, my dear listeners, is why I hate mornings!"

The booth door finally gave way to Rusabelle West's pushing and pulling, and the red-faced producer exploded out of the door. She stood there for a few moments, broiling in her own anger. Tabitha stood up and spoke quickly into the mouthpiece.

"Here's *It's All Gone Wrong* by The Strip Boys. It's been nice talking to you all, but I don't think I have a job anymore. So, have a good day everyone!"

Before the producer could say or do anything, Tabitha flicked on the track, ran out of the room, located the pole, slid down to reception (landing on her rear end, of course) and fled the building.

Belisha

"It was almost worth all of that pain and humiliation to get to the pub by four o'clock," said Adrian, grinning at his pint as if it were a welcome friend.

"Speak for yoursel' laddie." Gerry rubbed the small of his back with his fists and stretched. "It's gonnae take me a week to recover from that ordeal."

Belisha peered over the rim of her glass and observed Tabitha's colleagues, rosy-cheeked, relaxed and sharing a sense of relief between them. They seemed unquestionably closer than they had the previous evening, downing their various beverages and discussing the horror of the day's events. Belisha could not help but feel amused. She tried to imagine the broadcasters, crew and administrative staff at the Euclidean Building working through such an experience. She couldn't. Belisha had not so much as been out for a souprano with Oranjer or Elliot after a shift, let alone attended team-building torture days and chosen to reconvene en-masse in buildings named after extinct animals.

Her thoughts drifted to the stranger who had visited her at Cottonwood Close. How had he known who she was? What exactly was he expecting her to do to earn her passage home? Was he watching her now? She looked around her, her gaze flitting from person to person at the other chairs and tables. She strained to look through the window, searched the rafters for any sign of a security camera.

What was Tabitha doing on the Möbius Strip? What would she be doing if she was here in this public house? Would she be making polite conversation, joining in the camaraderie, or making excuses to leave? If what Ellie had said was anything to go by, Belisha expected that Tabitha would be requesting her help to survive the evening, to talk to Adrian, maybe. Or would she just drink enough alcohol until the words came to her naturally? Belisha wasn't quite sure that she had Tabitha figured out yet. She wondered whether Tabitha had figured *her* out yet. She was amused by the idea.

"What do you think, Tabitha?" Adrian's words slammed through her thoughts.

"What?" she turned to look at the handsome man next to her.

"About the company's plans to move? If they move to the other side of the city, then it'd be too far for most of us to travel. But then I guess there would be some kind of redundancy pay-out."

"The company's relocating?" Belisha asked, startled. "When is this happening?"

"Didn't you read the email?"

"Email? Doesn't something like the uncertainty of our livelihood warrant at least a formal meeting?" Belisha was utterly aghast. "Honestly, that company is like none other than I've ever had the experience to—"

"That's exactly what we're saying," Tricia broke in, "But in an age when good jobs are difficult to find, do we really have any choice, really? There may not be anything better out there."

"Nothing better out there?" spat Gerry. "There cannae very well be many places that are worse!"

"Are you saying that you're not happy at Miss Ree Loves Co., Gerald?" asked Jamil, laughter playing on his lips.

"Well, let me put it this way. When I was a wee'un, I didnae exactly imagine mysel' toiling behind a desk attempting to organise a bunch of feckless engineers in such an incompetent business as—"

"Are you saying we're incompetent?" gasped Tricia.

"Not us as individuals, exactly."

"You're right, Gerry. The management put profit before people far too often for my liking," Jamil piped up. "They're just going to run us into the ground."

"But if the offices move to bigger premises and Miss Ree invests more into the business, surely that's a good thing?" another colleague chipped in.

"Cheaper offices, more like, with fewer overheads and fewer transport links to boot," said Adrian glumly.

"Look, you're all speculating about what may or may not happen. Surely, we can do something about this," said Belisha. "There are more of us. Plus, workers make up the company, surely, not the management? They would be nothing without us!" She could feel the frustration building inside her.

Adrian laughed, not unkindly. "If only things were that way."

"But why aren't they?"

"Ever thought about going into politics, Tabitha?" Before she could think of a response, he added with a smile,

"You're not as quiet and unassuming as you make out, are you?"

Belisha, words momentarily failing her, looked longingly into those big, grey eyes. Those eyes that said one thing but promised something more.

"I always knew there was some passion in there somewhere!" said Jamil with a wink. Belisha felt that Jamil had ruined what could have been a special moment between her and Adrian. She wished, and not for the first time, that it was only the two of them in the Black Swan that evening.

"Anyone want to play pool?" came a shout from the other end of the table. It was a young man with blonde hair and spectacularly bad skin. Belisha had noticed him at the leisure centre. Particularly, how much he had been perspiring during the team-building exercises. The two sodden patches under his armpits had spread during the afternoon, turning his pale grey t-shirt dark and soggy. Belisha grimaced at the memory.

"Ooh, me!" Tricia called out, as though someone had offered her the chance to announce the next winner at an awards ceremony. There were some positive reactions from some of the others as they got to their feet. Only Belisha, Adrian and Gerry remained.

"I'm aching too much to move even a pool cue," Gerry admitted. "I can barely lift me pint. Another drink, anybody?" He stood up and cricked his neck. Both Belisha and Adrian nodded and, finally, Belisha's wish had been granted. She was alone with him.

"Let's talk about something else. Nothing work related for a change," said Adrian, a smile playing about the beer foam on his lips. Belisha, her head fuzzy with the effects of her drink, had to stop herself from leaning in and licking it off. "We got out early, so let's make the most of it."

"What did you have in mind?" asked Belisha, taking a sip, her eyes never leaving his lips. What was she doing? Was she trying to flirt with him? She had seen others do it, but it wasn't really Belisha's style. She had a professional image to maintain after all. But here, where there were no fans, no press, where she was residing in the body of a plain-looking wallflower, would anyone notice? Would anyone even care? While she was here, she may as well just *play the game*. The warmth of the alcohol inside her reaffirmed the notion.

"So, what is it that makes Tabitha Turner tick? There's obviously a lot more to you than people know about. People at Miss Ree's anyway." He looked down at his glass and his eyelashes swept up once more as his gaze connected with hers. "Is there anyone special in your life? I'm sorry. That sounds so cheesy." Adrian laughed awkwardly and took a large gulp to hide his embarrassment.

"No, not really," she replied truthfully. "It's all pretty dull if I'm honest with you. But this…this is nice."

"Yeah, it's not a bad place, is it?" he said, looking around the comfortable room with its beamed ceiling and quaint Georgian windows.

"I didn't mean the room. I meant the company." Belisha smiled and went to take a large slug of her drink to drown her words, until she realised that her glass was empty. Adrian smiled at her small misfortune as he drained the last of his own glass.

"I don't have anyone particularly special in my life either." He sighed, toying with the empty glass. "My brother Richard is always telling me to get out of the house more since Julie and I broke up last summer. I've never really felt motivated enough. I've been more focused on work and getting some money behind me, you know?"

"Oh, I can completely understand that," said Belisha, knowingly. Work had been her life for so long. It was nice to get out and socialise. Even if she was somewhere so alien to her.

"I mean, I don't want to live with my little brother for ever. He's fun and all, but there's only so much I can take of his dirty washing everywhere and his console football games on full blast. It's like living in the middle of Wembley Stadium sometimes."

Belisha smiled in amusement, although she couldn't understand a word he was saying. She was transfixed by his expressive eyebrows and those grey eyes. Her ears were tuned into the rising and falling intonations of that deep, intense voice. "Anyway," he said. "What about you? You're still quite young. Do you live at home? With flatmates?"

Of course I live at home, Belisha wanted to say. *Unless he means, do I still live with my parents. Yes, that must be what he means.*

"I have my own house," she told him.

"Nice one. Rented, or bought?"

"I. er..." Belisha had never heard of the concept of buying one's own home.

"Sorry, that's none of my business."

She changed the subject. "I'm not that young, by the way. I turned thirty this year." She knew it was true. When she had been standing idly at the bar, she had looked at Tabitha's driving licence. She had realised that her and Tabitha not only looked similar but were exactly the same age.

"Really? Well, you look much younger."

Belisha didn't know whether it was a compliment or a statement. It wasn't the kind of thing she was used to people saying in her circles. You either looked fantastic or you looked like you hadn't seen a hygiene cubicle for a week. There was no in-between. And Belisha hadn't felt that she looked anything but the latter since she arrived. She responded with a simple smile.

"Sorry I took so long," said Gerry, placing down three glasses that were brimming with amber liquid. "Michael had to change the barrel. Always happens on my go. Typical, eh?"

"I know the feeling," said Belisha, who didn't, of course.

"Michael?" asked Adrian.

"The landlord."

"Do you know him?"

"I've never met him before in my life. It always pays to know the name of the guy who pulls yer pint." He thought for a moment, then added, "You two were looking pretty cosy, though. Want me to go away and come back later?"

"Of course not," said Belisha. She took one of the cool glasses, took a sip and winked at Adrian.

He's definitely interested, she thought as the fizzy lager slid down her throat.

Tabitha

Tabitha didn't relish the feeling of going back to an empty apartment. There were so many questions and vexations in her mind; her brain was in absolute turmoil. She was about to step onto the conveyor when she noticed Elliot making his way to the Euclidean Building. He was carrying a bunch of purple and white flowers.

"Belisha, what are you doing out here?" he asked, aghast. "I brought these for you to congratulate you on your trial day on the…" His eyes widened. "Why aren't you inside?"

Tabitha explained what had happened in the finest detail. She even mentioned the conversation with Belisha's super fan. Despite Elliot's protestations, she refused to step back inside the building.

"No. I just can't do it."

"But the opportunity! You can't mess this up, Belisha! Don't you realise how lucky you are?"

"I understand that, but I just can't go back in there. Not…not today. Look, there's something I need to talk to you about." Tabitha could stand it no longer. She had to tell someone. And Elliot seemed to know Belisha well. Perhaps he was as good a choice as anyone to confide in.

"It's about your uncle. Elliot, can I trust you?"

"Of course."

"Look, I'm not who you think I am. I'm not actually your co-presenter, Belisha Beacon. Everyone here seems to think I'm some kind of queen of the airwaves and celebrity interviewer extraordinaire. But it's not that simple. Elliot, I think I might be connected to the Experiment that the professor was working on when he went missing."

"What?"

"I think I've got mixed up in it somehow. I never asked for this to happen, I can assure you. So, can I trust you?"

Elliot nodded. "Look, I have to rush off and run a few errands on the Strip this morning, but how about we meet at Kello Lumpy's this afternoon before my shift? The Hayfen Capital branch."

"Kello Lumpy's?" Tabitha shuddered, the image of Mumma Toille's fresh corpse slumped over the table in the souprano house still haunted her. "Can't we meet somewhere else?" She then added quickly, "It's the smell of souprano. It makes me feel sick."

"I thought you loved the stuff. Did you have a recent bad experience with it or something?"

"Something like that."

"Crashing hell, that must be tough. I don't think I could survive without my seven cups a day!"

"I don't mind if I never drink the stuff again."

"OK. Well, you can come 'round to my apartment if you like." He squirmed rather awkwardly and quickly added, "My flatmates will be in too, but don't worry. They won't bother us. They're normally busy playing virtual pong in the other room. They're obsessed with that game," he fumbled. "Anyway, is about two o'clock OK?"

"That sounds fine." She smiled. "Where do you live?"

Elliot gave her his address along with the flowers, which she happily received, before he embarked on his errands.

Tabitha felt bad for leaving the Euclidean Building in the way that she had. She didn't quite know why she had behaved like that. It had felt like everything had finally got too much for her; the humiliation on top of the succession of unfortunate events had just been too much for her to cope with. Tabitha normally tried to take things in her stride, or at least appear to. She liked to present the image of the proverbial duck gliding through the water while her feet paddled away beneath the surface. Although this was rarely the case. She was aware that she never appeared calm and collected. How did other people do it? Tabitha felt as though she was constantly fighting to assume an air of normality. But, in reality, she knew that people saw her as the odd one, the kooky one or the quiet one.

If only she had Ellie to talk to. Just being around Ellie made Tabitha feel slightly normal. She could hide behind her friend's generous head of golden hair, look up at those big, blue, happy eyes of hers and all would be right with the world. If only she could call Ellie now. If only she could explain her predicament to someone who would understand. There was no guaranteeing that even Elliot, the nephew of the fabled Professor Pagter, would truly understand. Would he be able to help her, or was he looking for something from her? Tabitha shuddered. It had to be worth trying, she supposed. *What else could she do?*

The conveyor took Tabitha past Kello Lumpy's and still she held on to the rail in front of her. She didn't want to be anywhere near the place where the incident with Mumma Toille had occurred. She noticed, as she whizzed past, that the souprano café wasn't cordoned off for investigation or anything; it seemed to be business as usual. She had been partly paranoid that someone would come after her and ask questions, but so far no one had. She wasn't sure what she would tell them if they did.

Tabitha had noticed that there was a marked difference between the fashion on the Möbius Strip and Hayfen IV itself. Most residents on the Strip seemed to have wardrobes similar to Belisha's, but Shan's clothes were decidedly shabbier. They were less tight fitting and duller in hue. Was Belisha's fashion an indication of her occupation on the Strip?

I don't think you have a job on the Strip anymore, thought Tabitha. *Sorry, Belisha. It might be time for a new wardrobe.*

If she had lost the job, then she doubted that her thumbprint would allow her back on the Strip again. She resolved to make the most of her time up here while she could. So, she decided she needed chocolate.

Tabitha's hands soon ached from hanging on to the rail so tightly for so long, so she stepped across to the median lane, onto the slow lane and finally onto the disorientating glass ground. She saw a hatch on the side of an eatery a few doors down and made her way there. Hoping that her thumbprint would still work at the businesses on the Strip, she ordered a glass of milk and the largest slice of quadruple chocolate cake on sale and sat on a bench a few feet away. She consumed the cake with large, grateful bites. *I don't care,* she thought. *It's not my body, anyway. I'm sorry about all the calories, Belisha! I'm sorry for a lot of things.*

As she rested, Tabitha watched a group of runners through the transparent floor, their trainers pounding the glass between them. A class of schoolchildren followed, all dressed in smart uniforms. She gazed at the commuters whizzing along the conveyor, both in front of her and through the floor. Her brain was still having trouble making sense of the place. She finished her cake and ordered another drink, a fruit juice this time, for the chocolate had made her extremely thirsty. Tabitha rested a while longer.

Eventually, the group of runners passed her again, although this time they were rather sweatier and the right way up. Tabitha decided that it was time for her to leave the Strip.

Hoping that she had come to the right place, Tabitha knocked on the door to Elliot's apartment. The door was one of many in a grey, long, squat, concrete apartment block.

"Belisha!" Elliot squealed as he let her in. She was still carrying the flowers that he had given her earlier that day.

"That's the first thing that you need to know," said Tabitha. "My name is actually Tabitha."

"It sounds like we've got a lot to discuss. Come in and I'll put the machine on. Do you want a souprano?" Before she could answer him, he quickly added, "Oh, no, of course you don't, sorry. Is there anything I can get you?"

"No, I'm fine, I had a drink and a snack not long ago. You carry on," she said, taking a seat on a low settee. He nodded and took the two steps that took him into the kitchenette.

As he busied himself with the machine, Tabitha took the chance to look around her. The main living space was smaller than Belisha and Shan's, perhaps even half the size. There was one door off it, which she assumed was where Elliot and his three flatmates slept. She could hear the background buzzing of a computer coming from the bunk room, with overtones of random bleeps, sound effects and spurts of music. How did three grown men cope with living in such a small space? Where were all their possessions? The main room seemed oddly tidy for a bachelor pad.

When Elliot sat down, his hands cupped around his mug for warmth, he asked Tabitha to start at the beginning. She started with the day that the egg had hatched, which seemed so long ago, and ended with her ruining Belisha's career, consuming far too much chocolate cake and her arriving at the settee in Elliot's small apartment.

"That's quite a story," he said when she had finished. Tabitha's throat was now dry, and she wished she hadn't refused the offer of a drink. "The to-do with that Mumma Toille woman – that sounds pretty scary. No wonder you're all over the place, soul!"

"So, do you believe me then?" she asked.

"Of course! Who on Hayfen IV would make up something like that? Belisha Beacon certainly wouldn't. No, she wouldn't be sitting on my mouldy sofa telling me some made-up story like that. But, Tabitha Turner, you do seem as though you're telling the truth."

"Now it's your turn."

"I want to help you, Tabitha. If my uncle has anything to do with this and if that poor deceased, but rather crazy, woman was right, then he must be able to help!"

"Do you think he'd be able to send me home?" she asked, excitedly.

"Well, if he was the one who was responsible for bringing you here, then he should be able to send you home. He can't keep you here can he?"

"Maybe he'll give me some ruby slippers," she said quietly. "If I am part of an experiment, then I don't even know what I'm supposed to do. What does he expect me to do?"

Elliot drained his mug and carefully placed it on the table in front of him. He ran his hands through his spiky blue hair in apparent deep thought. His excitable nature had slowed, and his words became more considered. "And you definitely don't remember volunteering for anything?"

"No. It's just not the kind of thing I'd do. I live by myself in a quiet cul-de-sac in suburbia. I have nosy neighbours and a mundane job, and I go to the local shop and the local pub, and don't do anything even mildly out of the ordinary without discussing it with my best friend Ellie first. Blimey, I don't even try a different lager without asking for her opinion beforehand," Tabitha realised. "I certainly wouldn't sign up for something like this!"

"OK, so you're not normally the adventurous type then?"

"Not at all," said Tabitha, shaking her head.

"Is it something you would want to volunteer for?"

"I'm way out of my comfort zone here, Elliot. I just want to go home."

"I see. I wonder about Belisha. She is, or was, a successful broadcaster living in a nice area of the world, working up on the Strip, showcasing new outfits on a daily basis and working her way towards the top of her career ladder."

"Which I completely ruined," Tabitha said glumly.

Elliot continued, "In her own way, she also led a small life. Select friends, a modest home, no partner, not travelling further than, say, a few miles a day."

"Yet …400 years apart from my time. 400 years exactly! That has to mean that all of this was purposefully engineered."

"But I don't think that this is something that my uncle would get involved in. He's a scientist, an inventor. He wouldn't hurt a moth, let alone do something that would potentially ruin a person's life – *two* people's lives."

"Then who is involved? He must know something!"

"Someone obviously doesn't want you to find out. Whoever killed Mumma Toille."

"She didn't seem to like me much, either. This could be dangerous. Are you sure you want to help me?"

"I have to. I have to find out whether my uncle's OK. Anything could have happened to him. He's been missing for so long now. Even my mother – his sister – hasn't heard from him."

"Maybe your mum knows something, though."

"No," said Elliot solemnly. "She calls me from her home on the other side of the capital every week and she always asks *me* whether I've heard anything. They were really close growing up."

"Where did they grow up?"

"Eastern Esk. About a hundred miles from here."

"Would it be worth going there? There might be some clues."

"Not really." Elliot shrugged. "Before he went missing, he lived alone for thirty years in Hayfen Capital."

"Do you think that anything relating to his work would still be there?" asked Tabitha hopefully. "Maybe you should go and have a look."

"It's unlikely that anything confidential would have been left on show, Tabitha. I did go 'round there once, you know, just to check whether he had actually physically gone. It took four weeks to apply for my thumbprint access for the property. They don't get any quicker with these things, do they? Well, I don't suppose you know about those things, being from a different time and place and everything. Anyway, I thought that perhaps there might be some clues there, but..." Elliot paused.

"But what?"

"Quite frankly, I didn't know where to start."

"What do you mean?"

"You'd understand if you saw the place, soul. I've been putting off going back there. But now...now it's been so long, Tabitha. Perhaps I *should* go back there. There must be something."

"Well, if there are two of us, it might be easier," Tabitha suggested. "With a fresh pair of eyes along with you, then you never know. We might find something connected to his whereabouts. We could see if there is anything relating to Smoky Hollow. There might be some directions or something. Smoky Hollow is about all we have to go on at the moment."

Elliot's eyes glinted with delight. "With that in mind, the place might be deserving of one more look, I suppose. It has been a while since I last went to his home."

Tabitha opened her mouth to speak, but Elliot raised a finger to her lips and shushed her. "Have you noticed something?"

"What?" Tabitha mouthed.

"There's no sound coming from the bunk room. All I can hear is that dreadful title music of that daft game going 'round and 'round in a loop." He got to his feet. "AJ! Rojer! Are you all right?" He approached the bunk room door and pushed it ajar. "You haven't knocked each other out, have you? I've told you before, you guys take that game far too seriously..."

He fell silent and slammed the door closed, holding on to the handle tightly, trying to contain whatever was inside.

He clasped a hand over his mouth in an oddly dramatic way as his legs gave way beneath him.

"What is it?" Tabitha leaped up and ran to his side.

"Don't go in there. It's horrific." He retched and looked up at her with watery eyes. "It's AJ And Rojer. They've been killed."

Belisha

"Turn it off, Shan!" Belisha cried out in annoyance as the alarm clock shrieked. "Shan! Please!" Her head was throbbing, and her skull felt like it was going to shatter. The alarm clicked into silence.

"Your wish is my command," came a deep voice that definitely did not belong to Shan. Belisha peered over the top of her bed sheet. Except it wasn't the silver bedsheet she expected, but Tabitha's musty cream one. She hauled herself upright and pulled back the covers to expose the naked imposter.

"Adrian?"

"Morning, Tabs," he said softly and tugged the covers back over himself, mocking a shiver and smiling cheekily. His face looked more rugged than usual. A whiskery shadow had crept across it during the night, and his hair was ruffled and messy. It obscured one eye completely. An image flashed into Belisha's mind. She had ruffled that mop of hair, tugged on it in a passionate embrace, she had…she gasped.

"Did we…" she started. Part of her wanted to get up, to jump away from the scene of confusion, but her head hurt so much, and her muscles ached at just the idea of any kind of rash movement. And she yearned for his embrace. She longed for those arms to be around her again. Another image flashed into her mind of their bodies pressed against each other, perspiring and warm. There was another image and another. She tried to look sternly at the man lying in her bed, but as the memories came back to her, a growing smile betrayed her. "I suppose we did," she said finally, answering her own question and settling back down under the warm blanket.

"I'm glad it was so memorable!" Adrian pretended to be offended. "There's nothing I'd like more than to stay in bed with you all day, but we do have to go to work." He startled her by suddenly leaning over and planting a kiss on her lips before jumping out of bed. As he casually pulled on a pair of boxers he said, "Shall I put the kettle on?"

"What?"

"Would you like me to make you some tea?" he asked as he began to do up the buttons of his pale blue shirt. Her gaze fell on the neat column of hairs that crept down from his navel.

"Tea? No!" she protested.

"I only asked if you wanted a drink, not whether you wanted to marry me!" he laughed. Spotting her confusion, he ruffled her hair and kissed her forehead. "I'll leave you to wake up properly. I know you're not a morning person." He winked and left the room.

"Just pour me a glass of water, please!" she called after him. Belisha looked around the room through dazed eyes. What a state Tabitha's room was in. How could she have brought a man like Adrian back here? She didn't even remember bringing him back! The last thing Belisha remembered was buying a round of drinks for Adrian, Gerry, Jamil, Judith and even Tricia, who didn't seem to like her very much. What had she been thinking?

The rest of her memories were a series of haphazard images that came back to her sporadically. It was all a jumble of light, sound, faces, laughter and sweating. A lot of sweating. There was a dancefloor and then the living room floor and then the bedroom…

Is this what that fizzy drink did to you – cause you to act out of character and then make you forget everything you'd done? Why hadn't anyone told her? If she had known, then she never would have tried it. And she vowed never to drink it again. And her head, oh, how her head throbbed.

Belisha finally summoned up the strength to leave the rumpled bed in favour of the bathroom. The chicks were hopping around the bathtub and tweeting loudly. She told them, fruitlessly, to be quiet. She was as unsuccessful as ever in her attempts to make the shower water run at the optimum temperature – it was either searing hot or icy cold.

Both extremes caused her to yelp and leap in and out of the water stream. Tabitha's array of products for hair and skin confused her, so she used the same bottle of gel cleanser for everything. Shivering, she went about drying her hair with a damp towel that was hanging on the back of the door. After finding a vaguely smart purple top and a fresh pair of navy work trousers in Tabitha's overcrowded wardrobe, she visited the cluttered dressing table, slumped onto the stool and sighed. Living in this century was far too exhausting for her liking.

The door opened, and Adrian walked in, all smiles and oozing adorable charm. "How are you getting on?" He placed a glass of water beside her.

"Not well," Belisha admitted. "How do people do this every day? The antiquated hygiene water cubicle is either too hot or too cold, there's a cupboard full of clothes, but nothing that anyone in their right mind would wear in public and I don't even know where to start on my face!" she buried her head in her hands.

"You really *don't* like mornings, do you?" Adrian asked. "Poor Tabs." He knelt next to her and pulled her towards him. His strong arms made her feel safe. It was something that Belisha had not really experienced before. Men that she had known had not been like Adrian. They certainly wouldn't have let her use the bathroom first, made her a drink and known all the right things to say. They would normally just nod and pretend they understood her or quibbled with her over the slightest thing.

"Do we *have* to go back to that place today?" Belisha grumbled, pulling away from him. "We could just stay here. Or go somewhere a bit nicer."

"You're not still apologising about your house, are you? You kept doing that last night!" Adrian recollected. "And, as I kept telling you, you should see the state my brother leaves our flat in. This is luxurious in comparison! Besides, I didn't notice all the mess that you kept referring to. I was too busy looking at you." He grinned.

"You flatter me," said Belisha with a smile. "But I wish you wouldn't look at me now. I must look a worse mess than the house!" She buried her head in her hands once more.

"I would give anything to bunk off work today. But it would look a bit bad, wouldn't it? I mean, everyone knows that we were out drinking last night, half of them know we went to that dodgy disco at the social club into the early hours and I'm sure Gerry and Tricia saw us sneak off together. And as for old Dragon Chops…"

"She wasn't there was she?" she asked, panic stricken.

"No, no. But she knows we were at the team-building day and she'll find out that we went out and had one too many last night. I'm sure Judith was her eyes and ears!"

"Too many what? What do you mean?"

"Drinks, of course. Well, not so many in your case, but it seemed to go to your head quite quickly. Then again, none of us had had anything to eat, had we? Apart from that kebab of course."

"Kebab?"

"Have you really forgotten that much of last night?" Adrian laughed. He reached for a comb that was on the floor by the dressing table and pulled it through his hair. "I wish I had my shaver with me," he murmured to himself. "You don't…you don't regret anything, do you?" he asked, suddenly serious. "Us, I mean. I don't mind if it was a one-off, but we seem to get on so well and last night was…" His eyes twinkled, his cheeks reddened, and his lop-sided grin widened. "…impressive. Fantastic, even!"

"I don't regret it," she replied as more of the flashbacks came back to her. "Not at all. But I have a headache and it's difficult for me to process anything properly at the moment." She picked up a brush and began pulling Tabitha's hair out of the overloaded bristles. "I'm a complicated person, Adrian."

"I understand, it's OK," said Adrian. "Maybe we can talk about it when we've both properly sobered up, eh?"

"It would be nice to be able to think properly again. How long does this feeling normally last? It's not permanent is it?"

"Anyone would think that you've never had a hangover before!" he said with a smile. "I don't think even those shots we had at midnight will do any permanent damage. You'll be fine after a few more glasses of that stuff," he pointed to the glass of water, "a decent breakfast and a few hours to recover. The way I see it is you may as well get paid to have a hangover."

"You could be right," she agreed as she tried to use Tabitha's hairbrush to make sense of her hair.

"Who's Shan, by the way?" he asked with curiosity.

"What?"

"When the alarm went off, you called me Shan."

"Oh, I was half asleep. Shan's my flatmate."

"Flatmate?"

"From when I was at university," she added quickly. "Help yourself to some breakfast and I'll be down once I've found something to put on my face. Oh, and can you put another slice of bread in the bath for the chickens?"

Tabitha

"How did… who would do that?" Tabitha's lips mouthed more words – nonsensical and soundless. She didn't know what to do. She was out of her depth. What would Ellie do? How could this be happening? She stared at Elliot, who had now joined her on the sofa. She couldn't stop looking at the horrified expression on his face.

"Oh… my… soul…" Elliot swallowed hard and closed his eyes. "Rojer's body was slumped over AJ's like a sack of vegetables and… their eyes…their eyes were bulging out of their bloody sockets like two pairs of pickled onions. Their faces were twisted into looks of sheer terror, Tabitha! And that's not all – masses of bloody guts were oozing from Rojer's body and dripping down onto AJ's face. It's... it's revolting. His hair was caked in the stuff." Elliot swallowed again.

Tabitha pleaded with him to stop, feeling sickened by the description he was painting. Nausea was spreading through her body and the chocolate cake was trying to make its way back up her gullet. She grimaced. She didn't run this time. Her feet wouldn't let her, even if she had wanted to. And she couldn't leave Elliot to deal with this on his own. She probably shouldn't have left Mumma Toille. But she hadn't really known her. This was different. This was definitely murder. Wasn't it?

"Shall I call the police? An ambulance?" she offered, panic in her voice.

"Press the red Mergencies call button on the wall by the front door. Speak into the grill and tell them the bodies of two inhabitants have been found dead. They'll know where to come."

Tabitha located the button and did as Elliot had asked her. A disembodied voice immediately informed her that help was on its way.

"Have you had to use that before?" Tabitha asked Elliot, if only to keep him distracted from the horrific scene in the bunk room. He nodded.

"Once. For my grandmother. She was elderly. There was nothing sinister about her death though. I expect you haven't called for the Mergencies before, being from a time before the emergency services merged."

"I've never even dialled nine nine nine," she admitted. "I've never witnessed nor been the victim of crime until that group of chavs..." she said, half to herself. "Anyway, are you all right?"

"Not really," said Elliot. "I just want to check something." He pulled himself to his feet and pushed the door open once more. He leaned in and peered inside for a few moments. Tabitha kept her distance, not wanting to be confronted with the murder scene. "The ventilation shaft cover in the ceiling is hanging off. The shaft is easily large enough for a person to pass through. It must be how they got in. They're probably still up there somewhere, scurrying through the ventilation system as we speak. Those animals!"

"But who would have done something like this?" asked Tabitha, aghast. "Did AJ and Rojer have many enemies? They weren't coming after you too, were they? Whoever it was…"

"I know as much as you do!" he protested. "I have no idea what's going on. I…I can't process this. I don't know what to do." He clutched his blue hair with his fists and began to pace the room.

"All we can do is wait for the Mergency people to get here," Tabitha said with a shrug. She turned away from the morbid bunk room scene and made her way back to the settee.

"They're not people, exactly," said Elliot. Before Tabitha could respond, a door at the back of the kitchen area that Tabitha hadn't noticed before slid open. Two metallic man-shaped forms entered. They wore metallic clothes that Tabitha supposed were uniforms. Tabitha surmised it was perhaps on account of the fact that they were fire fighters, paramedics and police officers combined. They were reminiscent of the ArrRobot, but more crudely built, and their speech programming favoured a digitised version of received pronunciation, rather than the information robot's confusing pirate speak. It had a somewhat chilling effect. It made them seem even less real, somehow.

"Direct us to the crime scene," said the one nearest to Tabitha. She nodded and pointed in the direction of the bunk room.

"They're in there."

Without another word, the Mergencies clunked past her and entered the bunk room. Tabitha had no desire to see the dead occupants, so she waited nervously in the main room with Elliot. The sound of digital photographs being taken, faint humming noises and bright, yellow beams of light came from behind the door.

"They're scanning the room," Elliot informed her. "I doubt it'll take long. They're so cold, so calculating. Emotionless. I suppose that's why they're good at what they do."

"Will they be able to tell what happened just from the room scan?"

One of the Mergencies clunked back into the room and addressed the two of them.

"I am Mergency unit number seventeen. The Mergencies appreciate the fact that you informed us of this incident," he said coldly.

"So, what happened?" Tabitha blurted. "Are you going to go after them? Elliot's poor flatmates have been murdered. They could have killed us too! Why–"

"The means and motive will be determined back at the Mergency headquarters," he stated. "Mergency unit number three-seven-five is currently clearing up the crime scene in order to return the living quarters to suitable habitable standards."

"But aren't you going to cordon off the area until the investigation is complete? This is a crime scene, after all!" Tabitha protested. "Elliot can't just carry on living here alone!"

"He will be assigned new flatmates accordingly."

"That's not what I meant!"

"Ssh, leave it, Tabitha," Elliot said out of the corner of his mouth. "They know what they're doing. They are working to normal protocol. Just let them finish their job."

"And what do they mean by *clear up?*" Tabitha looked at him. "What'll happen to their bodies?"

"Mergency unit number three-seven-five is currently clearing up the crime scene in order to return the living quarters to suitable habitable standards," unit seventeen repeated. It approached Tabitha and Elliot once more. "Please press your thumbprints to the panel in my chest," he instructed them. "Although your thumbprints are already on file, it will help to differentiate the criminal's prints from yours. They obeyed.

"Elliot Pagter. Identity confirmed," said the unit. Tabitha followed suit. "Belisha Beacon. Identity confirmed." The words unnerved her. She hadn't expected it to say her own name, of course, but it was the toneless, soulless way it had uttered the name of the body she was occupying that made her feel more uncomfortable than ever. To her surprise, the unit addressed her again. "Miss Beacon," said the unit. "Following this disturbance, your celebrity status entitles you to a bodyguard unit at a reduced rate of just fifty credits per day. Would you like me to send one?"

"What? No!" Tabitha protested. She didn't want another one of those bots following her every move. She did not plan on being around for much longer.

"But Tab – Belisha!" cried Elliot. "Why not? You said yourself that the murderer could have killed us, too!"

"Under the circumstances, it is advisable," the robot said in monotones.

"Under the circumstances, I think I just want to go back to my quarters and sleep. I really don't want any more drama." Tabitha could feel tiredness catching up with her. Any enthusiasm and energy she had had for searching for Professor Pagter had been sapped by the recent events. She just wanted to shut it all out.

"It is your decision," said the unit.

"It is." Tabitha realised that she had just been the most decisive and insistent she had ever been in her life. It was just a pity that it was with a lump of metal rather than her boss or anyone who would actually appreciate it. *Maybe I'll progress to the electric can opener and work my way up to humans,* she mused.

The Mergency unit turned and clunked back out of the door through which it had come, leaving Tabitha and Elliot alone once more.

Elliot turned to her. "Whatever happened in there could have happened to–" he paused and gulped.

"Look, if whoever it was had wanted us dead too, they would have come in here and got us, wouldn't they?"

"That's not what you said before," huffed Elliot.

"I didn't think of it before."

"But why would anyone want to do that to AJ and Rojer? Oh my soul, I don't think I can cope with this!"

"I don't know," she said solemnly. "How long do you think it'll be before the Mergencies let you know the results of their investigation?"

"I don't even know whether they will," shrugged Elliot.

"What? They won't tell you what happened or why or who did it?" Tabitha gasped.

"They have no reason to. I'm not related to them. We just happened to live together. As long as the Mergencies are satisfied that we were not involved, then they have no reason to contact us at all."

"We haven't even given a proper statement!"

"It's just the way things are done now."

"So, Mumma Toille in the café – there won't be anyone trying to find me and ask me questions? When those things came in, I suspected that unit seventeen would know somehow and quiz me about it, believe me!"

"The Mergencies obviously know you're not implicated. If they suspected anything, you'd know about it."

"Elliot," said Tabitha softly. "What if there isn't anyone with a grudge against AJ and Rojer at all? What if it's the same person who killed Mumma Toille? What if all of this is some kind of warning?"

Belisha

Belisha's morning was filled with knowing glances and colleagues nudging one another and giggling like school pupils whenever she passed by. But she pushed it all out of her mind. There wasn't much room in her head for much else apart from her pounding headache and flashbacks from the night before. Every time she glanced across at Adrian, she noticed him smiling to himself.

She waded through emails, which were seeping into her inbox faster than she could mop them up. She felt competent enough with most of the work, referring now and then to her manual or to the internet. But with remnants of alcohol still swimming around her system, her cares were slightly suppressed, and Belisha couldn't help but occasionally offer less than professional responses, particularly to the more bothersome complaints or customers who asked mundane or ridiculous questions. *What's the urgency anyway?* she wondered. *An engineer finishing the job one day later than originally estimated is hardly an apocalyptic disaster.*

As the hours passed and the painkillers did their job, Belisha pondered her situation. Was Adrian pleased that he had spent the night with Belisha or with Tabitha? Had he secretly always admired Tabitha and finally had the opportunity to do something about it, or had he only made a move because she was so different to the Tabitha he had known? If only she could tell him. But he might think she was crazy and wouldn't want anything more to do with her.

"About that email you just sent," barked Veronica, suddenly appearing beside her desk, startling her. "I don't know whether you realised, but you copied me in on it."

"Which email, Veronica?" Belisha asked, feigning innocence, but suspecting the worst.

"The one responding to our client down in Sussex. The one which advised Mr and Mrs Petticoat that the reason the response to their complaint was delayed could be put down to the fact that most of the office was out on a *torture day* yesterday! Really, Tabitha, that is most unprofessional and impolite. And quite frankly I find your attitude regarding the team-building day downright ungrateful!"

"Ah…" Belisha looked down at her desk and then back up at Tabitha's manager. "I didn't mean to copy you in on that one. My sincerest apologies," she said with mock sincerity.

"Is that all you have to say?" she snarled. "Your sloppiness, insolence and devil-may-care approach to your role has not gone unnoticed, Miss Turner."

"Excuse me, Miss Vaughan, but I think that you'll find that I'm a very conscientious worker!" Belisha dared to say.

"Consider this to be a verbal warning, Tabitha! And if I hear anything more about my staff fraternising with one another in... *inappropriate* ways, then..."

"Fraternising?" cried Belisha, standing up. "If you don't like the fact that your employees actually talk to one another outside of this dreadful, repressive place, then you're living in the dark ages! I appreciate that this is a backwards society, but at least these poor people know how to enjoy themselves!" By now a crowd had gathered around in a kind of nervous semi-circle. Veronica opened her mouth to speak, but Belisha continued. "You may not have been aware that your staff members called the team-building day 'torture day', but that's exactly how it felt. And you wouldn't know, because you weren't even there! Yet you are evidently the one person who would benefit from learning how to get along in a team. And, if I may speak candidly, every day is like torture in this place. It's no wonder Tabitha – I – have got no self-confidence. Well, madam, enough is enough!"

Leaving Veronica utterly speechless, Belisha swiftly gathered her belongings and marched towards the door. She halted, turned around and addressed the group as a whole. "And as for whatever *fraternising* Adrian and I engaged ourselves in in our own spare time is no one's business but our own!"

She was shaking so much that her legs were wobbling beneath her as she stood in the doorway, clutching her bag and looking crossly at the dragon and her brood. To Belisha's surprise, Gerry started to clap. And then Jamil and Tricia and some of the others. Adrian, too, and his grin was wide, and he was laughing, actually *laughing*.

"Well said, lass!" Gerry cheered. Even Judith's smile betrayed her usual stern exterior.

"Indeed," said Belisha and swiftly left the building.

She wondered whether Veronica would follow her, but she didn't look back as she hurried across the car park to Tabitha's little Fiesta. She opened the door and threw her bag onto the passenger seat.

"Wait!" It was Adrian. "I'm really proud of you. Slightly embarrassed about the bit about us, but–"

"She started it!"

"I know," he said and rested a hand on her shoulder, his lop-sided grin warming her. "Let me finish. I'm really proud and surprised, and you, well, you were amazing! No one has ever spoken to old Dragon Chops like that. And certainly not mousey little Tabitha! Where did you suddenly get the guts to do that?"

"I suppose she just pushed me too far. There was only so much I could take. That and this dreadful hangover."

"So, are you really going? For good?" he placed his other hand on her other shoulder. His big, watery grey eyes pleaded with hers.

"I don't know. Probably. I don't know what I'm going to do or where I'm going to go. I just need to take some time out and think things over for a while."

"Well, can I have your phone number? Just in case?"

Driving back through the city was markedly easier during the day when most people were at work, but Belisha had still been beeped and flashed at from all directions.

Now she found herself at Ellie's residence with a glass of orange juice. A plate laden with every kind of biscuit imaginable had been set between them. Belisha crunched her way purposefully through a chocolate Hobnob. She hadn't wanted to be on her own and had driven to Tabitha's friend's house on the off chance that she was in. She had to tell somebody what had happened that day, and Ellie had been the only person she could think of.

"I can't believe you did it, Tabs. You actually finally did it." Ellie pulled up a chair and took a sip of tea. "All those evenings at The Black Swan where you'd be going over what you would say to the old bitch if only you had the backbone. After years of bullying and torment. I'm pretty proud of you. Shocked, but proud."

"That's what he said, too," said Belisha. "Adrian. He said he was proud of me. I don't think anyone's ever said that to me before."

"Adrian? Did something happen between the two of you?"

Belisha smiled and told Ellie all that she could remember, including some graphic details.

"Tabs! I don't believe it!" Ellie almost choked on her pink wafer. "You've really come out of your shell, haven't you? And, well, he sounds amazing!"

"Yeah, he really is." Belisha beamed.

"I don't know, Tabs, you spend years working at a place you hate, being treated like crap, pining over some bloke you have barely even spoken to, and then when you finally spend the night with him, you go and leave!" she laughed, throwing back her head of curls. "Mission accomplished, huh? Was that your big plan all along?"

"There never was any big plan," said Belisha. "At least, not on my part. It was just right, I think. It felt right. And no one should be made to work in that place. I tried to make it work. But life's too short to be penned up like that being made to feel like–"

"I get it, Tabs," said Ellie, pouring herself a second mug of tea. "You don't need to explain yourself to me. I know how unhappy you were there. And I'm glad I had this afternoon off. I was at a loose end before you turned up, and, well, it's good to see you. It seems like a lifetime since our last real catch-up." She settled back down on her chair in the brightly lit kitchen. "So, what are you going to do now?"

"I don't know. Something different. Get a job broadcasting at a radio station, maybe!"

"But you hate radio DJs," gasped Ellie. "Particularly the cheerful morning ones. You're always ranting on about how unnecessarily happy and loud they are."

"Ah." How dare Tabitha dislike them? *She's really not going to be enjoying working at Möbius Strip Airwaves,* thought Belisha. Would she have a job to go back to when she returned? If she ever returned? "Even evening ones?" Belisha probed.

"What? I don't know. You tell me."

"Perhaps something else then."

"There's always hospital radio. But I'm not sure you'd get paid for that. I'll have a think. But you need to find something quickly, Tabs, or you won't be able to afford to pay the mortgage. Of course, if you were really stuck, you could always go back to Miss Ree and grovel."

"Never!" Belisha proclaimed. "There's no chance."

"It's your choice."

"Exactly. Don't worry, I'll think of something."

Tabitha

Tabitha considered telling Shan what had happened that day when she arrived back at the apartment. Perhaps she should tell her everything. But would she take it in her stride like Elliot had? Tabitha wasn't sure that Shan was capable at looking at things too deeply or laterally. She didn't come across as dumb, exactly, but she would never be a match for Ellie. Had Ellie believed Belisha, she wondered. Had Belisha even met Ellie?

The pair of corpses blinked into her mind. And then came the slumped figure of Mumma Toille. It was all too much. Way too much. Tabitha had to get out of this nightmare future.

"Hello?" Tabitha called out as she entered the empty apartment. "Shan?" *She must still be at work,* she realised with dismay. She really needed to see a friendly face.

Emotionally and mentally drained, Tabitha flopped onto the settee and closed her eyes.

"Belisha!" An abrasive voice pierced through the darkness. Barely conscious, Tabitha waved an arm dismissively. "Belisha, wake up!"
"What time is it?"
"It's five o'clock in the morning."
"You mean, five o'clock in the middle of the night," she murmured and forced herself upright, her back aching from lying curled up on the settee for so long. She looked up into the face of Rusabelle West. Tabitha's eyes widened.
"Rusabelle…"
"I have been trying to call you, but it seems that your communicom is out of service, so I thought I'd come and speak with you directly. Your flatmate let me in."
"I'm sorry that I walked out yesterday." Tabitha couldn't think of what else she could say. She bit her lip.
"Walked? You practically flew out the door, Belisha!"
Tabitha's cheeks flushed. "I didn't think you'd want me to stay there after I was so late and after all the stuff I said and–"
"I must admit that I was horrified. Mortified, even. What did you think you were doing?" Before Tabitha could muster up a response, the prim producer continued. "The truth of the matter is that the listening figures for the First Sunrise Show yesterday morning were higher than ever. For some reason, the listeners love you, Belisha," she said with obvious reluctance.
"What? How? I ranted and moaned into the mouthpiece for five minutes and then played that awful boy band at them!"
Rusabelle sat down next to her. She closed her eyes slowly and purposefully and when she opened them she stared hard her.
"It appears that there is a large proportion of the listenership who are awake early enough to listen to the

First Sunrise Show who share your perspective on mornings."

"There is?"

"It pains me to say this, but it seems that listeners do not wish to be greeted with cheerful broadcasters and aural souprano at six AM after all. In fact, yesterday's feedback indicated that listeners who are up and about at that time of day actually felt reassured by the fact that their radio broadcaster was not enjoying the early start either. They felt they could relate to you. Indeed, your ridiculously dreadful list of calamities actually made them feel better about their own day. The number of listeners rose, and, when you left, there were actually complaints of your absence."

"I see. So, what you're saying is that you were *happy* with my performance yesterday?"

"My own beliefs aside, it's the listeners that need to be kept happy. If they're happy, our advertisers are happy, and if our advertisers are happy, then I'm happy." She didn't sound particularly happy, but she certainly didn't seem cross either. Perhaps this was as much emotion as Rusabelle could express.

"I have said this all along," Tabitha said, partly to herself. "Nobody wants to hear how great everything is out there at that time in the morning. No cheerful DJs, no happy clappy competitions and sunny dispositions at six o'clock in the morning. Broadcasters need to be able to relate to their listeners."

"Quite. So, will you come back?"

"What, now?"

"Your shift starts in less than an hour."

"But…" The memory of yesterday's experience at Elliot's apartment was still fresh in her mind. There were so many more important things she could be doing. She needed to see whether Elliot was all right. She needed to get home.

"If you secure this position, your living quarters will almost certainly be upgraded." The producer looked around the sparsely furnished room and sneered. "Bring in enough revenue to Möbius Strip Airwaves and you could very soon be living up on the Strip."

"My flatmate too?"

"Does your flatmate work on the Strip?"

"No." What did Shan do for a living? Tabitha realised she had still not even asked her.

"Then you don't need me to answer that one for you." Rusabelle stood up and dusted down her skinsuit as though she had been sitting on a compost heap. "Get yourself into the hygiene cubicle and I'll see you at the Euclidean Building by six o'clock."

Belisha

A loud trill broke into Belisha's dreams. *I thought I'd turned that damn alarm off,* she thought as she scrabbled blindly to press every button on the alarm clock. It took her a few attempts to finally realise that the clock was not responsible for the racket. She reached across the bedside table and picked up Tabitha's mobile phone, which continued to bleep and flash impatiently in her hand.

"Hello," she said groggily.

"Tab, where are you?" It was Adrian.

"I'm in bed. I was enjoying a lovely dream, actually. I was back on the Möbius Strip and I was interviewing a new—"

"Something's happened," he said. There was urgency in his voice. She propped up a pillow behind her and pulled herself upright.

"What do you mean? Are you all right?" she asked quietly.

"It's Veronica Vaughan. She's dead." The phone slipped out of Belisha's hand and plopped onto the carpet.

"Tab? *Tab?* Are you still there?" Adrian's voice floated up from the bedroom floor. Tentatively, Belisha reached down and picked up the phone with shaking hands.

"Yeah, I'm still here." She gulped. "What happened?"

"She was found dead in her home in Token Row." It was Adrian's turn to gulp. Belisha imagined his big Adam's apple moving up and down in his throat. She pictured a pair of large, grey, sad eyes. He continued, "Apparently there were signs of a forced entry and…oh, Christ. I know she was an old dragon, but she didn't deserve this."

"Are you there now?"

"Where? I'm at work. Miss Ree called from her home in the Maldives and instructed Judith to conduct a meeting right away. There's a police officer here. Anyway, Judith wants to see you and the police officer wants to speak to you, too."

"Me? Why me? I don't even know where Veronica lives. *Lived.* I don't know anything about any of this!"

"I know that, Tabs. But…it just…I suppose, after the way you blew up and walked out yesterday. No one in the whole history of Miss Ree Loves Co. has ever dared do anything like that before!"

"And no one murders their boss in cold blood just because they have had a bad day!" Belisha protested, thoroughly offended. "Do you really think that I—"

"No, of course not. And no one said anything about murder! But the officer still wants to speak to you."

"If I'm a suspect, then why aren't the Mergencies banging on the door?"

"The what? Look, no one is suspecting you. Don't panic. He wanted to speak to everyone. Just come into the office, speak to him, then I can give you a great big hug and then you can go home and forget all about it." His words offered little comfort.

Belisha sighed. "All right, I'll get ready. Tell Judith I'll be there in an hour."

Returning somewhere from which she had fled in haste and anger was never going to be easy, but this situation was on another level entirely. Belisha hadn't just walked out of a job, she had walked away from a manager who was no longer alive.

As she walked across the car park, Tabitha's scuffed shoes kicked up gravel into their holey canvas, making them more uncomfortable to walk in than ever. Every fibre of her being begged her to get back in the car and drive away. She looked up at the large, oppressive building. Her gaze fell on the green and gold sign above the door. The logo's creepy crow glowered down at her as though it was accusing her. She felt sick. Only the thought of Adrian being there for her spurred her on. As she stepped reluctantly into the premises, the stench of the white-washed walls hitting her, Belisha's emotions quickly rolled into a ball of anger.

What am I doing this for? she thought to herself. *I have nothing to do with whatever's happened here. So, the vile woman has been killed. Send out the Mergencies to deal with it, not Miss Ree and a bunch of incompetent police officers. What a backwards way of doing things!*

"Ah, Miss Turner," Judith's left eyebrow rose into her fringe. "I'm glad you could join us." Even in her supposed time of grief, Judith's tongue was tinged with poison.

"You do know that I've left the company?" Belisha couldn't help but say, her anger fuelling her. "I only came in because Adrian asked me to."

"Ah, young love," said Judith bitterly. Belisha suspected that Judith had no experience of the concept. She had probably been a grumpy forty-something her entire life. Her eyebrows knitted into a kind of ill-tempered caterpillar and she declared, "It is imperative that I speak to all employees. Until your P45 has been returned to you, then that includes you, Miss Turner."

"I don't have anything to say."

"Well, you certainly had plenty to say during yesterday's little performance."

Belisha stood her ground and glared at Judith. She was often frighteningly similar to Veronica Vaughan in disposition but couldn't have been more different in the way she looked. Judith turned, obviously expecting Belisha to follow. Her scrawny body was so slight that she practically disappeared as she did so.

Belisha followed the bony behind up the corridor and into the office that had been Veronica Vaughan's. The scent of wood polish hung in the air. Judith pulled out Veronica's desk chair, lowered herself down onto her skeletal posterior and rested her bony elbows on the table in front of her. Judith puckered her sour lips, peered through her thick lenses and gestured for Belisha to take the seat opposite her. Belisha reluctantly accepted. She was not used to being interrogated. She had been pleased to leave the office yesterday and had no intention of returning. This had not been part of her plan. Judith leaned in.

"When was the last time you saw Veronica?" Her soft voice thinly masked the spite behind her words.

"You know when I last saw her," Belisha told her. "Yesterday afternoon. I walked out when she confronted me about some email issue or other. At least a dozen people saw me leave. You were one of them."

"Indeed I was." Judith narrowed her eyes. "You didn't part on good terms."

"That is correct."

"And when Adrian followed you out of the building, what happened then?"

"Well, if you must know, he came out to congratulate me."

"To congratulate you?"

"For sticking up for myself. And then he asked me for my phone number. And I said I probably wouldn't be coming back."

"Probably? So, you hadn't left for good?"

"I had made up my mind never to return, but I didn't want to say that to him. Not straight away."

"I see. And why not?"

Belisha heard the muffled ringing of Tabitha's phone in her bag. She ignored it.

"Look, what has any of this got to do with Veronica Vaughan? Yes, I shouted back at her, but I didn't say anything that didn't need saying. And then I left. I didn't the go to her house, hide behind the curtain with a knife and wait for her to come home at six o'clock!" She all but laughed at the absurdity of the situation. "How did you know what time Veronica arrived home? And who said anything about a knife?"

The phone continued to ring.

"I don't. I just guessed. I don't know anything about the woman. I know as much about her as I do about you, and I don't even know your last name!" Belisha cried. She paused and lowered her voice slightly. "This is just absurd. Why are you accusing an ex-colleague who had a few cross words with–"

"I'm not accusing anyone, Miss Turner. I'm simply trying to get all of the facts. Please try and remain calm."

Belisha buried her head in her hands. "It wasn't me, OK?" The Mergencies would know straight away that it wasn't her. *What a ridiculous system,* thought Belisha.

"Will you silence that phone, Miss Turner?" snapped Judith. Belisha bent down, grabbed the phone and saw its flashing screen. Ellie!

"Judith," said Belisha with a smile. "I believe I have an alibi." She tapped the answer button. Without taking her eyes off Judith, she spoke into the phone. "Ellie. Perfect timing, as always! Can you tell Judith here exactly where I was yesterday afternoon?" Belisha passed the mobile across the desk.

Two minutes later, Belisha walked out of Veronica's office with a certain sense of triumph. Adrian wasn't at his desk. In fact, none of the employees were at their desks. It was evident that nobody was in the right frame of mind to work and that they had perhaps remained in the office to offer each other moral support. A few of them looked startled by her entrance.

"Relax, it's only me. Judith's in the dragon's old office. She looks far too comfortable in there for my liking."

"She's back!" Gerry greeted her.

"I only came in to clear my name." Belisha shrugged.

"Clear your name?" Tricia repeated.

"I know what you've all been saying. You told Miss Ree that Veronica and I had had words, and apparently that made me prime suspect, however–"

"No one said that!" protested Tricia. "I was just saying to Jamil that–"

"However, it does not matter what you all think," continued Belisha, waving the mobile phone in the air. "Because I didn't do anything to Dragon Cho– to Veronica. And my alibi has just testified for me."

"All right. So, which of us do you think did it?" asked Tricia, her lust for gossip as strong as ever.

"This is not some trashy murder mystery show, Tricia," sighed Belisha. "It doesn't have to be someone in this room. It makes no sense that it is. I'm sure someone like Veronica had enemies everywhere!"

"The lass is probably right," Gerry guffawed. "I'm sorry to speak ill of the dead and all tha', but she was hardly Mother Theresa now was she?"

"I've had quite enough of this," whimpered another employee, who was clearly upset. "Someone has died!" She scuttled out; her nose buried in a wad of tissues.

"How did she die, exactly?" Belisha whispered to Adrian.

"You mean Judith called you into her office and didn't tell you? She was found this morning by her sister Caroline who had called round to drop something off at her house. There was…Caroline called the emergency services. The ambulance and the police. There was glass all over the floor where someone had broken in and Veronica was found on the living room floor with…with blood all over her forehead." He paused and swallowed, as though trying to rid himself of the bitter taste of the mental picture. "The officer said that her face was bloated and puffy. Much more than usual, I suppose. And–"

"Stop it, Adrian. I think I'm going to puke!" wailed Tricia, who had obviously been listening in on their conversation. Belisha ignored her, her eyes remaining on Adrian.

"That's a pretty graphic description from a Mergency," Belisha observed.

"I thought that, too," Adrian said absently. "But then I thought, perhaps he was trying to gauge some kind of reaction from us to see whether they could spot any signs of anyone who might be involved." He swallowed again. "It did sound pretty gruesome."

"So, where are they now, the Mergencies?"

As though on cue, the door opened and in walked a tall man in a badly fitting dark blue police officer's uniform. He looked uncomfortable in his attire and ill-fitting in the situation as a whole.

"Ah, there you are, the absentee," he said with a cough. He strode over to Belisha. "I have a few questions I need you to answer for me."

"I've already spoken to Judith and given her my alibi," Belisha objected. "There's nothing more to ask me. And anyway, I wasn't an absentee, I had *left*. Why doesn't anyone understand that?"

"Follow me, all the same, Miss Turner," he said and turned on his heel. Belisha huffed after him, utterly appalled that she was to be questioned once more. She followed him into a small board room just off the main corridor. Inside the musty-smelling room were eight straight-backed chairs around a large wooden table.

It was only when she and the police officer had sat down on two of these chairs that she realised the man didn't work for the emergency services after all.

Tabitha

Once again, Tabitha was torn between duty and desire. Should she go to the Möbius Strip to discover whether she really could make it in the career that someone with her disposition was apparently destined? Or should she eliminate any notion of work in this future world and call round to see whether Elliot was all right? After all, they had planned to go and investigate his uncle's disappearance and hopefully find out just why Tabitha had been sent here in the first place. It was the only lead that she had. Was Professor Pagter anything to do with her situation? There was only one way to find out.

But now Tabitha was struggling with which of the options was her duty and which was her desire. The very idea of being good at something and adored by thousands was not an unpleasant one, and it was certainly an alien concept to her. But could she really remain in a city with murder happening on her doorstep? Could she really continue blithely through this life without Ellie and without her family even knowing where she was?

Was Tabitha slowly turning into Belisha or was she the same person that she had always been? Or was she becoming the Tabitha that she was always destined to be? She sighed. The transition was obviously having an effect on her mental health. Her crisis of identity was gnawing away at her.

Tabitha's worries had always festered at the back of her mind, never quite allowing her to be the happy, carefree person that she so longed to be. If she looked back through her life, even through the good times, the anxiety monster was always there, peppered throughout her memories. Would she ever be free of her worries if she stayed here? Would she be free if she returned home? Which was the right option?

Her mind reeled through her dilemmas as she cleansed herself in the hygiene cubicle and pulled on a bright red skinsuit and stilettos. By the time she had left the living quarters, Tabitha had made up her mind. She and Elliot would go to his uncle's house in Hayfen Capital, they would find any clue they could on the mysterious Smoky Hollow and go from there.

Tabitha stepped off the conveyor and traipsed up to Elliot's front door. She pushed the buzzer and waited. When it finally opened, a squat man who must have been in his eighties peered out.

"Can I help you?"

"Er... I was looking for Elliot."

"He's not in. Who are you?"

"I'm…I'm Elliot's friend, Tabitha. Has he gone to work?"

"Not today. He, er, he said something about going to see his uncle."

"Really?" *He's gone without me?* "Has he found him?"

"Why? Is he lost?"

"You could say that," said Tabitha solemnly.

"He didn't say. He just said he was going to his uncle's house."

"Ah, I see."

"Will that be all?" The man hadn't opened the front door any further than a few inches.

"Er, yes. Oh, are you Elliot's new flatmate?"

"I have just moved in this morning, yes. I'm Mr Crabness. There is another occupant being sent along later on today, I believe."

Blimey. They don't mess about here, do they?

"You do know what happened here yesterday?" Tabitha bit her lip.

"I do not wish to be rude, but I'm a busy man and I probably should not be wasting my time conversing with strangers. I do have things to do."

"But it doesn't bother you?" Tabitha asked him, ignoring the fact that the man was indeed being very rude. "The idea that they've just moved you into this place, with all the mess and after–"

"Look, miss, this place is a perfectly functional living space. And compared to where I was forced to live previously, this apartment is paradise. Not that it's any business of yours."

"Where were you living before then?" Tabitha gasped.

"That is also none of your concern."

"You're right," Tabitha agreed. "All right. Well, I'd better go to work. Or I'll be late. Again. If Elliot gets home before I see him, please tell him that Tabitha came 'round to see him."

"Very well." The man went to close the door then opened it again, a little further than before. "One thing before you go. I thought I recognised you from somewhere. Your name's Tabitha, did you say?"

Tabitha nodded and made her way to the conveyor. Perhaps she should go up to the Möbius Strip after all. It would at least kill a few hours and perhaps muffle her mind's mitherings about how Elliot was getting on.

On her journey up to the Strip, Tabitha imagined where Elliot's new flatmate must have been living previously. He wasn't a young man and anything less than a cramped and frankly squalid bachelor pad that wasn't even fit for student accommodation was hardly suitable for a gentleman in his mid-eighties.

Perhaps he had been living in a bunk room populated with ten men, or perhaps a prison cell. Maybe he had been living with a wife who treated him badly and therefore his new home was, indeed, a paradise, a sanctuary. Tabitha had always been interested in the fact that every person had a story behind them. Their own unique tale. Some were harder to guess than others. She doubted whether anyone would guess her own story.

"*Please mind the gap between the elesphere and the platform. Please mind the gap,*" rang the disembodied voice, which probably didn't care whether anyone minded the gap or not. Tabitha stepped out of the elesphere and into the transport hub. She made the now familiar journey on the conveyor along the transparent mathematical shape and into the Euclidean Building. Despite the detour to Elliot's home, Tabitha was still three minutes early for her shift.

Judging by the expression on Rusabelle West's face however, she was not quite early enough. Tabitha got the impression that Rusabelle simply tolerated her. If it hadn't been for the high ratings that she had inadvertently achieved, Tabitha knew that she would not be there at all.

"Good morning, Belisha," she said curtly as Tabitha arrived at her desk. "You do like to keep me on my toes, don't you?"

"It's not six o'clock yet," Tabitha informed her with a polite smile.

"The commercial break is almost over. Get ready for your greeting," said the producer as she made her way to her booth. "And remember, keep it consistent."

"Good morning," Tabitha chimed into the microphone.

"What is that?" Rusabelle hissed into her ears. "No fake cheeriness. Just be yourself. It's what the listeners want. Remember what we talked about?"

Tabitha nodded. How had she forgotten? There was so much going around in her head that Tabitha had forgotten how to be herself.

"I know how hard it is to get out of bed at such a daft time in the morning, let alone be sitting at your desk listening to the radio at this awful hour. While you make yourself another cup of souprano, here's another tune to help console you."

Tabitha pushed up the faders as she had seen Elliot do and searched her recent memory for something to tell the listeners. Why didn't she plan something on the way up here instead of worrying about Elliot's new flatmate? What could she talk to her listeners about? She couldn't tell them about her dreadful day yesterday, could she?

"Good morning, Obscurous," Tabitha said into the mouthpiece as she faded down the final bars of Mistress Halo's latest song faster than she probably should have. "I hope you're all having a better morning than I am." She wrinkled her nose. "I don't know how many of you use the elespheres on your way to work, but *phewy*. I can still smell the body odour from the underarms of some of those commuters! It's as though my clothes have absorbed all of their sweat." She recollected the rest of her journey. "And the conveyors were busier than ever. Even at this time in the morning! Honestly, having to get up this early should be a crime." She continued to moan and make small talk into the broadcasting equipment while setting up the next track.

When she was off air, Rusabelle West took the chance to speak to her through the headset.

"Not bad Belisha, not bad. Keep relating to the listeners. But remember, not many people are as fortunate as you are and don't work on the Strip. Keep it real."

Keep it real? Had she suddenly turned into a nineties rap artist? Tabitha nodded and gave her a thumbs-up, racking her brain for something to say in the next slot. *Don't think about it too hard,* she told herself. *Just say it as it is. Be Tabitha.*

"I had to call the Mergencies yesterday. There was a, shall we say, a pretty unfortunate incident at the house of a, well, I suppose I could call him a friend." She was careful not to name her ex-co-broadcaster. "It's ridiculous the way the Mergencies deal with things, though. I suppose it's because they're just robots and they have no empathy. Speaking of robots... that ArrRobot at the transport hub. He just speaks in riddles! When he's not malfunctioning, of course..."

Calm it down, Tabitha, she cautioned herself. *You're not a comedian on stage, doing observational humour. Get back to your moaning. Pretend you just woke up. Empathise with them like you did before. Be natural.*

Tabitha feigned a yawn and then realised how good a nap would feel. As tiredness washed over her, she struggled to suppress a second yawn. She shook her head vigorously, as though to wake herself up. She pondered for a moment.

Maybe if she couldn't think of anything to say today, then she should ask the listeners to do it for her!

"I've just had an idea, listeners. A new feature for my new show. Call in with your thirty-second rants. It can be about anything. Within reason," she added, looking over at Rusabelle, but it was hard to determine her reaction. She was simply staring at her through the glass booth with a stoic expression on her face. Tabitha froze. How did people contact their radio stations these days? Were there still telephones? The internet? Someone of Belisha's calibre would definitely know about these things. She suddenly remembered Rusabelle mentioning something about something called a communicom. She glanced around for a clue. Then she saw it. There on the wall was a sign. Underneath the brightly coloured holographic logo of Möbius Strip Airwaves was the letter C, a dash and the figures 1253MSA8. C for communicom perhaps?

She read the number on air, and within seconds the dashboard next to her computer screen began to light up like a cruise ship at Christmas.

"You've done it now, Belisha. You'll be wanting a switchboard operator to help you next!" came the producer's voice as the next track boomed through the speakers. But Rusabelle did not seem displeased. "There are obviously a lot of unhappy people out there, just begging to tell the world their stories. Let's just hope they make interesting radio, yes?"

Rusabelle had a point. What if they didn't have anything more interesting to say than she did? She supposed it was a problem that has plagued DJs for centuries. Tabitha was forever rolling her eyes at mundane phone-ins.

Tabitha faded out the track, wishing that she had the opportunity to vet the calls before they came in. She was disappointed that the technology wasn't as slick as it could have been in the future. Maybe she would need an assistant after all. It was obvious that Rusabelle was not going to volunteer her services. She tapped on the screen and one of the lights extinguished, before quickly lighting up again.

"Good morning, you're live on air on the First Sunrise Show. Who am I speaking to?"

"I got through! I'm so happy that I got through!"

This wasn't a good start.

"Congratulations," she said sarcastically, "And what is your name?"

"What? Oh, sorry. I'm just really excited. I have never got through before. And especially not on your show, Belisha! Penelope Buckton. That's my name."

"And how are you today?"

"I'm great! I feel great now! I can't believe I'm really speaking to you, Belisha!" the young lady squealed with delight. Flattered though she was, Tabitha shook her head. This wasn't going the way she had planned it at all. Penelope continued, "But what was my reason for calling? Oh, yes! My day did start off very badly. First, I received two wrong numbers on the communicom, which woke the baby both times. Then my eldest was sick all over his bunk and all over his little sister on the bunk below him. And then my husband couldn't find his uniform and the hygiene cubicle stopped working!"

"Oh, I can relate to that one," said Tabitha.

"And now I can't go anywhere, as I have one sick child, another to somehow clean up without a functioning cubicle and a very tired baby."

"That sounds like a bit of a nightmare," said Tabitha, who had never seen the appeal in babies and young children. "And what song would you like to request this morning?"

"We get to choose a song?"

"Well, if it helps to cheer you up, then it's the least I can do," she replied, honestly.

"In that case, can you play Mistress Halo's *Where Have All the Seahorses Gone?* It's my favourite."

"Are you sure that's the song you wish to choose? Out of all the songs in the world, this one is your choice?"

"Yes, oh yes!" the young woman enthused. Tabitha sighed.

"Very well. I hope your day improves."

After enduring the headache of a song for the umpteenth time, the next caller took her by surprise.

"Welcome to the First Sunrise Show. And to whom am I speaking?"

"My name is Mr Crabness."

"Mr…Crabness?" The words stuck in her throat. Elliot's new elderly flatmate? Her mouth dry, Tabitha continued. "And how are you today?"

"We met earlier, I believe. When you left, I realised who you were. But you said your name was–"

"You must have been thinking about someone else!" she interjected, quickly. "I've been here all morning! So, soul, congratulations on being the second ever caller in our brand-new slot." His response was a mere harrumph on the other end of the line. "So, Mr Crabness, do you have anything you wish to rant about live on air this cold morning?"

After a few seconds of incoherent grumbling, he muttered,

"I don't appreciate the younger generation. Those such as yourself. They have absolutely no respect."

"And what kind of day are you having?" Tabitha continued through gritted teeth, hoping that the communicom connection would somehow be lost. Her finger hovered over the disconnect button. She couldn't be sure that anyone would believe that the old man had seen her, but Tabitha did not want to risk her true identity being exposed live on air.

"Well, I have spent the majority of the morning, early as it is, being bustled from one living space to the next. I've since been bothered by a succession of unsolicited callers and nuisance-makers knocking on my door. Still, it's the price you pay for freedom, I suppose!"

Freedom? Had her suspicions been correct?

"I suppose you could always go back to bed," Tabitha suggested.

"I can't sleep late at my age. Once I'm up, I'm up. Besides, if my new flatmate finds me asleep in the middle of the day, they might mistake me for dead!" Mr Crabness punctuated his sentence with a raspy cough. "And there's been enough of that going on lately." Tabitha wasn't sure how to respond without getting anyone into trouble and raising yet more questions. "That's the front door again!" he barked. "I had better go and see who it is this time. Probably someone trying to sell me a new souprano machine or something else I don't need. Goodbye, Tabitha." And with that, he hung up.

"Thank you for your call, Mr Crabness," Tabitha said as she faded in the next track. "After this next song, I will invite the next caller to give me their own daily objections."

"Not a bad start," said Rusabelle West. "I quite liked the grumpy old man. Although he did seem a little confused. What did he call you before he hung up? Anyway, perhaps we should have him on the show again!"

Tabitha took the final bite of a slice of quadruple chocolate cake, mentally apologising once more to Belisha's body, as she stepped onto the conveyor. She was getting used to the strange transport system now, and, as she dusted away the final crumbs, she stepped across onto the median lane with ease. It hadn't been a bad shift at Möbius Strip Airwaves and, typically, she was feeling more awake than she had done when she had woken up that morning.

But what to do now? Should she go home and perhaps have the chance to relax for a while and chat with Shan? Or should she go to see Elliot and risk bumping into Mr Crabness, Rusabelle's new favourite caller? He had mentioned that Elliot had gone to his uncle's house. Should she go directly there?

But as she stepped out of the elesphere, it happened again. Recognition.

"It's her!" a bright-eyed boy of about eight advanced towards her, tugging his mother behind him. "Mummy, it's

Belisha from the radio. And she *does* have weird hair. Look, Mummy!"

"Oh, so it is, Mikey," the mother cooed. Tabitha's thumb print allowed her to exit the elesphere barrier and she smiled politely at the woman and her son. "Have you just come back from the Möbius Strip?" the woman asked her, full of awe, although the answer was obvious.

"Yes," Tabitha replied and brushed stray crumbs from her cheeks. She was still not used to this kind of reception from perfect strangers. She felt like such a fraud. "Did you enjoy the show this morning?" she asked, conversationally.

"Oh, yes, we love listening to the First Sunrise Show – now more than ever!" she gushed.

"When Mummy's making my breakfast in the morning and telling me over and over again to go into the hygiene cubicle, I'm always really grumpy and sleepy and you make me laugh. You're so funny!" said the boy, his big green eyes sparkling.

"Well, that's good to hear."

"And that new man, Mr Crab... Crabtree... Crabness? He's funny too. He's a funny man. He's so grumpy like granddad!" The child burst into a fit of giggles which tugged at even Tabitha's un-maternal heart. She could not help but smile back at the boy.

"Will he be on again tomorrow, that Mr Crabness?" the mother asked.

"It wouldn't surprise me if we hear from him again," said Tabitha.

"Wonderful. Well, we'd better go and find Daddy, Mikey. It was nice meeting you, Belisha."

"You too!" said Tabitha with a wave.

As she watched them disappear through the crowds, Tabitha spied the ArrRobot in the edge of her vision and a sudden thought struck her. If Belisha was so recognisable here, maybe she should see whether the ArrRobot's databanks had any more information on her. And while she was there, perhaps it could tell her more about Professor Pagter's previous abode.

Belisha

Belisha looked across at the stranger who had come to visit her at Tabitha's house a few days ago. She narrowed her eyes and pursed her lips in concentration as she tried to determine what was going on.

"Do you remember me, Belisha?"

"Of course I remember you. You're the only one around here who knows my real name and you're the only one who seems to have heard of souprano. I don't suppose you brought me a jar?" she asked, hopefully.

The stranger shook his head. "There are more important things to discuss."

"Like how things are back at Möbius Strip Airwaves," she said, half to herself. "Has Tabitha ruined my chances at ever moving to The Strip? Is she spending all day cluttering up my apartment with her... clutter?"

"Oh, Tabitha is doing very well at the station. Very well indeed."

"She is?" Belisha asked, unable to hide the disappointment in her voice.

"In fact, she's been promoted. Tabitha now presents the First Sunrise Show."

"What?" she gasped. "But... but that's *my* dream!"

"I suppose she's just playing the game, Belisha."

"So... so she knows that she's part of this... awful experiment? Stranger, did she volunteer?"

"No. It hasn't been possible for me to contact her. It's not safe there at the moment. Just as it's not safe here."

"Are you... are you talking about the murder?"

The Tall Stranger paused, looked down at the polished desk and back up at her. "Death hasn't just found you here, Belisha. There has been rumour of one on the Möbius Strip and of two in Hayfen Capital, too."

"Hayfen Capital? Near my home?"

"Fairly near."

"And what happened to Veronica Vaughan... is that somehow linked?" Belisha swallowed.

"I am trying to find out what is going on. It is not easy for me. But, yes, I fear that may be the case."

"But who would do such a thing. And how?"

"That's what I'm trying to find out, Belisha. You have played the game well so far. But things have got out of hand. I'm trying to figure out what's going on and bring you home."

"Why can't you take me with you?" she rose to her feet. "It's not safe here!"

"Is everything all right?" Judith entered, unannounced.

"I have almost finished here," the man informed her. He unfolded his long legs from behind the desk and pushed his chair behind him as he rose. He turned to Belisha. "Think about what I said. And stay safe." He turned, nodded at Judith and promptly left. Judith followed in his wake.

"But," started Belisha. "I still don't know your name!"

Belisha joined her ex-colleagues in the office, where she knew Adrian would be waiting.

"What was that about?" Adrian asked, his eyes full of concern.

She could sense that Tricia and some of her ilk had been talking about her in her absence. Belisha eyed them, suspiciously.

"He didn't say much, really. Just that if I had any information then I should let him know."

"Is that it?" asked Judith.

"Yes, Judith," said Belisha. "That is it."

"Well, that's alright then," said Adrian. "So, what are you going to do now?"

"I really just want to go home," said Belisha, meaning Hayfen IV. How she longed for her own bunk.

"Maybe you should be going to the job centre," said Judith, spitefully. "You know, before you get a criminal record. That's if Miss Ree will give you a reference since you deserted us all."

"Don't listen to Miss Sour Face over there," said Gerry. "She's just got her knickers in a twist because she asked Dragon Chops for a pay rise before she croaked."

"Maybe that's what finished her off!" piped up Jamil. Gerry high-fived him and they both burst into laughter.

"Really, I have had enough quite of this!" Judith scowled at the pair, walked to her desk at the other side of the room and flicked on her computer. Belisha could see her shaking her head and muttering to herself.

She looked at Adrian and then at Gerry and Jamil. "Other than you guys, there's not much for me here." Belisha shrugged. "There's no point in me being here. I'd better go."

"All righ', lass. Shall we let you know what happened to Veronica when we find out?" asked Gerry.

"If you like," said Belisha, her only interest being the fact that Veronica's was one of four murders which were too close for comfort for her liking.

"I'll see you on Crimewatch!" Tricia hollered as Belisha left.

"You know, under normal circumstances, I would never let anyone speak to me like that," she said to Adrian, who had followed her out to her car. "But, you know, I'm never going to see her again, so why should I waste my energy?"

"That's the spirit." Adrian looked at her. "She's such a gobby so and so, isn't she?"

"Are you all right?" she sensed a sadness behind his eyes.

"Yeah, I'm fine. It's just not every day that something like this happens, is it? It's going to be a very different place without you. And without her. I don't mean to be disrespectful, but I don't know whether the company is going to change for the better or the worst now that she's gone."

"Well, I don't expect that whoever Miss Ree employs to replace her could be as bad as Veronica was. Unless she promoted Judith. Seriously, though, were those two related?" They allowed themselves a giggle.

"You're probably right. But still, I imagine that the atmosphere in there is going to be really weird for quite a while. I'm surprised that they don't close for a few days out of respect. Then again, nothing surprises me about Miss Ree's anymore."

"Then I'll give you something to keep you going," said Belisha with a smile. She wrapped her arms around his neck, and they kissed.

"I'm so tempted to jump in my car and follow you back to yours," said Adrian as he drew breath.

"Well, you know where I am." She winked as she opened the driver-side door.

"You might regret saying that!" he called as he made his way back to the building.

Belisha drove back to Tabitha's house, but instead of walking up the tarred driveway, she walked back along Cottonwood Close and took the route to the Black Swan. Fifteen minutes later, she was nursing a pint of lager and staring into the frothy head as the bubbles dispersed.

If only she could speak to the tall stranger who had come into Tabitha's home and then her workplace. She had spoken to him twice and was no closer to getting home. If only she could call him or summon him somehow. If she really was part of a huge experiment, was there anyone monitoring it? And if they were, surely they could stop it now that people were getting hurt – killed, even! Or were the perpetrators connected with the murders? Was it their doing? And, if so, why? Was the stranger helping her through the experience or trying to stop the Experiment? If it was the latter, Belisha wished that he would try a little harder.

An hour passed and Belisha drained the glass. She grimaced, for the drink had become warm and flat during the long minutes that she had been staring at the amber liquid. She took out Tabitha's phone and considered calling

Adrian. As she turned the smooth device over in her hand, she was suddenly startled by its trill message tone. Adrian's name flashed on the screen. Belisha opened the tiny electronic envelope with a tap of her thumb.

"Wish you were here. Work is as dull as ever, which is pretty astonishing considering what has happened. Morale is at a spectacular low today. Hope you're all right. Text me back if you like and if you're not too busy." He finished the message with two Xs.

Belisha grinned. She was impressed with Adrian's eloquence. Especially considering the fact that he was probably tying to conceal his phone under his desk as he typed. Of course, she wanted to respond to his message. But she also did not want him to get into trouble with Judith, whose prevailing temper was approaching dragon-like proportions.

She stared into the middle distance, contemplating an appropriate and perhaps slightly flirty response, when the man that Gerry had referred to as Michael the landlord appeared in front of her.

"Are you interested?" he asked her.

"I beg your pardon?" Belisha looked up at him.

"In the position. It looked as though you were reading my shiny new sign." The middle-aged man gestured at a yellow and black notice that had been pinned to a post above the bar. He smiled smugly, as though he had just unveiled the Mona Lisa. The garish lettering said, *'Bar staff required for immediate start. No experience necessary. Ask the landlord, Michael Maxwell, for details.'*

"Do you have a job at the moment?" he asked her, his bare arms crossed over his broad chest.

"I, er, no. Actually, I don't as it happens, Michael." said Belisha.

"Have you had any experience in pub work? You're Ellie's friend, aren't you? Tabitha? You used to work at that big office in town, didn't you – that Misery place?"

"I won't correct you. It is pretty miserable there. Especially at the moment…"

"By my recollection, you're not the most extroverted of my regulars – unless you've had a few glasses of the good stuff inside you, of course – but I'm sure you'll fit in all right. You can be welcoming to the punters? Not easily stressed?"

"Does this count as an interview?" asked Belisha. "You are asking me an awful lot of questions."

"And a sense of humour to boot!" Michael laughed. "I'll tell you what, why don't I give you a trial period? If you come back this evening and help me out for a couple of hours, we can see how it goes. What do you think?"

"Well, I do need to bring some money in," said Belisha. She looked around the comfortable room. The place that had been Tabitha's and now her own little sanctuary. It was certainly a more preferable working environment than the stuffy corporate office.

"Don't sound too enthusiastic, will you?" His belly shook as he laughed. His arms stayed crossed as he turned to a customer who had just walked up to the bar and told him, "I'll be with you in a moment, Bob." He turned back to Belisha and opened his arms out in a shrug. "Well?"

Belisha stood up, lifted her fists to her collarbone and pointed both elbows towards the puzzled-looking landlord.

"I'll do it."

The opportunity to work in any job in catering or serving people directly had never particularly appealed to Belisha. But neither had being jobless in the wrong time, on the wrong planet, in the wrong house. Equally, the opportunity to fall in love had never really presented itself to her either.

It was now six o'clock. Belisha sent a text message to Adrian for the fifteenth time that day as she entered the Black Swan for the second. Smiling, she ducked underneath the bar and joined the landlord at his side. She watched as he served a red-headed girl who had ordered a round of six drinks and armfuls of snacks.

"Do you want a tray for those?" Belisha found herself asking as she searched around her for something suitable.

"Yes please," the girl said through teeth that were clenched around the corner of a packet of cashew nuts.

"There you go," said Belisha with a smile. The girl smiled gratefully and loaded her purchases onto the tray.

"Nice one," said Michael. "Well, that's customer service ticked off the list. How about you try and pour a pint?"

"Who for?" she asked, looking along the vacant bar.

"Me!" Belisha looked up to see Ellie closing the door behind her. "I could do with one. But what are you doing on that side of the bar, Tabs?"

"Bar Tab. That's not a bad nickname," mused Michael.

"I don't think so," said Belisha, curtly. She turned back to Ellie, who was looking rather distressed, her curls more frowzled than usual. "Well, I needed a job, didn't I? And Michael Maxwell is giving me a trial."

"Well, it'll help, I suppose." Ellie smiled weakly. She waited for Michael to turn to fetch a pint glass from behind him. "Are you going to be able to pay the mortgage on a bartender's wage?" she whispered. "It's great that you found something so quickly, but there is a reason that you've never bothered with bar work before."

"Well, it's better than nothing," said Belisha with a shrug.

"Here you go. Which one will it be?" Michael handed the glass to Belisha.

"Oh, Tabs knows what I drink, don't you, Tabs?" Ellie said, pushing a crop of stray hair out of her eyes and pulling herself up onto a bar stool. Belisha thought for a moment.

"Well, let's pretend that I don't. For practice, you know."

Ellie pointed to one of the pumps and Michael watched while Belisha placed the glass underneath the nozzle and pulled the lever. A few seconds later, she raised the glass a couple of feet above the bar and wrinkled her nose, for it was half filled with foam.

"Can I have a Flake in that?" asked Ellie with a laugh, "And some hundreds and thousands while you're at it?"

"Sorry," said Belisha, who was slightly frustrated and annoyed with herself. "I'll try again."

"You're doing fine. Just tilt the glass more and it'll work much better, you'll see," advised Michael.

Belisha's second attempt was much more successful, and she proudly handed a glass full of golden liquid to her friend. She shook the drips off her hand.

"Eurgh, it's so sticky," Ellie complained.

"You'll have to get used to that, I'm afraid," chortled Michael. "I'm sure it's good for the skin, anyway."

Ellie handed her a note and Belisha held it in her damp hand. She had no idea what she should do with paper money.

Belisha wished Ellie could just complete the payment using her thumbprint. She could probably handle the card slot device, but this ridiculous paper money…

"The till is behind you," Ellie said, helpfully.

"You'll need to enter a code to open it," Michael informed her. Step by step, he explained the process of entering the amount of money received, where the notes went and how to administer change. Belisha was grateful for his slow-motion way of teaching. It was as if he were teaching a child to tie their shoelaces. Anyone native to the culture might have found his methods patronising, but the whole system was so new to Belisha that she appreciated his guidance. When another customer swiftly followed Ellie with an order of three different drinks and handed her a fistful of notes and coins, she asked Michael to go through the process with her again. He was happy to do so.

An hour passed, and Michael evidently felt confident enough to allow Belisha to supervise the bar on her own for a short time.

"I know it's your first day, but it's a clear night, and I just wanted an hour to myself to attend to one of my favourite past-times." Belisha raised an eyebrow and Michael elaborated. "Astronomy. I've bought myself one of those fancy computer-controlled telescopes, and there's a good chance I'll be able to get a good view of the international space station this evening."

Belisha wished him luck and took the opportunity to ask Ellie about her day. Her eyes had practically been begging her to comment on her obviously agitated state since she had arrived.

"So, what's wrong, then?" Belisha asked. "Why did you so desperately need a pint? What's happened?"

Ellie leaned across the bar, looked around her and then whispered, "Tabs. Please can you explain to me why I was asked to give an alibi for you this morning?"

"Ah."

"You'd forgotten?" Ellie asked, thumping down her glass. "Really? Tabitha, what were you doing back at Miss Ree's? And why did you really leave in the first place? You've had plenty of opportunities to walk out of there before. Why now?"

"What are you trying to say?" asked Belisha crossly. "You of all people know where I was when it happened."

"When what happened? You still haven't told me."

"They didn't tell you?"

"No! All they did was ask me if I could confirm that I was with you yesterday and where."

"I see." It was Belisha's turn to whisper. "There has been a death at the office."

Tabitha

Tabitha wasn't surprised to learn that the name Belisha Beacon was not in the ArrRobot's databanks.

"I be a transport hub bot. My databanks do not have that information. Only transport and limited local history cognition. Arr."

"Of course," she said, rather exasperated. "Isn't there a Googlebot around here somewhere?" Tabitha implored.

"I don't be knowing of any directions to any Googlebot."

"Right." Tabitha composed herself. She tried to formulate the optimum sentence in her head before speaking out loud. It felt like she was trying to think of the precise magic words for a spell to prevent herself from turning into a frog. "ArrRobot, can you tell me the directions to the residence of Professor Pagter? And I don't mean this mysterious Smoky Hollow place. Where is Professor Pagter's registered address?"

"Professor Pagter be registered to be living at number fifteen Hawkins Terrace, Hayfen Capital."

"Finally," said Tabitha, with a degree of triumph. "So how do I get there?" *It's as though someone combined a sat nav with the yellow pages, but there is only one available for the whole population of the city,* thought Tabitha as she considered the ArrRobot. How could this place be so advanced, yet so backwards? She would do anything to have her mobile phone and internet access again. She felt blind without them. How did people here cope?

It took Tabitha a little under half an hour to reach the destination given to her by the ArrRobot. She looked up at the concrete block that had been home to the professor. It was as unremarkable as the rest of the living quarters that the inner-city district had to offer. She hoped that Elliot was still inside. If he was, then he would have been there an entire morning, she realised. And it didn't look any larger than where Belisha and Shan lived. If anything, it was smaller. There was no way he was going to still be here, she thought.

As she approached the front door, though, she noticed that it was slightly ajar.

"Elliot?" she called, tentatively.

"Tabitha?" Elliot's head appeared over the top of a stack of metal crates. "Oh, soul, I'm so glad that you came! I hoped that you would."

"Wow," Tabitha remarked. "There's more clutter here than in my house back on Earth. No wonder you've been putting off coming here. What is all this stuff?" Aghast, she looked around at the room. It looked more like a warehouse than a living space. The cream settee was just about visible underneath a pile of papers that were strewn across the upholstery. The floor was littered in crates, half-opened parcels and files.

"I just wish he'd filed all of this in some kind of logical order," complained Elliot. "Why did he fill all of these crates? It's such an archaic way of doing things."

It wasn't only paperwork that had taken over the living space. The kitchenette surfaces were home to all manner of bags, empty bottles and discarded wrappings.

"Elliot, is your uncle a bit of a hoarder, by any chance?"

"It's even worse than I feared," Elliot sighed.

"What do you think happened to him? Have you found anything to do with the Experiment? Any ideas on how to get to Smoky Hollow?"

"Nothing yet, soul." Elliot ran his fingers through his hair, which pinged back into an upright position almost immediately. He clicked his tongue a few times in thought. "I almost wish I hadn't started now. I've found a few of diagrams and scribblings, but nothing that makes a lot of sense."

"Where have you got up to?" Asked Tabitha, kneeling among the towering crates.

"You can have a look through the stack nearest to you if you like," said Elliot. "I haven't gone through that one yet. But I can't help thinking that if there was anything of any importance, he wouldn't have left it here."

"Well then, none of this stuff can be that important. Unless…unless he left in a hurry. Which would explain why he didn't have time speak to you and your mother before he left."

Elliot gulped. "Perhaps he was *made* to leave."

Tabitha said nothing. Instead, she prised open one of the boxes nearest to her and began to sort through it. A thought suddenly occurred to her.

"How come the professor doesn't share his home like everyone else seems to?"

"What do you mean?"

"Well, he doesn't appear to have flatmates like you or Belisha. It took you weeks to be granted access to the place and you're a close relative. But there must be someone else. Did he live alone?"

"I told you that my uncle is a recluse. He paid a premium in order to get his quarters to himself. He said that he didn't want any distractions nor anyone bothering him while he worked. That's why he couldn't afford to live anywhere bigger, even on the commissions he makes as a professor. There was no one else to share the cost of living in the city."

"So, he lived and worked here? Among all of this? Didn't he commute to a laboratory or something? He's a scientist, isn't he? Unless he's a theoretical scientist." Tabitha felt like she was getting carried away with her thoughts. "Something just doesn't add up here."

"No, he didn't commute. He has… bad nerves. He can't handle the strain of using the conveyor over long distances anymore. He always worked from home. Of that, I am sure."

Tabitha leafed through a pile of yellowing files, which looked old even by 2018 standards. *Whatever happened to computers?* she wondered. *Are they just used for games now?* Most of the notes she came across were illegible scrawlings or they were so faded that they were impossible to read.

She was halfway down the third crate when she came across a thick, oversized notebook, bound in red leather. There was a stretch of elastic keeping the pages closed and marginally flat. Tabitha pulled the elastic to the side and was surprised when it simply crumbled in her hand. The material had perished over time. She opened the heavy cover carefully.

"What's that you have there?" asked Elliot as he hauled a crate from the top of another pile.

"I'm not sure." Tabitha delved through the pages with interest, peeling back one immense page at a time. The text in the notebook was darker and slightly more legible than the reams of faded papers. There were extra pages that had been attached to some of the pages. One appeared to be a document for planning permission for an extra room.

"Elliot," she cried with a sudden surge of exhilaration. "Did your uncle ever mention an extension that he had arranged to be constructed here?"

"An extension?" Elliot asked, obviously utterly confused.

"Specifically, an extension for an underground laboratory?"

Belisha

"I can't believe what you've just told me, Tabs," said Ellie as she took the first sip of her second pint of lager. "All of that madness at Miss Ree's and here you are, casually pulling pints in our local. Aren't you the least bit freaked out?" She took another sip. "I mean, the Tabitha that I know would be rocking back and forth in a corner and crying into her mobile phone with either your mum or me on the other end. No offence…"

"Really?" Belisha frowned. Of course, she had taken no offence whatsoever from Ellie's observation. "I suppose the Tabitha you know and love has changed."

"I admit that you have grown up a bit lately, Tabs, which is great and all that, but you do seem to be taking all this in your stride rather too well. Are you all right, Tabs? Do you think that maybe you're in shock or something? It wasn't long ago that I had to take you to see Doctor Wok. You were all over the place after the mugging, do you remember? How are you keeping it together after all of this?"

Belisha shrugged. "I'm over the mugging incident, I'm glad to be out of that awful office and the murder is nothing to do with me. It's horrific, even if it was someone as vile as Veronica Vaughan, but what can I do? Apart from comfort those who still work there, of course," she said with a sly grin.

"Namely Adrian?"

Belisha grinned. Ellie raised her glass in a half-hearted toast and said, "Well, at least something good has happened to you lately. I'll drink to that!" She returned the glass to the bar top. "So, are you going to go to her funeral?"

"Er, I haven't thought about it," said Belisha, honestly. "I haven't been to one before."

"Really? What about your great uncle Bob's funeral a couple of years ago? Yeah, I remember now. I helped you choose something to wear. You were paranoid about standing out and you said that you had nothing suitable to wear, despite the fact that half of the clothes you own are black anyway."

"Of course. Anyway, I don't know. I mean, it's not as though I was a friend or family member."

"Well it could be a while yet, anyway. If the circumstance is suspicious then I suppose they still might need to do a postmortem."

"Won't they know how she died by now?"

"These things can take a while though, can't they?"

"Apparently so," said Belisha with a sigh. The Mergencies at Hayfen Capital would have been more efficient.

An elderly woman approached the bar and gave Belisha a toothless smile. "Can I have a Bloody Mary please, dear?"

"A what?"

"Tomato juice, a shot of vodka and Worcester sauce," piped up Michael who had appeared beside her. He already had a glass in his hand. "Here you go. The optics are over there, juice is stored in the fridge and the sauce is on the shelf."

"Are you sure this is what you want?" Belisha asked the elderly woman.

"Tabitha! Give the lady what she has asked for," Michael admonished her. He pulled her to one side and whispered, "Don't ever question what the customer has ordered. Unless they're too drunk to stand up, of course. Then that's a different matter."

"Sorry, Michael," said Belisha. "But it just sounds so unappetising. I wanted to make sure before I put all of those ingredients together."

"All right. Well, don't do that again." His tone lightened again, and he patted her on the back fondly. "Service with a smile, eh?"

Belisha nodded and went about making the drink.

"I probably would have thought it was a strange choice at your age too, dear," the woman said sweetly. "But as I get older, my taste buds just aren't what they were. I need stronger and more unusual flavours to be able to taste anything at all these days!" She laughed and handed Belisha a ten pound note between shaky, arthritic fingers. "Keep the change, dear," she said and shuffled over to a table by the window, where the last of the sunlight shone in through the glass. She took a sip of her drink, closed her eyes and savoured the warmth of the early evening sun.

"A perk to the job," said Michael, pointing at the fistful of change that Belisha retrieved from the till. "Just pop it in your pocket, Tabs. Plus, I'm in a particularly good mood. I had a great view of the space station. That telescope was definitely worth the money. I'm sure it'll pay for itself one day," he said, wistfully.

Belisha beamed. "I think I'm going to like it here. If you'll let me stay, of course, Michael."

"Well, you seem to be keeping the customers happy," said Michael. "I don't see why I wouldn't want you to stay. Would thirty-five hours a week suit you for now? It would mean working evenings and weekends, of course. And the occasional holiday cover."

"Thanks, Michael," Belisha grinned.

"Great stuff. I'll get a contract written up and make it official."

Belisha turned to Ellie, who raised her glass once more by way of congratulating her.

It was twenty to twelve when Belisha finally left The Black Swan that night. Her feet were aching from standing for such a long time and her ears were ringing from the sound of the jukebox and drunken carousals.

Ellie had left half way through her shift, but by then there was little time to talk to her anyway. Belisha was surprised at how busy the place had got as the evening had progressed. It had also been a little unnerving, all those people getting increasingly tipsy and raucous.

Several of the male regulars had noticed that she was a new member of staff and had made efforts to flirt with her, but Belisha had found their advances amusing rather than alarming. Michael had even commented on her ability to turn them down without turning them away from the pub. He had even left her to man the bar by herself for almost an hour while he took a long phone call with one of the suppliers. And Belisha had felt confident dealing with a room full of strangers. She had even learned most of the drinks. Belisha found herself embracing this new challenge.

Tabitha

Tabitha watched Elliot scrutinise the document. He glanced over at her as a smile spread slowly across his face. He ran his long, pale fingers through his iridescent hair in his usual quirky manner as he pored through the papers. Then suddenly, without a word, he stood up, picked his way through the littered living space and into the bunk room. Curiously, Tabitha followed him. She tripped over the clutter at least three times and twisted her ankle in the process.

As she clutched her left foot and muttered a string of expletives, she heard a hygiene cubicle door opening.

"Elliot?" she called. "Is it really the time to have a shower?" Tabitha hopped through the bunk room door. The room was empty. "Elliot?"

A minute or so later, the door of the hygiene cubicle opened and there stood Elliot, a glint of excitement in his eye.

"Come with me!" he commanded and held out his hand.

"You want me to follow you in there?" Tabitha wrinkled her nose.

"Just come on. It's not what you think. I promise you that."

Tabitha did as he asked her and stepped tentatively into the small, metallic room. But instead of beginning a cleansing cycle, the room lurched and pulled downwards. "Are we in a lift?" she asked, holding onto one of the walls. "You're not going to make me slide down a fireman's pole too, are you?"

"What?" said Elliot. "Yes, the hygiene cubicle does appear to double up as a lift. I pushed those buttons next to the door. Come on."

The door opened once more, and Tabitha gasped as Elliot led the way into a cavernous room.

"So, this is your uncle's extension?" She whistled, utterly impressed by the enormity of the space.

"It looks that way. It's fantastic isn't it? This must be where the professor spends most of his time," said Elliot. "Or, should I say, *spent*."

"It must expand underneath the street. This place is huge!"

Tabitha stared around them, consumed by absolute awe. The room was certainly astonishing. A line of benches banked the wall to the left, their surfaces festooned with canisters, bottles and strange-coloured liquids. To her right was all manner of machinery, the likes of which Tabitha had never seen.

"Some of these actually have blinking lights, like in the films!" she exclaimed. "And can you hear those ones over there bleeping? This is fantastic! What does all of this stuff do?"

"I don't know much more than you about this kind of thing, I'm afraid," said Elliot. "Some of this machinery looks positively archaic!"

"Archaic?" Tabitha snorted. "It looks futuristic to me."

"Well, you would say that," he said. Tabitha was a little taken aback by his tone, but she did not react.

"This looks interesting." Tabitha lay her hand on a white leather seat, which was set in the recline position. "What do you think it does? Perhaps it's some kind of deluxe massage chair or…or perhaps it's a dream-recording machine. Finally, someone invented one!" she cried, excitedly.

"That's a nice idea, but there's a cold cup of souprano on the table beside it," said Elliot flatly. "I think it's just where my uncle liked to nap."

"Oh," said Tabitha, disappointed. "Well, some of this equipment must do something interesting. What about the Experiment that he was working on? There must be answers here."

"It's a little tidier than his living space upstairs, but there's still a lot of stuff to examine," Elliot said.

Tabitha looked around her, desperately looking for clues. Clues relating to the Experiment and any explanation as to where the professor had gone. Perhaps he was still here somewhere, hiding among the equipment, busying himself with a project.

She ran a hand across one of the laboratory's many workbenches as though her fingertips were scanning the surface for even a tiny scrap of evidence. Her fingers fell on a book entitled *How to Build your Dreams and Discover the Future*. She flicked through its pages with interest. There was nothing about its contents that sparked any interest or relevance.

She felt Elliot's eyes watching her. Had Belisha's colleague taken a liking to her? Were his glances ones of desire, intrigue or something else? Either way, he was making her feel a little uncomfortable. She shot him a look and he immediately looked away. *Stop being so paranoid,* she said to herself. She replaced the book on the desk and, as she did so, accidentally pressed a button. A square of pale blue light hung in mid-air in front of her.

"Don't panic. It's only a blue board," Elliot told her as he picked up a piece of equipment from the floor and examined it carefully. "I doubt it says anything interesting. Or decipherable, for that matter."

"Oh, it's like one of those hologram screens they have at the radio station," she said as she observed a lengthy mathematical formula appear one character at a time on the floating screen. It was as though an invisible pen was being used on a whiteboard by an unseen entity. The language was beyond her, no matter how hard she tried to understand it. Suddenly, an invisible eraser made light work of the formula, which vanished in seconds, only to be replaced by a dialogue box that demanded a pass code of five digits.

"How frustrating!" puffed Elliot. "And, before you ask, I have no idea what that formula means, let alone the passcode."

"One, two three, four, five," Tabitha said aloud. A short, sharp low buzz indicated that she was incorrect and the screen promptly winked out of existence. "It was worth a try," she said with a shrug. She tapped the button again and the screen reappeared, but this time the dialogue box appeared straight away before deactivating itself almost immediately. She did not try a third time. "Hey, it didn't even give me a chance that time!" Tabitha heard Elliot laugh and she noticed that he was shaking his head. "Yes, I know your uncle's a genius and would probably have a more cryptic passcode than that, but you never know." Elliot, for once, said nothing.

Tabitha continued her journey around the perimeter of the laboratory, scanning every piece of equipment from the smallest alchemist's teat-pipette to the largest, most complicated-looking electronic instruments she had ever seen. She followed a trail of implements, which cumulated in a spaghetti of wires and tubes. Despite all the advanced equipment available to him, the professor seemed to revel in combining chemistry and electronics in the crudest manner.

"This all looks so fascinating," said Tabitha. "And somewhat dangerous. Are electrics supposed to be exposed to so much water?"

"It's pretty much how I imagined his laboratory to look," said Elliot. "I just didn't expect it to be here underneath his home. I still can't get over it."

"Have you found anything interesting? Are there any notes or anything relating to where he might have gone?"

Elliot shook his head, glumly. "If only I could find a diary or some equipment or even just a few notes that make any kind of sense."

Tabitha picked up a yellowing magazine entitled *Innovations and Opinions* and thumbed through it. She read out various article titles she found within its pages.

"*The Rise and Fall of the Internet* by Gill Bates, *The Holographic Revolution* by Professor R. Arnold, *Mergencies and Why Not to Trust Them* by Doctor Septic, *Teleportation Through Time and Space – Temporal Neural-Matter Transference* by…by Professor Pagter. Elliot, look! A whole article written by your uncle. And it sounds like it could be related to the Experiment. Have you read this?"

Elliot bounded over to Tabitha and all but ripped the publication from her hands.

"Careful!" she scolded him.

Elliot apologised and clutched the magazine. His eyes widened as he read the title for himself and drank in the words.

"This is interesting. This is very interesting."

"What does it say?" Tabitha pleaded with him. Her ankle still causing her some pain, she steadied herself on one of the benches. She accidentally knocked over a glass canister, which went crashing to the ground, scattering dozens of tiny glass shards in all directions. Fortunately, it was empty. "Oops!" Tabitha hopped out of the way on her good foot.

Elliot shook his head again and focused his attention back on the magazine.

"According to this article, the professor claims that he is at the helm of the preliminary stages of a brand new project with an unnamed commissioning client. The project proposes to address the position of the possible transference of two consenting bodies to two specific points through a man-made hole in the space–time continuum." Elliot looked up at Tabitha, who was standing open-mouthed. He looked back at the article and read, "Once the two consenting, like-bodied, like-minded beings are positioned thusly, only then can preparations for the neural-matter interchange commence. Of course, the largest challenge, and possible ruination, of the process is the prevailing inability of gaining consent from the secondary party."

Tabitha didn't know where to start. "Like-minded? Never! And consenting? I certainly didn't consent to anything like this." Elliot held up a finger. "Just wait until I've finished." He scanned through the text, turned the page and read, "Despite all of the scientific theories mentioned above, plus a significant cash injection to the project, I cannot confirm at this stage whether the project will be viable. Even in the remote event that the project was to be a success, there is the monolithic factor of the repercussions on the test subjects themselves. Firstly, how would they react to a new and potentially hostile environment? Would the subjects be accepted in this unknown habitat and would they recover from the uncertainty of the experience, which could be traumatic and possibly dangerous? There are many factors to consider before moving on to the next stage of my research." Elliot paused.

"That can't be it. What else does it say?" Tabitha silently pleaded with him. Her stomach lurched and gurgled.

"There's not much more," said Elliot with a shrug. "The last paragraph goes on to say: We are a far cry from transferring a physical being back through time to days past, but with modern scientific breakthroughs, switching consciousness between two bodies inhabiting two different temporal planes is theoretically plausible. However, before the dream of temporal neural-matter interchange becomes a reality, many tests will have to be undertaken, and a method of gaining retro-consent takes precedence. Until there is a way of gaining lawful consent, then the experimentation regarding this project will be limited."

"Limited to what? Animals? Amoeba? Or to slightly overweight brunette females?"

"It is a bit of a flat conclusion to the article isn't it?" said Elliot, wrinkling his nose and absently flicking through the remainder of the magazine. "I have read a couple of issues of *Innovations and Opinions* before. Their articles on new projects and proposals promise everything and deliver nothing. It's all opinion and speculation with no satisfying conclusion. Most frustrating. I bet half of that article isn't even in my uncle's own words."

"But if any of the experiments mentioned in there were ever successful, they'd print it, wouldn't they? Think about how many copies they would sell then! If the Experiment worked, then why isn't it in the magazine? Or the following issue*? Why isn't it common knowledge?"*

"Isn't it obvious, Tabitha? Because the industry hasn't been able to gain retro-consent."

"It was obviously a very expensive experiment," said Tabitha, eyeing the magazine. She began to pace, the broken glass crunching underneath her soles. "So, if I am part of it, then why am I allowed to walk around freely, unobserved? And where is the professor now?"

Tabitha jumped as the door to the hygiene cubicle lift suddenly opened. The silhouette of a slight man stood the doorway. He was carrying a torch, which he flicked on and pointed directly into her eyes, dazzling her. Despite his small stature, the man's voice boomed through the cavernous laboratory.

"So, you think you've been walking around unobserved, do you? Well, I can tell you that that is not quite the case!"

Belisha

Oh, tall stranger, where are you?" she pleaded with the front door, staring at the patch of flaking paint near the latch. "Just turn up again and tell me what's going on. This needs to end! If there are any more deaths…if Adrian is next, then…then…" The tear that had been threatening to fall tumbled down her cheek, followed by another and another. She felt utterly helpless.

There was a sudden loud knock on the door. Belisha looked up and wiped her eyes with her sleeve, for once not caring how she looked. Could this be him?

To her surprise, the letterbox opened, and a voice cooed through the gap, "Hi, Tabitha, it's only me. Melanie from number twelve. I know it's late, but I just saw you get home. I have some more farm produce for you. My mum has been 'round again and she asked to ask around the neighbours' to see whether anyone wanted anything."

Belisha pushed herself to her feet and opened the front door with a sniff and a stifled sob.

"Whatever is the matter?" Melanie placed a large wicker basket down on the doorstep and wrapped an uninvited arm around her shoulders. Belisha shied away. She did not appreciate sudden, unwelcome kindness from strangers. "I'm sorry. I was only trying to comfort you." Melanie took a step backwards and pulled her oversized shirt awkwardly around herself. "Well, whatever's wrong, maybe my fresh crusty baps will help!"

"What?" Belisha looked at Melanie's toothy smile, upturned nose and small green eyes. Her face was weathered and freckled. Belisha assumed that it hadn't been exposed to any conditioning products in its life. Melanie's lined forehead and crow-footed eyes sat unashamedly underneath an unruly bob of mousy brown curls. Belisha thought that her clothes were best suited on a male who was three sizes larger.

Melanie from number twelve delved into the basket and held out four round, floury loaves. "Here," she said. "Greg from number thirty suggested that the eggs I brought 'round to everyone last week were a little on the fresh side." She stopped to cough. "But there's no danger of anything like that with these. In fact, they'll probably only last until tomorrow. They should be fine if you put them under the grill for a few minutes, though. Perhaps with a slice of cheese!"

"Perhaps," said Belisha, curtly.

"I will give you the last four for a pound."

Belisha's stomach grumbled and her mind mentally surveyed Tabitha's pitiful cupboards. With a sigh, she picked up her bag and sought the correct change. Her time at the pub had helped her get used to twenty-first-century coinage.

"I knew you wouldn't be able to resist. And cheer up, Tabitha, it might never happen!" Belisha dropped a pound coin into the top pocket of Melanie's checked shirt, took the loaves and forced a smile. "Thanks again, Tabitha. See you soon, I expect."

Belisha kicked the front door closed, proceeded through the house and placed the baps onto the only free kitchen surface, which became immediately covered in flour. She dusted the white off her sleeves and switched on the grill.

As she sat staring into the middle distance, chewing the slightly stale cheese on toast, Belisha noticed that there were half a dozen young chickens pecking at crumbs around her feet.

"Oh, hello," she said softly and crumbled a chunk of bread onto the floor for them to share. "You finally managed to get out of that tub, did you? I bet it was that Melanie's fault that you're all here in the first place. I'll give her 'slightly fresh'! Maybe I should have sold you back to her." She sighed and looked down at her bland meal. "I can't believe I paid for this. I can't believe what I'm putting up with. I was practically robbed on the doorstep, wasn't I, little chick chicks? The old Belisha wouldn't have put up with any of this. Maybe I'm not thinking straight. It's all too much without the added inconvenience of mad people turning up on the doorstep demanding money." She looked down at the chirruping young chickens. They had lost some of their yellowness but were as fluffy as ever. "What shall I do, eh?" she asked them with a sigh. "Of course, I want Adrian and my new job at the friendly pub, and even Ellie seems like a good person to have on my side, but I want my home and I want to get away from the murder and the terror and…oh, I'm so confused." Belisha placed the half-eaten meal down on the sofa next to her, much to the birds' delight. She grabbed the nearest cushion, curled up and cried herself softly to sleep.

Belisha's dreams were filled with confusing and frustrating images. She was back on the Möbius Strip. The tall stranger was standing on the fast lane of the conveyor and she was stuck on the slow lane. She tried to step across to catch up with him, but every time she made an attempt, something stopped her. She called after him, but he didn't turn around; he simply held onto the rail in front of him and looked straight ahead. She called out again and tried to step across in vain. Why wasn't he listening to her? She tried to run along the conveyor, to catch up with the fast lane, but the other travellers were stopping her and telling her to move across, not forwards. They were pushing and jostling her, and soon the stranger was out of sight.

Next, she was sitting at her desk in the Euclidean Building, wearing her headset. Although, it wasn't her desk, it was Oranjer Bannawoo's. Through the glass, she saw what looked like herself from behind. She appeared to be interviewing someone. Was that Veronica Vaughan? To her horror, Veronica's neck suddenly snapped backwards with a sickening sound, and Belisha saw that her face was covered in blood. Her dead eyes were wide open and stared at her through the glass. Blood trickled down her bloated face, her lined forehead, through her hair and onto the floor. Her other self seemed to be oblivious.

Belisha cried and wailed and banged on the glass, but she could not be heard. Through her tears, she noticed that Adrian was also sitting there. How long had he been there? Had he been there during the whole gruesome scene, or had her sick, tortured mind conjured him up to frighten her? She looked away. She didn't want to see the same thing happen to him.

When she finally looked up, she was back on the slow lane of the conveyor, and it was now Adrian who was in front of her, staring stolidly forwards. Her cries were, once more, unheard, her movements fruitless. She pleaded with him to turn around.

She screamed as a large green and gold crow appeared from nowhere and landed swiftly on Adrian's shoulder. It cocked its head and delved its beak deep into his ear. Blood gushed from the orifice. The bird was soon met by dozens more crows.

"No!" Belisha cried out. She was suddenly awake. The midday sun was flooding into the room and one of the chickens was pecking at her cheek. In a flourish, she pushed it off the sofa and quickly got to her feet. She ran out through the kitchen and opened the back door. "Get out. All of you!" She picked them up one by one and closed the door behind them.

She sat back on the sofa and buried her head in her hands. A moment later, she looked up again.

"No. I've done enough weeping. I need to find out what's going on. Enough is enough."

Tabitha

"Professor?" Tabitha called out to the silhouette. "Can you please stop dazzling us with that light?"

"That's not my uncle," said Elliot.

"Then who is it?" asked Tabitha.

"I have been waiting for you," said the figure, knavishly. He walked slowly and purposefully towards them, the dazzling light growing in intensity as he did so. Tabitha screwed up her eyes.

"I have been waiting for *you,* Tabitha Turner. *We* have been waiting for you."

Tabitha opened her eyes a little and noticed that the light was not shining in Elliot's face, only her own. Elliot was looking at her. Something was different about him. It was like he was someone else. There was a gleam in his eye that made her feel extremely uncomfortable. A cruel smile crept across his lips.

"Elliot, what have you done? Who is this?"

"He's led you to exactly where we need you to be. That's what he's done."

The man flicked off his torch. It took a few moments for the light spot to disappear from Tabitha's vision. There was something familiar about that voice. She had heard it at least once before.

"Do I know you?" Tabitha asked, quietly. Suddenly feeling vulnerable, she hugged herself and realised that her arms were covered in goose bumps.

The man gave a raspy laugh. Tabitha's vision finally cleared, and she could see plainly who was standing in front of her.

"Mr Crabness?" She gasped. She heard Elliot laugh, but kept her eyes on the old man, whose features sat contentedly within the folds of his aged skin.

"He's not really Mr Crabness," said Elliot, matter of factly.

"If he's not your flatmate, then who is he?"

"Oh, he is my flatmate, Tabitha. He has been for ten years now. Tabitha, I'd like to introduce you to Smoky Hollow."

"What? But Smoky Hollow is a place, isn't it?" Tabitha's voice wavered.

"You only assumed that it was. And Mr Crabness was just a name that he made that name up on the spot when you turned up at our home, and then he subsequently called you at the radio station."

Elliot was right. How had she been so stupid?

"So…so you really know where the professor is?"

"Of course!" Smoky grinned a gummy grin.

"Then…then why were you pretending that you were trying to find him?" Tabitha turned to Elliot. She felt utterly betrayed and completely confused.

"I wasn't. All I had to do was get a job working at the station, flatter Belisha's ego and yours, scare you a little and lead you exactly where I needed to. And you're so easy to manipulate, aren't you?"

"Scare me?" Tabitha's mind was whirring. Nothing was making any sense. She closed her eyes and tried to piece together all the pieces of the puzzle. She gasped. "Rojer and AJ? Was it you who killed them?"

"Rojer and AJ don't exist. I invented them and their deaths entirely for your benefit. To frighten you. Think about it. Did you meet them? Did you even see their bodies?"

"Their murder, all that about a killer escaping through a ventilation shaft, the blood on the ceiling, everything – all of it was made up by you to scare me?" Her throat felt dry.

Elliot nodded in a self-satisfied manner.

"But the Mergency robots! They came when I called them and investigated the crime scene."

Elliot laughed, "Ha! They weren't real Mergencies, merely a pet project of mine. The beauty of you having not trodden on this world for very long is that you're so very clueless about such matters. Anyone else would have noticed that my lovely creations, as clever as my robotic skills are, could never be mistaken for real Mergencies. Mergency unit seventeen and his metal companion were knocked up right here in my uncle's laboratory. They have been kept in my back storeroom ever since. Did you not notice that they entered my home via the back door?"

"But I thought you knew nothing about technology!"

"It seems that you thought a lot of things which turned out not to be true," said Elliot.

"But why send your robots in at all?"

"Two reasons. One, to validate my story. And two, to get Belisha's thumbprint," said Elliot. "Once we had the thumbprint and once we were certain that you did indeed refer to yourself as Tabitha Turner and not that egocentric radio DJ, we continued to the next phase."

"The next phase?"

"Which was to lure you here, of course," said Elliot. "It wasn't difficult to persuade a compassionate, caring person such as yourself to come and help me find my dear long-lost uncle," he said mockingly and feigned the act of wiping away tears. Tabitha narrowed her eyes. How dare he do this to her?

"I trusted you!"

"I know you did. Poor girl. All alone in the world. A little lost fishy, all alone in a big, wide toxic swamp. You didn't stand a chance, really, did you?"

"But I still don't understand why, Elliot."

"Haven't you understood any of the information that was fed to you along your breadcrumb trail to this laboratory?" Smoky said as he walked around her, as though he was trapping her inside an invisible circle.

"What do you mean?"

"If my uncle had really been lost, don't you think that I would have found all this stuff by now? I planted the leather-bound book in the pile that *I* suggested you search. Then I lead you underground to the laboratory, which I had known to be here all along, knowing that you would find that article in *Innovations and Opinions,*" Elliot sneered.

The truth hit Tabitha like a breeze block. She turned to Smoky Hollow. "You…you are the unnamed commissioning client. You just want to try and gain retro-consent!"

"Oh, the ancient coin has finally dropped has it?" Smoky gave the loudest and raspiest laugh that Tabitha had ever heard. The sound of it burrowed right through her very nerves. She was boiling with anger and encumbered with fear. "And there's no question of trying, Tabitha. We *will* get that consent. From both of you!"

"I won't give it to you!" Tabitha insisted, her adrenalin suddenly energising her. "By its very definition, you needed to have gained consent retrospectively – that is, *before* this terrible experiment ever happened. It's too late. And if you haven't got Belisha's genuine consent by now, then I doubt that you ever will!"

"Oh, we will find a way of harvesting your consent, don't you worry, soul." said Elliot. "And as for that smug little radio broadcaster – well, the professor himself is well on his way to getting close enough to her to acquire exactly what he needs. She'll soon be begging to tell him."

"Sign it!" Smoky Hollow bellowed.

Tabitha could barely see the faces of the two perpetrators through her tears. She tried desperately to remember what had happened. She recalled Smoky circling around her while Elliot taunted her. Then she had felt a sudden pain in the back of her head. The next thing she knew, she was tied to the white leather seat she had mistaken for a massage chair. She could not have been more wrong about its purpose.

Her limbs were bound down by coarse, leather straps that prevented her from moving more than a millimetre. An angle-poise heat lamp was pointed at her face and, even with her eyes closed, she could feel its warm glare burning her skin. Her throat was dry, and her bladder was full. The discomfort was unbearable.

"It's simple, Tabitha. Just agree to go back and sign your consent with that lovely moniker of yours, and you will no longer be tied up," said Elliot. His soft tones mocked his vulnerable prisoner. He seemed to be enjoying the power that the situation offered him. Tabitha felt sick. She wanted to vomit and pee and shout. The only part of her that wasn't bound up was her mouth. So, she screamed.

"No one can hear you down here, soul." Elliot reached down and stroked her hair. "Relax! Perhaps you'll find this a little more comfortable?"

"What are you doing?" she shrieked.

She felt the chair recline further and further back, until she was almost upside-down. She could feel the blood rushing to her head. The lamp had moved with the chair and was burning her more than ever.

"No, no!" she begged.

"Like your young man friend said, just agree to sign your consent and we will let you go," said Smoky.

"He's no friend!" Tabitha spat.

"I fooled you for a while though, didn't I? Just like I fooled my uncle into thinking I was helping him."

"What have you done to the professor?"

"Oh, he's quite safe. As long as he complies with me, then he'll be quite comfortable."

"Oh, comfortable like I am, you mean?" spat Tabitha. She squirmed, and the more she did so, the more the straps tightened against her skin.

"This is such a primitive form of, er, persuasion, Smoky. I wasn't convinced to start with. But I must admit that it is quite effective," she heard Elliot say with a callous laugh.

"Please, Elliot. Just let me go to the toilet at least!" she begged, hoping that she could appeal to his better nature – if Elliot even had one.

"Oh, I'm not stopping you, sweetheart," he said quietly and stroked her hair once more. "You go ahead. We won't watch."

She shook her head free from his caress and scowled at him. He withdrew his hand and crossed his arms.

"You already have my thumbprint, don't you?" Tabitha reminded him. "I am not saying that I consent to any of this cruel, wicked experiment of yours, but I don't understand what you need from me."

"We only have Belisha's thumbprint, remember? It's her body you're rattling around in. You two may be strikingly similar in body type, but you're not identical. And, unfortunately, any signature taken from you here and now would not suffice," said Smoky with a sigh. "I will instruct you exactly how to word the document, which you can write out in good old-fashioned ink at your own desk in your own cosy little home back in 2018. All I need is your agreement to sign your consent on your return." The heat from the lamp burned too brightly for her to see or think clearly. Nothing was making any sense.

"That's quite a nice tan you're getting there, Tabby," observed Elliot. "When this is all over, maybe we should do this again."

She cried out. "I won't do it. You're completely insane!"

"Perhaps. Perhaps I take after my uncle."

"I think that gene skipped his generation," said Smoky Hollow. "The professor is just too nice sometimes. A little too trusting. A bit like you, Tabitha."

"Please, please, just let me go."

"You don't understand," said Smoky. His tones were serious now. "I have spent my life's earnings on this project. When I discovered that Professor Pagter was working on temporal neural-matter interchange, I knew that I could persuade him to work for me."

"And by 'persuade' I suppose you mean 'threaten and torture'," Tabitha growled through gritted teeth.

"Oh, neither of those things were necessary. His mounting costs of running this place and the threat of debtors' prison was enough to sway him. I was able to pay him handsomely," he said proudly.

Belisha squirmed. Her bladder felt as though it was going to rupture. "What would you do to him if he refused to help you now?"

"Then he would experience a very unfortunate demise," he said, matter of factly. "And there were the others, of course. Doctor Molly Wok, Veronica Vaughan, Tricia Mason…"

"What? These are all people I know!" Tabitha gasped. She suddenly forgot all about her bladder. "They have nothing to do with any of this. You killed them? All of them?"

"Oh, it hardly matters now whether I did or did not kill them," said Smoky. He gave a gravelly cough.

"They're all dead, anyway. You see, everyone you ever knew back on Earth is dead, Ellie, your family, the Queen of merry old England! It was all so very, very long ago."

"You killed Ellie?"

"Did I say that?"

"But..."

"Although it's not without question. How about you agree to sign your consent and I'll spare her life?"

Tabitha gulped.

"And you'd let me go home?"

Smoky laughed so loudly that the cacophonous sound echoed throughout the cavernous room. "Do you really think that I went to all of this trouble so that you can continue with your miserable little life back on Earth? No, no, no. Signing your consent would simply allow us to continue. On your return here, you will be released from your restraints, of course. Oh, Tabitha. Did you really think that it would be that easy? This is only stage *one* of the experiment."

Belisha

Belisha heard Tabitha's phone ringing inside her bag. It was Gerry. He wanted to know whether Tabitha could cover the lunchtime shift. It had been barely twelve hours since she had left the Black Swan and her first instinct was to tell him that she couldn't work today. She had more important matters on her mind, after all. But maybe she had more chance of seeing the stranger again if she went about her daily business and went along with things. Maybe there was someone she could talk to about what was happening. Perhaps she could trust Ellie, Adrian or even Gerry. But would they be able to help her? Would they believe her? Even Tabitha's doctor, a supposed professional, had dismissed her proclamations as falsehoods. Without even attempting to understand her plight, she had looked down her nose at her and fobbed her off with primitive, low-level painkillers.

"So, is that a yes, then? It would be really helpful if you could do a few hours just to cover the lunchtime rush."

"Well, I was going to go to the shop and see if I could get some supplies," she said vaguely. "I haven't eaten yet."

"Well, if you get here within the next half an hour, I will ask the chef to cook you up some pub grub. On the house. Is that a deal?"

"All right," she said.

Whatever 'pub grub' was, it sounded like some kind of strange insect.

Belisha had a few hours to spare between the lunchtime shift and the evening shift, so she decided to go for a drive in Tabitha's Fiesta. She had only ever previously driven to

Miss Ree Loves Co. and Orly Leisure Centre, and curiosity was getting the better of her. After all, what harm could she do by exploring this strange and unfamiliar world? Without the aid of the satnav, she drove blithely through suburbia, humming along to the radio, which she had never figured out how to switch off. She listened with interest to the broadcaster, who introduced one primitive tune after another, peppering their programme with asinine chatter.

Some of these broadcasters do talk a lot of drivel, she thought to herself. *And my grandmother's, grandmother's, grandmother probably listened to some of this music.*
It seemed odd that they were promoting these songs as brand new. Belisha wondered what new music she was missing back on Hayfen IV. She supposed she would be completely behind in the latest releases by now. She would feel so out of touch when she got home. If she ever did get home.

A brief fanfare bridged the gap between a song and the afternoon news bulletin. A serious-voiced male reported,

"The body of the Acting Director of Birmingham company Miss Ree Loves Co., Miss Veronica Vaughan, was found in her home in Token Row two days ago. The police are viewing the incident as suspicious. Judith Highbury, also of Miss Ree's Loves Co., describes the deceased as 'a charming, warm person' and she 'can't understand why anyone would want to harm such a delightful lady'. More on that story as the investigation continues. Meanwhile, over in Leicestershire, a dog owner has discovered the benefits of–" Belisha the dial on the radio and it stopped.

Veronica Vaughan, a 'charming, warm person'? A 'delightful lady'? She knew people used to say not to speak ill of the dead in the olden days, but this was going a bit far! *Besides, I don't think that whoever is behind this killing will stop at Veronica. Who will be next?* She thought, horror-struck.

She thought about the other people at the office. Gerry, Jamil, Adrian. She thought about the others who were closer to home. Michael, Ellie. Belisha held back her tears so that she could still see the road. She did not want to stop driving. She had a mission. She wanted to find the stranger.

Oh, where are you?

Tabitha

"So, what's stage two?" Tabitha asked, bravely. The more she spoke, the easier it was to keep her mind off her full bladder and the heat of the lamp, which, despite her protestations, had been pushed an inch closer to her face.

"Tell me, Tabitha," said Smoky Hollow softly, "If you had commissioned a temporal neural-matter transference, what would you use it for?"

"I don't know." It was not something that Tabitha had ever thought about before. She had fantasised about travelling back through time in a time machine as much as the next person, but this was different. She had had no choice in her destination and her body had been left behind.

"Well, I'm assuming you'd want to use it yourself wouldn't you?"

"Well, I wouldn't force two complete strangers to swap places – people who weren't aware of what was happening to them!" she cried. "It would be obvious to me that they would feel disorientated and confused and...no. *Confused* is not a strong enough word. Look, I have been going out of my mind! I didn't know where I was, who I was, whether I was in the middle of some terrible nightmare...I still haven't adjusted properly and, to be honest, I don't think I want to! All I want is to get out of this horrible place where people live in tiny houses, listen to terrible music, lie about who they are and...torture people!"

"But don't you see? Your world is not so different from ours. You were alone, you worked at a job you hated, and you were attacked and mugged in your own neighbourhood."

"How did you know that?"

"You don't think we just plucked someone randomly from the surface of that doomed planet, do you?" laughed Smoky. "No, we had been carefully observing you for quite some time." Tabitha visibly shuddered at the thought of the intrusion into her life. "We wanted to see how a person like you would respond to the transference. If the brain of a person who was oblivious of what was about to happen to them could cope with the transference, then it would make sense that the mind of someone who was aware - myself for example - would stand an even better chance."

"But I still don't understand why you chose me. And I didn't hate everything in my life you know. I have a mortgage and friends and—"

"And all of those things were tying you down," said Elliot, intoxicated by his own words. "You were trapped in that little world of yours. By your own admission, you didn't get dressed in the morning without first consulting your best friend. You didn't leave the job you hated because you had bills to pay and you never had the confidence to try and get a better one."

"But I would have…eventually. I had plans, you know. I had plans to travel one day…"

"With Ellie, I suppose?"

"Perhaps, but what's wrong with that?"

"I don't think you planned to travel much further than the local tavern," spat Elliot.

"Whatever my plans were, it was my life and it doesn't justify you snatching me from my home and bringing me here just to…to broaden my horizons!"

"You credit me with too much compassion, Tabitha, sweetheart," cooed Smoky Hollow. His false sentiments made Tabitha feel sick. "That was a mere by-product of the Experiment; one which made observing you so entertaining. The reason that we chose you, Tabitha Turner, is that you are very similar in shape and size as our dear Miss Beacon. If we had managed to transfer your bodies as well as your minds, then few would have noticed the difference. You are of the same build, your hair is of the same colour and length, your features are remarkably akin and your neural systems matched perfectly. The only deviation being, of course, is the way in which you inhabit your bodies. Belisha makes the best of hers and walks around as though she doesn't care whether anyone else approves. Although, of course, she does care. She cares very much. She wears her skin like a fashion accessory. But you look so awkward in yours, whichever body you occupy! It's as though you're apologising for your own existence, for that tiny bit of room that you take up. The difference between the two of you is, in fact, quite extraordinary."

"He's right, of course," said Elliot. In a strange, forced voice he croaked, "And even though you have access to all of the best garments, paid for by the hard work of one of the biggest celebrities on the Strip, it's as though those clothes are wearing *you,* soul."

"I've heard that before." Who had said that to her before? Tabitha gasped. "Mumma Toille. You were there! It was you!"

"Of course it was him!" Smoky laughed. "You don't get any women that ugly up on the Strip."

"The old-lady makeup and padded clothing was pretty effective, if I may say so myself," said Elliot, proudly.

"Toille…Elliot…" she mouthed silently. Tabitha scowled. How could he do this to her?

"You didn't hang around for very long did you? You sky-rocketed out of Kello Lumpy's didn't you?"

"You're disgusting, both of you."

"I think the word you're looking for is 'clever'," said Smoky.

"You two do seem to have some kind of crises of identity. First Mumma Toille and then Mr Crabness—"

"Just sign the form and we can move on!"

"But why? You've already got me here. You've proved that the experiment works. I've survived Hayfen IV for days and I'm still alive. Why do you still need me to sign anything? Just send me back."

"Because if I don't get your consent, Professor Pagter will not let me use the neural-matter transference machine for myself and I will not get any of the glory!"

"I'm surprised that you haven't just used it anyway," Tabitha scoffed, despite herself. She wondered what deeds he had in mind for the year 2018.

"Unfortunately, the professor is the only one who knows how to operate it," said Elliot. "My uncle is sly like that. The crucial operational instructions are kept where no one can see them – inside his brain. And, unfortunately, I have no way of retrieving them. He is remarkably resilient to my persuasion techniques."

"But how will you go about getting the consent of whoever you swap places with?" asked Tabitha. "I still don't understand."

"Oh, that's simple. You will get it for me. And then the professor can't refuse my requests. Not while I'm keeping him out of debtors' prison. And alive."

"What if I refuse?" asked Tabitha, who was still squirming against the rough leather straps. Her ankles and wrists were red raw. "Can you please get that lamp away from my face and let me use the toilet?" Her pained expression only served to make Elliot to smile with smug satisfaction at her increasing discomfort.

Smoky ignored her pleas.

"If you refuse, then my servant back on Terra Firma will pay a little visit to Ellie's house just as she's getting home from work." He continued, casually, "Perhaps he'll welcome her home with a knife or a blunt instrument…"

"Stop, stop!" she begged.

"So do we have a deal, Tabitha Turner?"

"If this monstrous person has the wherewithal, then why don't you get him to do your dirty work for you?"

"Don't you want to go back home, Tabitha?"

"Yes, but–"

"Besides, sending instructions back in time is impossible. My dear servant has been advised that if I don't bring his consciousness back to Hayfen IV within twelve hours, then his instruction is to kill your friend."

Tabitha gasped.

"Therefore, when I send you back, you will get the consent for me and take it to a safe place, where it will remain until I collect it four hundred years later."

Tabitha shook her head, attempting to make some sense out of what the deranged man was telling her. Dehydration, pain and discomfort were causing her to become confused. Her conscientious was becoming hazy. "But that doesn't make any sense. You would need to go back to Earth to retrieve it. It won't be here on Hayfen IV."

"It will be if you take it to the right place and entrust it with the early founders of Project Borrowed Time. I have worked out all of the logistics, don't you worry about that. Think about it. Who would willingly travel forwards through time to see how things turn out? Someone with great influence and power? Someone quite important, perhaps?"

Tabitha realised the enormity of the situation. She gulped, her throat as dry as glass paper. "You…you want to swap places with someone like…like the Prime Minister?"

"Someone *like* the Prime Minister, yes…or the man himself," said Elliot, nonchalantly. "It didn't take her as long to work out as I had expected. I underestimated her. Perhaps her being here has enhanced that small mind of hers."

"Be quiet, Elliot," Smoky Hollow admonished him for the first time, which came as a surprise to Tabitha. Elliot had stepped to the side of the heat lamp, so she was able to see his thunderstruck expression. In an act of defiance, he pushed the heat lamp closer to Tabitha's face, momentarily. The bulb hissed as it touched her skin. She screamed out in pain. There was the sudden stench of burnt flesh.

A raspy laugh erupted from the depths of Smoky's throat and he continued, "And should I enjoy my new position as ruler of Great Britain, then perhaps I'll make it more of a long-term post and remain there."

"If you can send me back, then why can't you go back yourself, retro-consent or not?" she tried to shout, but her mouth was too dry. She tried to turn her face away from the searing heat.

"As we have already told you, because your neural coordinates are already set up," answered Elliot. "We can send you back and forth as we please. Smoky already told you that he needs to gain retro-consent before the professor will sanction any further transference pairings."

"I'd rather die than let you be in charge of my country," squealed Tabitha. The pain was unbearable, and she felt as though she was nearing death.

"Would you really let Ellie die?" boomed Smoky.

"You said yourself, she's already dead. They're all dead… and… and I'm not far behind them…" she said, weakly.

Tabitha's body seemed to be shutting down in an attempt to escape the pain. Her eyes were closing, and she was powerless to stop them.

She could barely feel the straps being loosened and her limp body being carried to another room.

Belisha

Tabitha's old Ford Fiesta jolted and jumped along the tarmacked street. Belisha steered it instinctively towards the kerb and it came to a halt. She wound down the window to let the fresh air cool the interior. She cried out in anguish.

"What's wrong with you, you obsolete, rusty old piece of–"

"Are you all right?" A young man with blonde hair and the beginnings of a beard was standing on the pavement.

"This corroded piece of rubbish just stopped!" she exclaimed.

"It just came to a halt?" he asked and scratched his chin. "Hmm...at the risk of asking the obvious - has it got enough fuel in it?"

"Fuel?"

"Yeah, you know, petrol." Belisha's puzzlement must have been obvious, because he reached an arm through the open window and pointed at the dashboard. "See that red light there? It's warning you that you're low on petrol. It looks as though it has been on for some time, because your gauge is on zero."

"How do I fix it?" she asked.

"You have passed your test, haven't you? This is your car, isn't it?"

"What are you, some kind of Mergency? Of course it's my car. Well, it belongs to someone whose house I'm currently staying in. I have been using it for ages."

"Well, it looks as though you've emptied the tank. Has your friend got a petrol can in the boot?" Belisha looked at him blankly. The man shook his head in dismay and walked around to the back of the car. He opened the boot and returned with a green canister with a black pipe attached to it. "Fortunately for you, they have. There's a garage about a quarter of a mile away," he said and pointed further along the street on which she had been driving. "If you fill this up there, then you should have enough to get you back on the road again."

"Right."

"Are you all right? You didn't knock your head when you came to a sudden stop did you? You seem a bit-"

"I'm perfectly fine," snapped Belisha as she wound the window back up. She took out the key, picked up her bag and stepped out of the car. She took the can from the man and muttered, "Thanks, soul."

Belisha started along the pavement and left both man and car on the kerbside. "Stupid, antiquated old transport pods," Belisha muttered to herself. How was she supposed to know it needed feeding? You didn't have to pour petrol into a conveyor on Hayfen IV to make it work. She never understood why Earthborns didn't harness the power of the oceans. They had enough of them on this damn planet. It was no wonder it was doomed if they couldn't look after it properly.

Belisha looked around for a building that might be referred to as a garage. She recollected going to O'Reilly's Garage to collect the car from after its service, but she was far from that neighbourhood now. If only Connor O'Reilly had told her about petrol, she thought.

She passed a short row of shops, then came upon an immense sign standing proudly on the edge of a forecourt boasting the cost of fuel. This must be the place the man meant, although it looked very different from O'Reilly's.

Fortunately, there was an assistant at the pumps at this particular garage, who spotted Belisha and her bright green can.

"Oh dear, did you have to walk far?" asked the assistant.

"Far enough," grumbled Belisha.

"Diesel or petrol?"

"Er, petrol please," she said, handing him the can. It didn't take long before it was full.

"It's going to be a fiver. I'll hold on to it while you pay inside." The assistant smiled at her under his red cap.

When she was finally on her way back to the car, Belisha noticed someone on the other side of the street. It was someone tall and familiar. He was standing next to a blue, battered van. The stranger!

Belisha ran across the street, petrol can swinging in her hand, and narrowly missed being hit by a Range Rover.

"Be careful now, babe," the stranger said. But as he lowered his hood, he she realised that it wasn't who she had expected. Gone was the Hayfen Capital accent, gone were those benevolent eyes. Instead, the voice was gruff and the eyes unkind. He looked her up and down, lustfully.

Before she realised what was happening, Belisha was being bundled into the back of the rusty blue van and the doors were slammed shut behind her. Seconds later, the vehicle began to move at such a speed that Belisha was sent crashing headfirst into a large, metal toolbox and was knocked unconscious.

When Tabitha awoke, her head was pounding, and her body ached all over.

Did they hit me over the head again? she thought, feeling more panicked than ever. *What did they do to me? Where am I?*

Wherever she was, she could tell that she was moving at quite a pace. Suddenly, she was being hurled so forcefully into a metallic wall that she saw stars. Tabitha swore loudly as she clutched her throbbing head and felt around for purchase in the dark space with the other hand. She managed to hold onto a ridge in the metallic framework of her immediate surroundings. As her eyes adjusted to the dark, she realised that there was not enough room to stand up. She was in the back of a vehicle of some kind.

"Help! Let me out!" she cried out and banged at the hard metal shell.

Without warning, the vehicle came to an abrupt halt. Moments later, a door was opened and the light from the setting sun glared into the compartment.

"Get a bit battered, did we, babe?" asked an unfamiliar voice. "Get out. Now!"

Tabitha whimpered. Was she dreaming? Before she could respond, a tall youth had grabbed her wrist and dragged her outside onto hard ground. She fell to her knees and cried out in pain. The young man grunted, grabbed something from inside the van with one hand and her wrist in the other. He yanked her to her feet and dragged her along the stony ground to a dilapidated building. She quickly realised that she was indeed awake and that she was no longer wearing Belisha's clothes and shoes. She was no longer even wearing Belisha's skin. Tabitha put her free hand to her face. It didn't hurt. The burns had gone. They had remained on Belisha's skin! Her bladder was no longer throbbing with fullness. She was home. Or was she?

"Where are you taking me?" she pleaded. "Are you…are you the servant of Smoky Hollow?" she gasped.

"I'm not nobody's servant!"

A moment later, the man stopped. He looked her up and down, which made her feel very discomfited.

"I recognise you now, babe. You're that girl. You don't talk like you did last time I saw you, outside Orly offy. And you look different somehow. More, I don't know, common. No, awkward. Weird."

You wouldn't feel fantastic if you'd been rattling around in the back of an old van, she thought.

"What do you want from me?" she begged.

"All in good time, babe."

Her memory returning to her, Tabitha recalled something. "Please don't hurt Ellie," she begged.

"What?"

"She's my friend. He said someone was going to hurt her if you hadn't received further instruction or been transferred back within twelve hours."

"Who have you been talking to?"

"Ouch! Where are you taking me?" she squealed as he grabbed her arm once more. She looked around. Perhaps there was someone she could shout out to for help.

"In here," he nodded towards the crumbling building. It looked as though it had once been a warehouse. Every single one of its windows had been smashed and the stench of stale urine permeated its very walls.

"No!" she protested. But the skinny stranger was deceptively strong.

Once inside, Tabitha wrinkled her nose and tried not to breathe too deeply, for the smell was making her feel nauseated. The room was immense and seemed to take up most of the first floor of the building, yet the stench filled it. She squinted in the dimness and could just about make out two filthy, sodden mattresses in one corner of the room, which were surrounded by piles of syringes and foil paper. In another corner, a bucket overflowing with excrement and urine sat among a stack of greasy empty takeaway cartons and paper bags. She put a hand to her mouth and tried not to vomit. She half expected a rat to scurry past and wondered whether the room had been recently vacated or whether its occupants were due to return at any moment. Or perhaps it was where this vile man lived. Either way, Tabitha hoped that she didn't have to be there for much longer. She thought of the heat lamp and the leather straps almost longingly.

Don't be silly, she admonished herself. *You're not in pain anymore. You're home! You just need to get out of here and everything will be fine.*

But she knew that this was not true. She had never been so terrified in her life. She was out of the frying pan and into the fire.

The stranger pushed her to the floor. She yelped and examined her soiled hands with disgust. She still felt confused and disorientated since the neural transfer, and the stink of the place was not helping her to see things clearly. She coughed and forced the contents of her stomach back down with a swallow.

"So, miss high and mighty. You think it's OK to get my sister carted away in the back of a police car do you, babe? Some kind of grass, are you?"

"What?"

"My sister. Keeley Jackson. Her best mate was about to give birth and the Old Bill turn up just as the ambulance arrives. Yeah, nice one, bitch!"

"I don't know what you're talking about!" Tabitha proclaimed. "It's got nothing to do with me!"

"They were only messing around when they borrowed your ID, you know. There was no need to call the Old Bill."

"I...I'm sorry, I don't remember calling them." Who had called them? Mr. Aurora the shopkeeper? Ellie? Belisha? Oh, no.

"Get over there!" spat the youth, pointing towards one of the stained mattresses.

"No way. It's disgusting," she pleaded.

"*You* disgust *me!*" he yelled. He reached for the petrol can he had carried in with him and proceeded to pour its contents onto the already sodden mattress. Before she could escape, he grabbed hold of her, pushed her onto its saturated surface and slammed the door closed. Now that dusk had arrived, the only light that she could see was the sudden flicker of a match, which blazed into life. She screamed.

"I wouldn't move if I was you," he said softly.

"You wouldn't, would you? If you drop that match, the whole place will go up."

"Then don't move. It's just you and me, babe. You and Kenzie Jackson by candlelight. Ahh, how nice." Tabitha saw the flame move across the room and ignite a candle, which he waved around, its trail ghost-like and threatening in the gloom. His dark features and long hands were just about visible in the spooky glow. She heard the scraping of something heavy being pushed against the door. She was trapped. Again.

"This is insane. If these fumes ignite then we'll both-"

"But I'm invincible, babe! At least, I feel invincible."

He was more crazy than Smoky and Elliot put together. She needed to get out of here. The smell of the fumes was by now overpowering the odour of excrement.

"You're quite safe. This room is massive, and all the bloody windows are smashed so there's plenty of air." He laughed cruelly. "Stop coughing, will ya? Look, I need to know that you know Elle. She's your bestie, ain't she?"

"I'm not telling you anything about me. Who are you? Some kind of hired assassin?"

"Assassin?" he exploded into laughter. "No, babe, I'm more of a, er, trader." He paused to cough and spat something bright green onto the ground. Tabitha cringed and tried to figure out a way past him that didn't involve dying in a blazing inferno.

He knelt down so that he was at the same level, but not too close to the fuel-soaked mattress. Kenzie waved the candle around as he spoke, dripping wax all over the filthy floor. Her eyes didn't leave it.

"You're off your face, aren't you, Kenzie?" she sniffed.

"I am feeling pretty good, yeah. But not as good as I felt last weekend. Last weekend was something else! I've still got some of those jellies around here somewhere." He reached into his shabby tracksuit bottoms and retrieved a small bag of pills. He grinned and gave a strange, disconnected laugh. "Ah, there's still some left. Quality. Want to try one, babe?" Tabitha shook her head and pursed her lips in defiance. Kenzie shrugged and pocketed the bag once more. "Last time I had one of these bad boys, it was like I'd been transported to another place. It was so freaking different from, well, anything I've seen before. I've not told no one about it, but you're lucky, 'cause I'm gonna tell you all about it." His eyes had glazed over as though he was recalling a particularly surreal and vivid dream.

Tabitha pulled herself slowly to her feet, but he pushed her immediately down onto the mattress again. "Let me talk!" he barked. His voice softened again. "You shoulda felt what I felt, babe, seen what I could see. There were all these flashing lights and there were these people dressed in weird clobber, and…and they were all talking to me, proper friendly, like. And it was like I was some kind of rock star or summat, 'coz there were these people and they wanted my autograph and they were chanting at me, over and over again, to sign my name. '*Sign it, sign it, sign it.*' Yeah, that was it! All I remember thinking was how funny they looked with blue hair. At least, this one guy did, anyway. Didn't wake up until two days later. Mental, ain't it?" He paused and laughed to himself. "With my iPod banging me tunes in me ears for hours on end while I was high, like. Me brain probably thought I was in some kind of nightclub or concert or summat."

Tabitha's eyes widened as the delinquent's words filtered through. Had this person been to Hayfen IV? Had Kenzie unknowingly undergone neural-matter transference and unknowingly given consent? And, if so, what had he done with the consent form? Would he have been with it enough to remember? It was difficult to know if what he was talking about were real memories. If he had been taking all manner of drugs from a young age, his brain was probably already fried from substance abuse. He most likely didn't know what was real and what wasn't any more. She was beginning to know how he felt.

She looked up at the windows. Their broken panes were so small that she would never be able to climb through them.

"Did I blow your mind, babe?" Kenzie asked, obviously entertained by his own story, real or not. He waved the candle about more slowly now, dazed and transfixed by his own movements.

Tabitha gulped. If this man had indeed undergone neural-matter transference, it didn't sound as though he had been there for very long, but the question was: who had come down in his place? And how had they gone through the procedure without the aid of the professor? Was Kenzie really dangerous or was he just a twisted junkie? Which was worse? She could feel the petrol seeping through her clothes and skin. She tried to get her head around what was happening.

Had Elliot and Smoky used Kenzie to threaten and kill people? Were those people that Smoky and Elliot mentioned really dead or were they just trying to frighten her? Tabitha was having doubts now. Did this man even know how to find Ellie? He seemed so out of it that she didn't think he had much more of a grip on reality than she did.

"The guy with the blue hair. Did he say anything about me?" She had nothing to lose by asking him.

"Whoa, babe. 'Ave you been tripping too?"

"Humour me," she said. "What did he say about Ellie?"

"He told me where she lives and what to do to her if her friend didn't show up. But it looks like you have, so I might probably do those things to you instead, babe."

Tabitha flinched and crawled quickly backwards on the heels of her hands.

"Relax. We got plenty of time yet, babe. Oh, and he said…"

"What did he say?" she whispered, her words sticking in her throat, her heart pounding.

"That I was to give you this." He reached into his pocket and disclosed a crumpled piece of paper. "He said for you to put it with yours, safe like."

"I… I…" Tabitha reached forwards and snatched the paper from him. She stood up and tried to read what was on it in the dim light. The writing was almost illegible, but it looked as though it was signed in Kenzie's hand at the bottom.

"Whatever, babes. I'm bored now," Kenzie declared. "Want to have a bit of fun?" He reached into his left pocket and took out the bag of pills once more.

His gaze hovered over Tabitha's chest for an uncomfortable amount of time and then up to her face. "You know, there are ways you can pay me back for grassing up my little sister." Suddenly, his lips were lunging towards her. In revulsion, she pushed him back, lifted her right leg and gave him a swift kick between his legs.

"You bitch!" he cried out, recoiling in pain.

Tabitha made for the door. She held her breath as she heaved the bucket that was jamming the door closed.
The handle slipped out of her grasp and the putrid contents spilled across the floor and onto her shoes. She retched as she reached for the door handle.

"Wait!" Kenzie cried out. She heard him cough and struggle to his feet, scuffing his shoes on the dirty floor. She pulled open the door and welcomed the cool fresh air and milky moonlight. "Tabitha Turner, Belisha Beacon, whichever one you are!"

Tabitha halted. She turned slowly towards the junkie. What did he say? And what had happened to his voice?

"How did you…? I'm Tabitha…you're not…"

"Professor Pagter," his voice rasped and then levelled out. It was as though an older man were speaking out of the lips of a much younger one. He pulled himself to his full height and looked around the grim room. "Let's talk outside. This place is revolting."

Belisha

Belisha could feel her bladder emptying. The feeling of overwhelming relief was quickly followed by the sensation of great discomfort. Her face was burning, her lower half was sodden and her wrists and ankles were raw.

"Get that thing off my face!" she screamed. She could hear her skin sizzling under the heat. "What do you think you're doing? Get me out of this van!"

"What van? Smoky, I think she's finally cracked!"

"Ssh. Listen to her accent. Something's changed. This is not right." Smoky leaned in, swiped the lamp away from her face and asked, "Belisha Beacon?"

"Who are you?" she cried out, although her throat felt dry and cracked. When was the last time she had drank anything?

"It's a local accent all right," he said. "If you are Belisha, then you're back home. But I have no idea how. We were so close to getting that signature!"

"Home? Home where? Cottonwood Close or Hayfen IV?"

"*Home* home. Well, near enough," said Elliot. "But what are you doing here?"

"That's what I want to know. Untie me and get me some water."

"Not craving souprano then?" Smoky laughed. "I suppose the stuff's completely left Tabitha's, I mean, *your* system now. Only water now, eh?"

"Just get me a drink," she begged. "Please."

"Are you really the professor?" Tabitha walked along and wrapped her arms around her torso, defensively. She bit her lip and looked up at the man. The tall, filthy, scrawny body may now have been inhabited by another person, but it did not mean that Tabitha was no longer frightened. The man nodded.

"There's no need to be alarmed. Although, that's easier said than done, I'm sure." He looked down at the scruffy clothes, nicotine-stained fingers and chewed nails and visibly shuddered. He did not seem comfortable in the skin he was wearing.

"What are you doing here?"

"I'm sure you have many questions, but we don't have much time. I will explain as much as I can." Tabitha nodded and let the man speak as they walked slowly away from the abandoned warehouse in the direction of the main road. "As you have probably worked out, you are part of an experiment. One which I originally constructed. And I'm sorry. None of this was supposed to happen."

"I know. Smoky Hollow and your nephew told me. Smoky commissioned you to fabricate temporal neural-matter transference and perform the experiment."

"But it never should have been used. It should never have gone this far. Not without retro-consent. Which is, of course, impossible."

"Unless taken by force…"

"Again, I am sorry." The professor stopped and rested his hands on both of her shoulders. His breath was still foul, and she recoiled in recollection of Kenzie's advances and pulled away. He gasped. "Oh, what have they done to you? What did *he* do to you? Why couldn't I have chosen someone else to transfer with instead of that drug-fuelled delinquent?"

"Yes, why did you choose him?" she asked as they continued to walk. She recognised the road that would eventually lead back to her home. Her real home. She felt comforted by that thought, at least.

"Because he was nearby. And because we are physically closely matched. And Elliot was able to get his consent. Although, not in a manner with which I entirely approve."

"He was off his face on drugs. I don't think he knew what he was doing."

"That, my dear, is hardly the point."

"You're right," Tabitha agreed.

"And when I found out what Smoky and that deranged nephew of mine had planned for him, then I knew that I had to do something. Using an Earthborn for their own evil deeds, even such a man as Kenzie Jackson, it's unthinkable."

"They're trying to use me too," said Tabitha. "I don't think that Smoky meant to send me back when he did, but he wanted me to get consent for him. From the *Prime Minister,* of all people. Can you imagine?"

"I'd rather not!" coughed the professor. "My soul! He really is more unhinged than I thought."

"I think that's a bit of an understatement."

"So, you believe that you flipped back before Smoky had finished with you, do you?"

"Yes, I'm quite certain. He wanted me to agree to sign the consent form first."

"Then it's a good job that you flipped back when you did. Unknowingly to those two, the transference can be activated and deactivated in advance of the desired time. I set your transference to a specified amount of time."

"Two weeks? Is that all it's been? Well, I wish it had been shorter, but I'm grateful to be back now." She smiled weakly. "I'm not entirely sure how Smoky expected me to find the Prime Minister or do any of the things he asked me to do. Professor, he wanted me to locate the early founders of Project Borrowed Time. He told me that he had all of the logistics worked out."

"I've no doubt that he had. To some extent, at least."

"But how? If physical objects can't be passed backwards through time, then I fail to see how he is able to engineer anything."

"Who knows what plans he has in place? For all we know, a distant relation of his may have started this whole thing and when he discovered that someone – me – had found a way for the conscious mind to travel through time, then he threw everything he had at it. He's not a poor man,

Tabitha. They are not a poor family. He doubtlessly inherited quite a fortune."

"So, why did he need me?" sighed Tabitha. "That's the part I don't get."

"Because you happen to be part of the pair that I chose for the initial experiment. I wanted to switch the mind of someone thoughtful, kind and benevolent with the mind of someone who was confident, successful, celebrated…" The professor continued. "Of course, I never wanted to go ahead with it without retro-consent, and none of this should have happened. Your neural coordinates were already set up, and by the time I discovered that Smoky had gone ahead anyway it was too late. I tried to stop him, but he locked me away and threatened me."

"Yes, he told me that part. So, it didn't have to be me. It could have been anyone that he sent back to do his dirty work. How did you even know I existed?"

"Well, not just anyone, Tabitha, dear. We have archives of the people who made the most impact on our history, and–" he stopped and turned to look at her, wide-eyed. He clamped a hand over his mouth.

"*I* make an impact on the world?" Tabitha gasped. "In what way?"

The professor simply shook his head and mumbled something incoherent.

"You can't tell me, can you?"

The professor dropped his hand and shook his head again. Even so, her heart gave a little leap of joy at the notion.

"Well, I don't think I'm going to make much of an impact at Miss Ree's."

"Ah," said the professor, finally. "There's something else you should know."

"He's gone!" Elliot stomped into the room.

"What? Where could he have got to? He was tied down!"

"No, no, no. His body's still there. But that blithering junkie is occupying his brain again. He keeps mumbling about experiencing a bad trip."

Belisha rubbed her wrists and ankles and stretched her aching legs out in front of her. She was no longer restrained and had been handed a grimy mug brimming with tepid souprano, which tasted sour on her lips. She looked up from the makeshift seat onto which she had been pushed and listened to her captors.

"How did he do that?" growled Smoky. "And how did he arrange for Miss Belisha and Miss Turner to flip back too? What are we going to do now? We can't get them back without the professor being here!"

"Oh dear. Has it all gone a bit wrong?" asked Belisha in mock sympathy. Throwing the mug down with a mighty crash, she shouted, "Well, if your plan has gone haywire, then you may as well just let me go. In case you haven't noticed, I have urgent need of a hygiene cubicle and a pain suppressor patch!" She pointed to her tender cheek and scowled at the pair.

"That attitude is going to get you sent straight back to the chair, young lady," said Elliot. He stepped quickly behind her, restrained her wrists and pulled her shoulder blades back behind her. Her struggles only served to tighten his grip. "And I won't make you as comfortable this time!"

Belisha opened her mouth to protest, but Smoky interjected. "We need to step up our game. We need to find a way to get the professor back. Keep her secure," said Smoky as he left the room.

"He won't stay on the stinking homeworld forever will he?" Elliot called after him. Then he whispered thickly into Belisha's ear, "The moment the professor returns, I'll show him what pain *really* is."

Tabitha

"So, while I've been interviewing pop princesses on a mathematical shape orbiting another planet in the future, Belisha has left my old job at the office to work in my local pub?" Tabitha shook her head in amazement. "That's probably the craziest thing I've ever said. And I'm not sure whether to laugh or cry!"

"Let's not forget the importance of the other events," said the professor.

"And at least one person is dead. Yes, I know. It's horrifying. Look, I can't process all of this." Tabitha slid a hand slowly down her face and frowned. "But while that freak is in your body in the future…Ellie is safe now, isn't she?"

"He can't stay there forever, Tabitha."

"Why not?"

"Because it would completely mess everything up. Can't you understand? Besides, it would mean that I would be stuck here. Stuck inside the body of a wasted junkie, craving God knows what!" He paused. "Although, perhaps that would be a rather fitting punishment…" he said, humbly.

"Punishment? But you haven't done anything wrong. Not really. It was those two maniacs! And how are they going to get their comeuppance if we remain here? Listen, I've been thinking about it since we started talking, and I want to help you. Even if it means taking my consciousness back with you."

"I haven't got much time left," said the professor. "I programmed the transference to be reactivated after ten minutes."

"But why?"

"I merely wanted to poke my head 'round the door, so to speak. I did not wish Kenzie to be a part of this any more than I do you, no matter what his background may be. It would not be right for me to leave him there, being subjected to such torture."

"So, what shall I do now? Will I be transferred too?"

He shook his head, stopped and faced her. "I would need to activate your transference at the other end. Now that I've had a break from the pain that has been inflicted on me, perhaps I'll be able to think more clearly and put a plan together. Perhaps-"

"But what if you can't?" Tabitha grabbed him by the elbow and looked up at him. She saw his Adam's apple rise and fall. He looked down at her, and it was as though someone had suddenly switched on a different-coloured bulb behind his eyes.

Kenzie cried out in his own accent, "Turn off that bloody lamp, would ya?"

Tabitha's eyes widened. She loosened her grasp, turned around and ran as fast as she could, resisting looking back even once. Before Kenzie could fully comprehend what was happening, she had reached a bus stop just in time for the number eleven Route Cruiser to pull up, and she quickly boarded.

Her heart racing, she fumbled about her person for some change and paid the fare before taking a seat next to a grubby window. The bus stopped no less than four times during the five minutes that followed, and it was at the fourth stop that Tabitha recognised the little battered Ford Fiesta, which had been abandoned at the side of the road. She swiftly got to her feet, rushed down the aisle, waved to the driver and stepped onto the pavement.

Once across the road, she got inside and kissed the steering wheel. On turning the key, however, she realised what had happened. She glared at the petrol warning light.

"Oh, Belisha!" she screamed. With a sigh, she got out again and opened the boot. The petrol can was not there. Her heart fell. The abandoned car, the fuel-soaked mattress…now things were starting to piece themselves together. *It's a good thing that I have emergency breakdown cover,* she told herself. *Although, I'm going to look pretty foolish.* She reached for her mobile phone. *Now, let's just hope that Belisha thought to keep this thing charged.*

Belisha relaxed her muscles as far as she was able.

"I wonder what the professor is doing down there, back in 2018," she mused. She also wondered whether appearing calm was the best way to infuriate her captors. "Perhaps he's warning people, perhaps he's helping Tabitha, or maybe he's interfering with Project Borrowed Time."

"Shut up. You know nothing! You have no idea about anything apart from how to talk into a microphone," Elliot spat, pulling her shoulder blades closer and tightening his grasp on her wrists.

"Oh, I've learned quite a few more skills these past couple of weeks," whispered Belisha who made the most of the fact that her chest was jutting out proudly in front of her. She could feel his eyes on her. "Look, Elliot. Elliot, darling, with your breath-taking vibrant hair and your cute little sneaky smile. I'm sorry for shouting earlier, for being so angry. How about you let me go, and I go and talk to this junkie? I may be able to help."

"Why would I let you do that?" puffed Elliot.

"As I said, I've learned a lot. You may not be aware of this, but the professor visited me on several occasions while I was in Tabitha's body," she emphasised the word 'body'. In a sudden movement, she was free from his grasp and he was standing in front of her, a hand on her hip and the other on her shoulder, a lustful smile on his lips. Elliot's eyes fell to her breasts and Belisha placed a finger underneath his chin. She tilted his head so that his eyes met hers before leaning in and slowly whispering in his ear, "He may have told me of the secret to the transference."

"Did he, now?" Elliot faltered. He pulled back, his lips moist and longing. She dropped her hand and sashayed past him in the direction Smoky had gone.

"Wait, wait. I'll have to ask Smoky first."

She stopped, regarded him, her eyelashes sweeping upwards. "Oh, so *he's* the one in charge now?"

"Of course he's not. Not technically. After all, the professor is my uncle."

"Precisely," she said, softly.

Once inside the small room where the professor and his transference match had been kept captive, Belisha kept up her act and approached Smoky and Kenzie. The professor's body had been restrained in much the same way that she and Tabitha had been, complete with leather-strapped chair and heat lamp. Kenzie looked up at her through the professor's wizened eyes. He managed a croaky laugh.

"Looks like this trip ain't so bad, after all."

"You're the one who threw me in the back of the van, I suppose, judging by your accent and the way in which you screw up your face like that."

"You remember, do ya, babe? So you decided to take a pill with me, after all? Although, I don't actually remember taking anything since this morning."

"What are you talking about?" Belisha paused for a moment and then decided to play along. "Yes, yes. I'm enjoying this experience as much as you are… *babe*."

"When you two have quite finished, I need to get down to business!" Smoky harrumphed.

"And what do you propose to do?" Belisha asked him. "You can't do much without the professor's knowledge."

"But you have the professor's knowledge," said Elliot, who had appeared in the doorway, his pupils still wide with desire.

"Hey, it's you, blue hair!" rasped Kenzie. "You're the geezer who I saw on my last trip!"

"You are a vile excuse for a human being. I'm glad that project Borrowed Time opted to iron people like you out of the system!" Elliot spat.

"It looks like the gene pool still became tainted anyway." Belisha shot him a look.

"Hey, gorgeous, why the strong tone?" Elliot looked visibly hurt. "I thought you and me had something."

Belisha shook her head and muttered, "You're pathetic."

"What's happening?" bellowed Smoky. Belisha turned to Kenzie, who seemed to be convulsing. If it weren't for the restraints around his limbs, she was certain that he would have fallen off the reclined seat.

"Enough is enough!" cried a voice. It was the voice of professor Pagter. "Untie these restraints, Belisha!"

Before Elliot or Smoky could stop her, Belisha was at his side, tugging at the straps that held his body down.

"All right, uncle, you can have a rest from the chair. For now," cried Elliot. He turned to Belisha. "Go ahead, beautiful. Untie the professor. Perhaps he has suffered enough for now. But he will *not* leave this basement. He will not leave this laboratory until the next phase of the experiment is in motion."

"And what is the next phase, dear nephew?" asked the professor, through parched lips.

"You will flip Belisha and Tabitha back so that I can give Tabitha instructions on how to write out a consent form. You will then flip them back again in order for her to write the thing and leave it in the good care of the founders of Project Borrowed Time, where it will remain until the correct time for me to retrieve it. Then I will present the consenting signature to you, thus allowing you to reveal exactly how exactly you engineer temporal neural-matter transference."

The professor laughed. "Did you really think that that is how it would happen?" His eyes were wide, and a smile broke through his wizened, tortured face. "You thought you had it all worked out, didn't you? Elliot, did you actually believe that torturing and threatening someone to give retro-consent was the way around this paradox? And you thought that I'd accept that method as a valid procedure and grant you the power to do the same to anyone you wish? Good heavens. I know you didn't inherit the intelligence gene, but this is utter madness!"

"But you said—" Elliot fumbled.

"What are you trying to tell us?" growled Smoky Hollow. "Elliot, you told me that this plan was fool-proof, when in fact it is half an idea backed up by wishful thinking and deficient organisation. You told me that the professor would need little persuasion."

"I didn't know that the girls were going to swap back when they did, Smoky! If they hadn't, then I could have given Tabitha the instructions by now and the signed consent would be ready for us to collect whenever we wanted at the agreed spot. I could have handed over the consent and we wouldn't be in this situation."

"Don't you see that I still wouldn't have accepted it? Because genuine retro-consent is impossible."

"But perhaps it will still happen," said Elliot, his voice high, powerless and desperate. "Perhaps we will succeed, and she has left it where we agreed. Where we *will* agree."

"You do realise who Tabitha turns out to be, with respect to Project Borrowed Time?" asked Smoky.

"Of course, but—"

"I thought I recognised the name somewhere when I first heard it," broke in Belisha. Suddenly oozing with confidence and excitement, she glided up to the chair to which the professor had been tied and sat down. "A very unremarkable girl with a vaguely familiar name. Of course. Tabitha Turner and Michael Maxwell are the people who came up with the idea for Project Borrowed Time. Michael – ha! He was just a pub landlord with a telescope. Who would have thought it? And if it wasn't for me getting her a job there, it's unlikely that they would ever have had a conversation about it. So, in fact, it is I who should take the credit."

"What are you harping on about?" asked Elliot. "You shouldn't even be here. Uncle, flip them back. Now!"

"I shall do no such thing," the professor protested.

"Then make your choice. Is it to be the debtors' prison or the chair?"

"I think I'll choose the cells."

"What?" cried Smoky and Elliot. In unison, they fell as the floor beneath where they had been standing suddenly gave way. The two felons were suddenly lying on the hard floor at the bottom of a pit some ten feet deep.

"You could have broken my legs, you stupid old fool!" Smoky shook his fists up at the professor.

"It was a risk I was willing to take," the professor called down to them. "Thank you for making this so easy."

Belisha clung on tightly to the chair, almost unconsciously. She noticed a lever on the wall next to the professor. She grinned at him in pure admiration.

"Shall, I call for the Mergencies, professor?"

Epilogue: Tabitha

Tabitha Turner arrived at Ellie's house, her car now restored and working. She was relieved to discover that Ellie was alive and well and gave her such a long hug that Ellie had to eventually prise her away. Tabitha rid her mouth of Ellie's stray curls and simply grinned at her.

"Oh, how I've missed you!" she bleated.

"Er, are you all right, Tabs? It's only been about a day."

"And I've missed that name. My wonderful, normal name and my wonderful, normal life, normal friend. No, my *terrific* friend. And, oh, and apparently a new job."

"Normal is not a word I would ever use to describe you," laughed Ellie as she filled the kettle. "Particularly these last couple of weeks. But that new job does seem to suit you."

"I can't wait to get started. Er, to get to my next shift."

"Tabitha Turner actually looking forward to going to work? Well, that's something I never thought I'd hear."

"Yeah. I'm quite excited about tonight's shift, actually. The landlord, Michael, called me a few minutes ago to ask me whether I'd like to borrow some of his books on astronomy. He said he'd find them for me in time for this evening. I always wanted a hobby. I think looking out into the cosmos and discovering other worlds is something that I could really get into."

"So, you fancy yourself as a bit of an alien spotter, do you?"

"Not aliens, no. Habitable planets, perhaps. There could be somewhere right under our noses, Ellie, but we just can't see it yet. There could be whole worlds just perfect for human habitation, just obscured from view." Ellie poured herself a cup of tea. "Have you run out of mugs?" asked Tabitha with dismay.

"I thought you'd gone off tea."

"What, me? Never."

Ellie shrugged and took another cup out of the cupboard.

"I think you'll need more than a few books and a household telescope, Tabs," she noted, but not unkindly.

"Of course. But it's a start, isn't it?"

Ellie handed her a steaming mug of Tetley tea.

"Then I wish you all the best with it. Go for it!"

"Oh," said Tabitha, delving for her phone, which was vibrating in her pocket. She looked at the screen, puzzled. "It looks like I've got a missed call from Adrian from my old place. I wonder what he wants?"

Epilogue: Belisha

Belisha Beacon entered the Euclidean Building, fully rested, fully cleansed, wearing a sparkling hot pink body suit, six-inch gold heels, perfectly coiffed hair and a plenteousness of confidence, which radiated throughout the studio.

Several hours later, she left the same building, looking as glamourous as she had on entering it, but was confused to find that a freshly shaven Professor Pagter was waiting for her in the transportation hub down on Hayfen Capital. He handed her a carton of steaming souprano and smiled.

"What are you doing here, Professor? The last I heard, you were in debtors' prison."

"It was only a short spell. It wasn't anywhere near as bad as I feared. As I said before, in the end, I was willing to accept punishment after what my actions have caused. Or did I say it to Tabitha? Never mind. I'm a tough old fool, you know. Don't worry about me. Shall we get out of here? This place is far too chaotic."

Belisha nodded, and they stepped onto a conveyor that lead out of the hub.

"How is it going at Möbius Strip Airwaves?" he asked.

"It's going well," she told him. "But it took some getting used to when I first started at the First Sunrise Show. My usual style didn't seem to please Rusabelle West nor the listeners. Nothing I did could please them. It was most frustrating! It was my dream position, after all, and I did *not* want to lose that job, Professor. And then I discovered the new style that Tabitha had adopted and was expected to follow on from her. At first, I found it difficult, but then I realised that if I relaxed a little and observed the world around me, there was plenty I could complain about on national radio! And jibing at some of those so-called pop stars without them realising is more fun than I could have imagined! No more faking it for me. I can be myself for once."

"So, you've managed to keep with Tabitha's broadcasting style then?"

"Kind of, but I've added my own twist, of course," she smiled wickedly.

The professor laughed.

"I never did find out – whatever happened to Smoky Hollow and your nephew?"

"When you left, I threw some pain suppressors and some basic sustenance into the pit and left them for the Mergencies to deal with," he replied. "That's when I gave myself up too, of course. I then vowed not to let those two anywhere near my laboratory ever again. But I suspect that it's not the last I'll see of either of them. My nephew is a sly one, so I shall be sure to keep an eye on him when he's released."

Belisha scoffed. "You make him sound like a naughty child with a chemistry set. What he and Smoky did to all of us was barbaric. And they tried to change history!"

"There's enough evidence of their activities in my laboratory for them to be incarcerated for quite some time. They are both fully aware of the consequences of their actions."

The professor stepped onto a conveyor that lead out of the city and in the opposite direction of Belisha's home. She unconsciously followed him, click-clacking after him, souprano in hand, her curiosity getting the better of her.

"One thing that I have been worrying about, though, is those people back in Tabitha's time. Those people who were killed. What happened? Did Tabitha get the blame?"

The professor frowned. "During the few weeks I spent in debtors' prison, I took it upon myself to engage in some research. There was little else to do. The archives on Tabitha Turner explain her work history, her marriage, her descendants, her legacy, but they mention nothing of any of those so-called murders. I have no reason to believe that Molly and Tricia died of anything but natural causes later on in life. More of my nephew's lies, I expect. All part of the torture process."

"But what about Veronica Vaughan? I know for a fact that she was killed. I heard first-hand after all."

"The circumstances around her death were suspicious at the time," explained the professor. "Veronica died of a heart attack and split her head open on her glass coffee table as she fell. The shock of someone breaking in literally scared her to death."

"That someone wasn't our friend Kenzie Jackson, was it?" gasped Belisha.

"It is very possible, Miss Beacon. Although, no one was ever convicted for the crime. That young rogue had a lucky escape. In fact, he ended up living a lavish lifestyle in an exotic country on the homeworld."

"Don't talk nonsense, Professor. I can't imagine he'd have grown up to be businessman of the year," she sneered.

"He was in the Times Rich List three years running, according to the archives. He married into a very wealthy family."

"Well, no one ever said that life was fair, I suppose," Belisha said with a frown. "And talking about marriage, you said the archives discussed Tabitha's work history and her marriage. I'm curious…did Tabitha marry Adrian?"

"The archives mention an Adrian who came to work for her and Michael in their later career. Tabitha went on to marry someone called Mark Hollister, I believe. Why do you ask?"

"No reason," she said with a smile, happily accepting that her time with Adrian may have just been a special few days between the two of them, like a holiday romance. Unless they went on seeing each other after the girls had switched back, but Belisha refused to believe this to be the case.

She thought about Tabitha for a moment. Suddenly filling with enthusiasm, she said, "And what a career, eh soul? Who'd have thought that ordinary little Tabitha and a run-of-the-mill pub landlord could turn out to be not so ordinary after all?"

"There were many people involved over a substantial piece of history, Belisha," Professor Pagter reminded her. "But, indeed, it was Tabitha's visit here, her subsequent schooling and her initiative that drove Project Borrowed Time into the starting blocks."

Belisha smiled and said with affection, "And to think that I've been back there and stood in her shoes. Her very grubby, ugly, flat shoes!" Belisha giggled and raised her souprano cup in a kind of toast. She took a sip and looked up at the buildings around them, the lights, the colours and at the beautiful, impossible mathematical shape that hung above them in its everlasting orbit.

ALSO BY RUTH MASTERS

THE TRUXXE TRILOGY

Three novels following the adventures of Tom Bowler, a human who finds himself working in an intergalactic service station during his gap year. He discovers the secrets of the planetoid Truxxe, traverses the galaxy to rescue his alien friend from the prison planet Porriduum and ultimately defends the earth against an alien invasion.

A cast of colourful aliens good and bad, fantastic alien worlds and witty dialogue make this trilogy a great read for any sci-fi fan!

Vol 1: All Aliens Like Burgers
Vol 2: Do Aliens Read Sci-Fi?
Vol 3. When Aliens Play Trumps

AUTOGRAPH HUNTER SERIES

A pair of "paraquels", each covering similar events, from the perspective of different characters. In both books, attendees at the same sci-fi convention happen across a real working time machine, and set off on autograph-hunting missions through time.

The two pairs of friends cross paths occasionally, with Rosemary and Joanne intriguingly being one step ahead of Alistair and Jeremy. Along the way they meet the great and the good of history, from Shakespeare to the inventor of the modern toilet. Friendships are tested and life will never be the same again…

Vol 1: Extreme Autograph Hunters
Vol 2: Ultimate Autograph Hunters

BELISHA BEACON & TABITHA TURNER

Tabitha Turner is a complaints executive from contemporary Birmingham. Belisha Beacon is a celebrity DJ working on the illustrious Möbius Strip, orbiting the planet Hayfen IV, 400 years in the future.

Inexplicably finding themselves inhabiting each other's bodies and living each other's lives the two women must survive in a strange new world.

How will they get back to their own realities… and do they want to? Nothing is ever as it seems as Belisha and Tabitha's lives begin to change forever.

Order from www.ruthmastersscifi.com or on Amazon.